REBELLIOUS BRIDE

ADRIENNE DAY

AVON BOOKS ◆ NEW YORK

REBELLIOUS BRIDE is an original publication of Avon Books. This work has never before appeared in book form. This work is a novel. Any similarity to actual persons or events is purely coincidental.

AVON BOOKS
A division of
The Hearst Corporation
1350 Avenue of the Americas
New York, New York 10019

Copyright © 1995 by Linda Andersen
Published by arrangement with the author
Library of Congress Catalog Card Number: 95-90099
ISBN: 0-380-77413-5

First Avon Books Printing: October 1995

AVON TRADEMARK REG. U.S. PAT. OFF. AND IN OTHER COUNTRIES, MARCA REGISTRADA, HECHO EN U.S.A.

Printed in the U.S.A.

RA   10   9   8   7   6   5   4   3   2   1

"WHAT ARE YOU DOING HERE?"

"I couldn't sleep," he answered tersely. "Obviously, neither could you." Adam's blood was running hot. He wanted her. Regina could *feel* the tension that emanated from his body.

"I'm curious about something, Miss Langley." His hushed words hovered in the cool air between them. "Does your brother know you sneak out at night?"

"As far as you or my brother or anyone else is concerned, I spent the entire night in my bed. Now if you will please let me go—"

Adam slipped an arm around her waist. "Since you never left the house," he said huskily, ignoring her efforts to free herself, "you have no proof I ever saw you. Nor do you have proof that I did this . . ."

He lowered his head to hers . . .

Praise for Adrienne Day's
A GENTLE TAMING

"Exquisite.
Snappy dialogue and raging sexual tension . . .
A must read for romance fans everywhere."
Rendezvous

"An entertaining read"
Affaire de Coeur

Chapter 1

June 7, 1716
Virginia

Regina Langley squirmed on the hard pew and suppressed a yawn as Father Tidewell droned on and on in his mosquito-hum voice about Betsy Staunton's indelicate condition. The air inside the church was hot and stifling, causing Regina's clothes to cling to her damp skin and her dark hair to curl around her face. She wished the priest would talk about something else. This was the fourth Sunday in a row that he had made poor Betsy the target of his sermon.

"However," Father Tidewell continued, looking straight at Kyle Jamison, "if someone takes Betsy as his wife *before* the baby is born, I will consider dismissing all charges of fornication and will implore the vestry to waive the fines that have been imposed upon Mr. Staunton as a result of his daughter's misconduct."

Regina chewed on the inside of her cheek and stared at the spot where several gray hairs sprouted from the middle of the portly priest's otherwise bald head. *Hypocrite*, she thought. Everyone in Westmoreland County knew where Father Tidewell spent his Saturday nights, and it certainly wasn't in his study at the parsonage preparing for the next day's church service.

1

"One more thing," Father Tidewell buzzed. "A disturbing rumor has reached my ears that there was an excessive amount of drinking and cavorting at a particular social gathering earlier this week, resulting in more than a few tarnished reputations among the female population of this parish."

A titter rippled through the church.

Regina choked on a laugh and turned her head to look toward the Randolph pew.

His face turning several shades redder than his hair, Arthur Randolph, Senior, one of the most influential members of the vestry, glowered at Father Tidewell, while Arthur's wife began fanning herself harder, her ivory and lace fan making a swishing noise that could be heard several pews away. Arthur, Junior, a nineteen-year-old replica of his father, right down to his flaming hair and bright blue eyes, grinned sheepishly.

And Beatrice Randolph, two years younger than her brother and Regina's best friend, caught her bottom lip between her teeth and glanced in Regina's direction. Beatrice was so red that it was impossible to make out a single one of the two hundred and forty-four freckles that adorned her face.

In spite of herself, Regina felt her own face grow warm, and the giggle that she had previously managed to swallow suddenly erupted in an unladylike snort.

"Regina, behave yourself!" Caroline Langley whispered.

Regina turned back to the front and glanced at her aunt from beneath her lashes. In spite of her stern tone and the fact that her lips were compressed into a disapproving line, Caroline's eyes sparkled with mirth. Regina felt the corners of her mouth begin to twitch, and it was only a fortuitous peek at her Uncle William's countenance, rigid and grim beneath his snowy wig, that sobered her enough to prevent her from bursting out laughing.

Utterly unrepentant, Regina fixed her attention on Father Tidewell and wondered if it were possible to *will* someone into silence. She, for one, had had a delightful time at the Randolph party. The food had been delicious. The music and dancing were marvelous. And James Fitzhugh was a positively wonderful kisser.

On the far side of William Langley, Regina's two cousins, twelve-year-old Robert and eight-year-old Timmy, began fidgeting and twisting around on the pew. Caroline leaned around her husband and hushed the boys. Just then, the spotted lizard that Timmy had sneaked into St. John's Church wriggled out of his pocket and darted over the Widow Waite's lap.

Mrs. Waite gasped.

Timmy scrambled off his seat and dove after the lizard.

"William!" Caroline whispered.

William Langley, his thoughts abruptly interrupted, scowled at Robert and growled ominously, "Settle down."

Robert's eyes grew round and wide. "I didn't do nothing!"

Mrs. Waite slumped back on the pew and pressed her hands over her heart.

A murmur rumbled through the church and heads began turning as everyone strained to see what was happening.

Father Tidewell stammered and seemed to forget what he had been about to say.

Timmy, who had disappeared in a sea of silk skirts, suddenly cried out, "I got him!"

William Langley surged to his feet and stepped over Robert, then over Mrs. Waite, then over the Bartlett sisters, steadily working his way to the end of the pew.

Regina's shoulders began to shake with unconstrained laughter.

Caroline Langley groaned.

Seizing the opportunity, Regina turned and looked behind her, her eyes scanning the crowded church until she spotted James Fitzhugh's wheat-blond head.

As if feeling her gaze on him, James glanced in her direction.

Regina's pulse began to race as she remembered the night of the Randolph party, when the two of them had slipped away from the crowded ballroom. Not only had James kissed her, he had unlaced her corset and put his hand—

"Regina!" Caroline whispered sharply.

Regina snapped back around.

William Langley, his face flushed and his snowy wig askew, was working his way across the church with the squirming eight-year-old in tow. When they reached the Langley pew, William lifted Timmy by the back of his collar and planted him firmly on the seat.

For the first time in the seventy-six-year history of St. John's Parish, the church service—which always lasted precisely twenty minutes—ended early.

* * *

Regina cast a furtive glance over her shoulder at her family gathered on the freshly cut lawn in front of the church, exchanging gossip and news with friends, before she slipped around the corner of the parsonage.

James Fitzhugh caught her around the waist, nearly lifting her off her feet as he swung her around. He backed her against the house and covered her mouth with his, smothering her squeal of surprise. She moaned softly and wrapped her arms around his neck. She slid her fingers up his nape, burying them in his silky blond hair, and surrendered willingly to his kiss.

Finally she tore her mouth away. "James, stop," she said, blushing and trying to catch her breath. "I only have a minute. Aunt Caroline thinks I'm going to the privy. If I don't return soon, someone will come looking for me."

James moved his lips down Regina's throat. "Let them come," he dared. He nipped at the soft flesh with his teeth.

"Ouch!" Regina twisted out of his arms. "Don't do that! It leaves marks."

James caught her wrist and pulled her back to him. "When can I see you again?"

Regina placed her palms on his chest, delighting in the feel of his firm muscles beneath her fingers at the same time that she kept him at bay. The expression in his blue eyes was closed and unreadable, but the determined set to his jaw sent a thrill of excitement spiraling down her spine. "I don't know. Uncle William is still angry over what happened at the Randolph party."

"I'll meet you at the mill this afternoon."

"I can't. Richard arrived home last night, and he's bringing guests to dinner."

"Then let Richard entertain them."

Regina ignored the sarcasm in his voice. The animosity between James and her brother had been smoldering ever since that ridiculous duel over Leticia Sandhurst. "He's been away two years," she said. "I was asleep last night when his ship docked, so I haven't even seen him yet."

James kissed her again. "When?" he murmured into her mouth.

"My aunt and uncle are going to Williamsburg at the end of the month. They'll be gone two weeks."

"I need to see you tonight, after the others have gone to bed." James threaded his fingers into her hair, causing the pins to dislodge, and covered her mouth with his.

Regina's knees felt as if they would give out.

Suddenly they were interrupted by a loud cough.

James released her and took an abrupt step backward, and Regina found herself staring over his shoulder at Uncle William. She hastily dragged her hand across her mouth in an unconscious attempt to erase what her uncle had just seen, but she knew it was too late.

William tapped his riding whip against his polished black boot. Beneath his wig, his face was taut with barely-suppressed rage. "We are ready to leave," he said stiffly.

Regina's gaze slid to the whip in her uncle's hand, then jerked back up to his face. It was no use trying to talk her way out of this one. Uncle William had already warned her what would happen if he caught her again with James Fitzhugh.

Her stomach knotting, she cut a wide path around him and started back to the church.

James started to follow her, but William stuck out the crop, blocking his way. "Young man, you and I are going to have a talk."

Regina stopped. She glanced at James, and then at her uncle, and her heart began to pound with the slow, steady beat of a death knell. There was a hard glint in her uncle's eyes that frightened her. She didn't know what he intended to do to James.

She took a step toward them. "Uncle William—"

"This has naught to do with you, Regina," William snapped. "Go back to the others."

"But it wasn't James's fault. I was the one who—"

"*Now!*"

Regina's face flamed. Gathering up her skirts, she whirled around and ran back to the church.

"All three of you deserve a thrashing!" William Langley bit out.

Regina followed him intently with her eyes as he paced the length of his study. When he moved away from her, she noticed the white knuckles of his left hand, which clasped his right behind his back, and his right hand, which was fixed firmly around the stock of the riding crop.

Regina, Robert, and Timmy stood by the massive oak desk that William had had shipped from England, their gazes nervously following the ominous twitch of the crop when William's position provided a view of it.

"You disrupted a solemn service," William continued. "You embarrassed your mother and me, and you've disgraced the Langley name."

Robert whimpered. "But I didn't do nothing!"

William Langley rounded on his son. "I didn't do *anything*," he bit out, a pained expression on his face. "Good God! Didn't Melville teach you anything while he was in my employ? I certainly paid the man enough!"

"Uncle William, Mr. Melville was a Scot," Regina said matter-of-factly.

William Langley stared at her as if seeing her for the first time. Regina never knew what went through her uncle's mind when he looked at her like that, but she suspected it had more to do with the Powhatan blood that flowed in her veins than he was willing to admit. With the dark hair and dark eyes that she had inherited from her mother's side of the family, she bore little resemblance to her fair-haired, fair-skinned English cousins. More than once, William had remarked that she looked uncannily like one of the ill-bred savages he sometimes feared his own children would become.

After a few seconds, some of the starch left William's countenance, and the Langley brood breathed a collective sigh of relief as the threat of punishment became less imminent.

"You're right," William conceded, sounding unusually distracted. "Had I not been reduced by circumstances to hiring a bloody foreigner to tutor you children, none of this would have come about. Your manners are deplorable, not a single one of you has a head for business, and your diction would cause your grandfather to turn over in his grave." William wagged the crop at Robert. "And if you, young man, wish to study at Oxford, you must first learn to speak the King's English. Let us hope there is an educated man among the indentures who arrived last night on the *Lady Anne*. I don't want you children to go another month without a suitable tutor."

Regina fidgeted. She wasn't the least bit interested in her cousins' education. She wanted to find out what Uncle William had said to James. Both men had emerged from behind the parsonage with unyielding expressions, tension crackling between them like lightning. James had not so much as glanced in her direction, but had gotten on his horse and ridden away from the church at a furious pace.

William now waved his hand in dismissal. "Get out of here. And try to remember that we have guests. I would like to get through this day without any more incidents."

All three of the younger Langleys bolted for the door.

"Regina!"

Regina skidded to a stop. "Yes, sir?"

"I wish to have a word with you. Close the door."

Regina clenched her teeth. She should have known her uncle would not let her off so lightly. She prayed silently that he would at least be quick about it. Beatrice and Izzy were probably already at the cliff, waiting for her. The three of them met there every Sunday afternoon.

She pushed the door shut. "Uncle William, if this is about James—"

"James Fitzhugh is betrothed to Lucy Carlisle. Or have you both forgotten that?"

"Uncle William! Everyone in the county knows

that James is trying to end the betrothal. He doesn't want to marry Lucy."

"Of course he doesn't want to marry her; he wants to marry her money!"

"You're not being fair! James had no say in the matter. His father and Mr. Carlisle were the ones who negotiated the betrothal. James is being forced to marry Lucy."

"Bah!"

"It's true! He told me so!"

"And I suppose you're gullible enough to believe everything that young whippersnapper tells you?"

Regina felt herself growing defensive. "Whatever else you think of James, he is not a liar."

William's face turned dark. "You had better by God hope he's a liar, young lady, because he's been telling everyone at the Boar's Head that he's had his way with you!"

Her uncle's words struck Regina like a physical blow. "That's not true!" The words came out as a strangled gasp.

William placed the tip of the crop beneath her chin and tilted her head back, exposing the bruise on her neck. "Isn't it?" he asked meaningfully.

She jerked her head away. "No, it's not! I never lay with James. All I let him do was kiss me."

"I want you to stay away from him. I'll be damned if he's going to plant his bastard in your belly while he puts a ring on Lucy Carlisle's finger."

"You can't stop me from seeing him."

"Oh, I will stop you, young lady, if I have to lock you in your bedchamber until your wedding day."

"Then you might as well throw away the key,

since that day is not likely to arrive during my lifetime."

"Stop exaggerating, Regina. You've already had three offers of marriage. Three *good* offers."

She groaned. How Uncle William could consider any of the offers she'd received to be good was beyond her.

"I gave Charles Toliver leave to call on you."

Regina's eyes widened in horror.

William clasped his hands behind his back and resumed pacing. "I know you don't care for young Toliver, but I insist that you seriously reconsider his marriage proposal."

"I'd rather throw myself in the river!"

"Toliver stands to inherit a sizable fortune," William continued, ignoring her outburst. "He will be able to provide well for you and for any children you may have with him. You'll want for nothing. Furthermore, the young man's eagerness will weigh heavily in your favor when we negotiate the prenuptial contract, something you must consider since you have no dowry."

Regina bristled at the unwelcome reminder that she didn't have a shilling to her name. When her father died, he had left Summerhill to her brother, Richard. Preferring the amusements of London to the responsibility of running a plantation, Richard had promptly turned Summerhill over to Uncle William to manage during his absence and had booked passage on the next vessel bound for England, taking with him the five hundred pounds that was to have gone to her.

She did not need to ask what had become of the money. Letters of indebtedness, attesting to her brother's lack of business acumen and his fondness for the gaming tables, had arrived at Summerhill with distressing regularity during Richard's two-year absence. Not only had he squandered her inheritance, more than once he had come dangerously close to losing his own as well.

"Since my happiness obviously means so little to you," she said, masking her hurt with sarcasm, "why don't you just put me on the auction block and sell me to the highest bidder?"

"Which is precisely what your brother is likely to do," William shot back. "I've kept my word and said nothing to Richard about the proposals, but now that he is home, he is bound to learn of them. When he does, he will take it upon himself to select a husband for you, and his choice will more likely benefit his purse than your well-being."

"I won't marry Charles Toliver. I don't care what you say, I would prefer to be locked in my bedchamber until the day I *die* rather than marry that pompous ass."

"I refuse to continue this discussion with you, Regina. You will do as you are told. Now, go. I have work to do."

Anger and an overwhelming sense of hopelessness swelled inside her, building to dangerous proportions until it threatened to explode if she didn't get out of there fast. Tears stung her eyes, but she refused to give her uncle the satisfaction of seeing her cry. Audibly releasing her breath in a hiss of frustration, she whirled around, yanked open the door, and nearly collided with her brother.

Richard Langley stood in the hall, surprise frozen on his face and his hand extended toward the door knob that had just been jerked out of his grasp. His hair was still damp from a recent washing and his white shirt, open at the neck, contrasted startlingly with the tan he had acquired at sea.

Regina glared at him through a haze of angry tears.

He had changed little in two years. If anything, he had grown more handsome. Like her, he had black hair and dark eyes and their grandmother's high cheekbones. Her throat constricted. As children, they had been allies, two black sheep in a flock of pale English faces. Yet Richard had betrayed her. Had he not frittered away her inheritance, she would not now be facing the joyless prospect of marriage to a man she couldn't abide.

Richard grinned at her. "Hello, Reggie."

His face swam before her eyes as whatever joy she had felt at having him home quickly evaporated. She shoved past him and bolted out of the house, leaving Richard to stare after her in bewilderment.

Richard gave his head a sharp shake as if to clear it, then sauntered into the study. Crossing the room to a side table, he removed the stopper from a clear flint decanter and poured himself a glass of port. "What's wrong with her?"

"It's a personal matter," William said brusquely. He pulled himself up to his full height. "I was beginning to think you intended to sleep all day. You should have gone to church with the rest of the family."

Richard brushed off his uncle with a wave of his hand. "That's not your concern."

William's hand crashed down on his desk with a force that caused his nephew to drop his drink. The glass hit the floor and shattered. "And Summerhill?" William demanded, the distended vein in his neck visibly beating. "Is that, too, none of my concern?"

Richard shot William a glance of annoyance. "That's right," he said coolly.

The two men eyed each other evenly for one long, deadly moment. William was the first to break the silence. "Caroline and I will be gone at the end of the month," he bit out.

Richard turned away from his uncle and calmly poured himself another drink. "Good."

Chapter 2

Beatrice Randolph and Izzy Fitzhugh were waiting for Regina at their usual meeting place in a secluded glade overlooking the Potomac. At the top of a cliff and surrounded by trees and honeysuckle vines, the spot provided a shaded lookout from where the girls could watch for ships sailing upriver. Two were anchored offshore today, the *Lady Anne* and the *Triumph*, merchant ships that Richard Langley owned and that had set sail from London forty-seven days before.

"You certainly took long enough," Izzy said. "We were beginning to think you'd forgotten about us."

Regina collapsed on the soft grass. Her face was flushed from running, and the remaining pins had fallen from her hair, causing it to spill down her back in a mass of unruly curls. She struggled to catch her breath.

"Why were you so late?" Beatrice asked. In the sunlight, her red hair and freckles gleamed like polished copper. "We were worried about you. And why didn't you tell us Richard was home? We've been sitting up here for the past hour, trying to catch a glimpse of him."

Regina had forgotten that before Richard's departure for England, Beatrice had fancied herself in love with him, even though the object of her affections had never so much as acknowledged her existence. *Wait until you're a little older*, she had told the then fifteen-year-old Beatrice, trying to soothe her friend's bruised feelings. She had hoped that Bea would have outgrown her hopeless attraction to Richard by now.

Apparently, she hadn't.

"Uncle William was lecturing me on the benefits of considering Charles Toliver's marriage proposal," she said, trying to avoid discussing Richard.

"King George's codpiece! I hope you didn't accept!" Izzy looked aghast. In spite of the fact that she was petite and fragile looking, like a tiny gray barn mouse, Izzy Fitzhugh could swear like a seaman, and often did, to the chagrin of her poor mother who was trying desperately to turn her into a lady.

"Of course I didn't accept. I'd rather stay a spinster than marry *any* Toliver."

"There isn't anyone in the parish I'd want to marry," Izzy said. "All the eligible men are either too old or too far in debt, or else they look like toads."

"Reggie would marry your cousin James if he wasn't already betrothed to Lucy Carlisle. You should see her make eyes at him." Beatrice batted her copper-tipped lashes.

Regina plucked a fistful of grass and flung it at her. "I don't do that!"

"Oh, yes, you do! I also saw the two of you leave the ballroom together at our party last week."

"We went for a walk!"

"Did he kiss you?"

Izzy snorted. "If I know James, he did a lot more than just kiss her."

Regina felt her face grow hot as she remembered what Uncle William had said James was telling everyone at the Boar's Head. She didn't want to believe it. She was more inclined to believe that Uncle William had told her that simply to drive a wedge between James and her, and she refused to let that happen. But until she heard from James's own lips that it wasn't true, there would be a niggling doubt in the back of her mind. "Yes, he kissed me."

Beatrice wrapped her arms around herself. "I wish someone would kiss me," she said, puckering her mouth. "Someone handsome and strong and—"

"Who doesn't slobber," Izzy finished for her.

"Or have false teeth," Beatrice added.

Regina choked back a giggle. "You two are awful."

Izzy, who was sitting closest to the edge of the cliff, peered through the foliage that shielded them from view below.

"Can you see anything?" Beatrice asked.

Regina suspected that what Bea really meant was *Can you see Richard?* She felt a twinge of guilt.

Although she didn't know exactly why she had snubbed her brother, her anger with him had been building for the past two years. Richard's inheritance had made him one of the wealthiest young men on the Northern Neck, if not in all of Virginia. Had Summerhill gone to her instead of to him, she would now have her choice of suitors. She would have James.

She fell back on the grass and lay staring up at the cloudless sky. The sun was warm on her face and the air was heavy with the scent of honeysuckle. James Fitzhugh's fair face and tall slender body flickered through her thoughts, softening the edge of her anger. "I wouldn't mind if James did more than kiss me," she said drowsily. She rolled onto her stomach and propped her chin on her hand. Bits of grass clung to her hair. "I wouldn't mind letting him make love to me."

Izzy turned back to the others. "I told you he did more than just kiss her."

Regina glanced from one friend to the other, wondering from whom she could get the greatest reaction. "He touched my breasts."

Izzy gaped at her. "Under your clothes?"

"Uh-huh."

Beatrice's eyes widened. "What did it feel like?"

A dreamy look crept over Regina's face. She smiled secretively. "It felt wonderful."

"That's only because you're smitten with him," Izzy said. "It wouldn't feel so good if Charles Toliver did it."

"I wouldn't even *let* Charles touch me. Just thinking about it makes my skin crawl."

"If your uncle makes you marry him," Izzy said, "you'll *have* to let him touch you."

Regina snorted. "I'll drown myself first."

"You could always make him get a mistress," Beatrice said.

"Jenny Robinson told me it hurts like hell a woman's first time," Izzy said. "She said that on her wedding night, she bled so much that George wanted to send for a doctor. The only reason he didn't was because she cried and begged him not to."

"That's because it wasn't her blood, silly!" Regina could not believe her friend believed that old yarn. "She took a pig's bladder filled with blood to bed with her, because she didn't want George to know she wasn't a virgin."

"I didn't know Jenny wasn't a virgin when she got married."

"She wasn't," Regina said.

A dreamy looked passed over Beatrice's face. "I wonder if Richard will notice me now that I'm older. Reggie, you must invite me to dinner while he's home. I'll *make* him notice me. I'll spill my food in his lap if I have to."

An idea suddenly occurred to Regina. She sat up. "Why don't you come this evening? Both of you. You can stay the night. The Sandhursts will be there, and the Lees, and God only knows who else. It'll be fun."

Beatrice's cheeks were pinker than usual. Even though her parents had declined their invitation, no one had said *she* couldn't attend. "I'd love to! Izzy, say you'll come too!"

Izzy grimaced. "Reggie, spending the evening watching every eligible bachelor in the parish fawning over you is not my idea of fun."

"Izzy! Not two minutes ago, you said there wasn't anyone in the parish you'd even want to marry. Besides, if you didn't always behave as if you might faint whenever men pay you any attention, they'd be willing to spend more time with *you*."

"That's not fair! I've just never met a man I felt comfortable talking to."

"Well, this could be your lucky night."

"I don't know . . ."

"Then it's settled. As soon as we get back to the house, I'll send one of the servants to tell your mothers you'll be spending the night at Summerhill."

Izzy peered through the bushes again. Suddenly she beckoned them with a wave of her hand. "Come here, and look at this."

Regina and Beatrice crawled to the edge of the embankment and peered through the foliage. Directly below them, seamen and slaves and indentured servants were loading wagons with crates and burlap bags that had been taken off the ships. A half-dozen dirty, raggedly dressed men had alighted from a small boat that had been rowed to the shore, and were being escorted toward the warehouses by men armed with muskets. A guard placed the stock of his musket in the middle of one man's back and shoved, causing the man to stumble.

"Those must be the indentures Uncle William was talking about," Regina said in a low voice. "He's hoping one of them knows how to read and write so he can press him into service as a tutor for the boys."

Beatrice shuddered. "I wouldn't want any of them in my house. I'll wager they haven't bathed sinced they left England. They probably stink."

"Not *them*," Izzy said impatiently. "Over *there*."

They looked in the direction that Izzy pointed.

At the auction block, where the slaves brought over from Africa were bought and sold, a man—a white man—was chained to one of the upright posts that supported the raised wooden platform.

He was shoeless and shirtless. His black hair hung in his eyes and down around his shoulders, and a thick black beard covered the lower half of his face. His hands were raised above his head and chained to the post, and his feet were manacled. He looked like a wild man.

And he was huge.

Regina's pulse quickened. He was taller and more muscular than any man she had ever seen. Even from this distance, she could make out the well-defined muscles of his broad chest and his powerful arms. She wondered if he was a nine-year indenture, a convict, sent to the colonies to do his time at hard labor. If so, he would probably be sent on to Barbados. The planters on the Northern Neck seldom took on nine-year indentures. They were too much trouble and required too much supervision.

"My God, look at those muscles!" Beatrice whispered. "I'll bet he could snap you in two with his bare hands."

"It's too bad the Bartlett sisters aren't here," Izzy said. "Can't you just see them looking him over the way they did with those slaves last month?"

"I'll never forget the expression on that one man's face when Frances felt his privates!" Regina said, and all three girls choked back fits of giggles.

"That's what we should do," Izzy ventured. "We should go down there and pretend one of us wants to buy his term of indenture."

Regina shuddered, although the reaction was less from distaste than from anticipation. The

thought of seeing the man up close was more tit-
illating than she wanted to admit.

Beatrice shuddered. "I'm not sure I even *want* to
get close to him. He looks crazy."

"If one of us goes down there, we all go," Regina
said. "We're in this together."

"I'll go," Beatrice reluctantly agreed. "But I'm
not going up to him, and I'm certainly not going
to touch him."

"Regina can touch him," Izzy teased. "Then,
when she's old and gray and married to Charles
Toliver, she can tell her grandchildren that she once
touched a real man."

Without warning, the man suddenly lifted his
head and stared straight in their direction.

The girls sucked in their breaths and pulled back
from the edge of the cliff.

"My God!" Beatrice squeaked when she finally
remembered her voice. "He saw us!"

"He didn't see us," Izzy assured her. "There
were too many branches in the way." She tugged
at Regina's sleeve. "Are we going down there, or
not?"

Mounting excitement had brightened Regina's
eyes and heightened the color in her cheeks. "I'll
go down there," she whispered, her pulse racing.
"But I refuse to touch his privates."

The girls made their way through the throng of
workers and planters who had come down to the
docks to meet the ships. The smells of fish and tobacco and unwashed bodies hung in the air. Although they were well upstream from the ocean,
Regina could taste the salt spray on her lips. She
saw several of Summerhill's slaves rolling hogs-

heads of rum toward the warehouses, their dark bodies glistening with sweat from the heat and from the exertion of pushing the huge wooden barrels. A half-dozen pigs, scrawny from the long voyage, escaped from their makeshift pen and ran, squealing and grunting, through the crowd.

The girls stopped a few feet away from the man in irons. If Regina had thought he looked dangerous before, up close he looked positively satanic. His black hair was matted, and beneath his thick beard, his face was lean and swarthy, with hawklike features. He was a giant, well over six feet, with the widest chest that she had ever seen on a man. His arms and shoulders bulged with muscle, and there wasn't an ounce of fat beneath his sunbronzed skin to soften the well-defined contours.

A tendril of fear snaked up Regina's spine, and she began to feel an overwhelming urge to turn and run as far away from there as she could get.

Coward!

She pressed her lips together. The man was chained, she reminded herself. He couldn't possibly hurt her. And after today, she would probably never see him again. Even if he wasn't sent to Barbados, the slaves and indentures who worked in the tobacco fields never set foot anywhere near the house.

"Go on," Izzy whispered in her ear. "Do it."

Regina shot her a startled glance. "Me! I thought we were in this together."

"We are. But *you* are the one who is pretending to buy his term of indenture."

She didn't remember agreeing to act on her own. "All right. But if you leave me, I'll never forgive you."

Beatrice gripped Izzy's arm. "We'll be right behind you."

"Careful there! Out of the way!" a man called out, and they scampered out of the way as a wagon rumbled past them, the large spoked wheels splattering them with sand and gravel.

Regina took a deep breath to steady herself, then started forward. She couldn't believe she had let Bea and Izzy talk her into doing this, yet she could not deny that she wanted to see the prisoner as badly as they did. Eventually, her curiosity would have gotten the best of her.

As she neared the man, her footsteps slowed. She glanced over her shoulder to make sure her friends had not abandoned her, then turned back to the man.

If he knew she was there, he gave no sign. He was staring toward the warehouse, his brows drawn together and his forehead creased as if he was brooding about something. *Or was planning someone's demise,* she thought uneasily. From where she stood, she could see his profile and was surprised to see that his features weren't as harsh as they had appeared from a distance. His nose was aquiline and his cheekbones high. Elegant, she mused. She might even go so far as to say they were aristocratic. Shaved and bathed, the man would look human.

Almost.

She suppressed a shudder. There was something about him that attracted and repelled her at the same time. Something indefinable, yet unmistakable. Like the scent of danger.

Behind her, Izzy whispered impatiently, "Go!"

Her heart pounding mercilessly, she folded her

arms over her chest. "Well, well, what have we here?" she said, careful to avoid the man's gaze. She knew if she looked him in the eye she was liable to panic and run. She nervously moistened her lips. "He certainly looks strong enough. Don't you agree?" She glanced back over her shoulder at Izzy and Beatrice, who were both struggling to keep straight faces.

This was easier than she had expected. She wondered what it would be like to actually purchase an indenture. Surely it couldn't be that difficult. Uncle William did it all the time. She turned her attention back to the man. "Straight bones. Good muscles. No doubt, he could clear several acres a day by himself," she said with an air of bored indifference. She feigned a frown. "Of course, the size of him could be a problem. He probably eats enough to feed an army of men."

Behind her, she heard a muffled giggle.

An uncertain laugh rose in her own throat, and she choked it back. "I wonder how much Mr. Langley wants for him," she mused aloud. "Of course, he will need new clothes. The ones he is wearing now aren't fit for—"

The words died in her throat.

She had inadvertently allowed her eyes to travel upward, and now she froze, her startled gaze trapped in his like a rabbit in a snare.

His eyes, wide-set and intelligent, were a startling shade of blue, and were fringed with the longest black lashes she had ever seen.

And they glittered with a hatred so intense it chilled Regina's blood.

She unwittingly took a step backward. Her heart pounded so loudly she was certain the man could hear it. Never in her life had she seen such loathing in anyone's eyes, or felt the pulse of such primitive, consuming rage.

"Reggie!"

She glanced behind her to find Beatrice motioning frantically, a worried expression on her face. Something had happened, but Regina didn't know what. She shifted uneasily. Izzy was nowhere to be seen. Suddenly Beatrice pivoted and ran, disappearing into the crowd.

Regina fought back a rising sense of alarm. "Blast you, Beatrice Randolph! Wait for me!"

Forgetting about the prisoner, she whirled around and came up hard against a black frock coat topped by a white cleric's collar and a broad face rigid with righteous indignation.

She gasped. "Father Tidewell!"

Chapter 3

Adam Burke was not comforted by what he saw. Entire shipments of cargo had been recorded as lost at sea, cargo on which Richard Langley had realized a handsome profit. Either the books had been deliberately doctored, or William Langley and his nephew suffered a deplorable lack of communication.

He closed the journal and looked around him at the office William Langley kept in one of the warehouses on the waterfront. Used strictly for business, it offered little in the way of comfort. Bookshelves along one wall held ledgers and journals bound in dark leather, as well as several law books and crates of documents. Because the sturdy timber-framed building was originally intended for storage, the interior had never been finished for use as an office, and sunlight filtered between the weathered wood planks that formed the exterior walls.

The single desk, at which he now sat, and two ladder-back chairs were the room's only furnishings. Tall sash windows had been opened to admit cooling breezes from the river, making the high-ceiling room surprisingly pleasant in the humid summer afternoon. But winter was going to be another matter entirely. With neither a fireplace nor a stove, he wondered how the elder Langley kept the office warm.

He leaned back in his chair and watched Richard Langley pace the length of the room like a restless cat, and he felt only contempt for him. In the past two years, he had watched the younger Langley squander a sizable fortune in London's most exclusive gaming halls. Ordinarily, he would have paid Langley scant attention, but since he did business with him, he had his own interests to protect. Langley had once gambled away a shipment of tobacco that his own office had already sold on consignment. The buyer was not amused.

It was the last time Langley made that mistake.

It was not, however, the last time that he lost his shirt at faro. It would have been an easy matter for Adam to just sit back and watch him, fully deserving of his fate, lose everything he owned. It proved to be even easier to step in and rescue him—for a price. A price that Richard still did not seem to fully grasp, yet which he had been all too willing to pay at the time.

"I want to see the real books, Langley, not just the ones your uncle maintains for the king's tax collectors."

Richard stopped pacing. "What do you mean?"

"I purchased five hundred bushels of wheat from you last year. There isn't a single entry in this journal to substantiate that purchase."

"Perhaps it's in another one." Richard's voice rose in frustration. "I've never gotten involved in Uncle William's bookkeeping. I don't know how he figures his entries."

"Perhaps it's time you learned."

Richard's face reddened. "Listen here, Burke. My uncle is allowing you access to the books, but don't get the idea that you can start telling me how to run my business."

Adam pushed back his chair and stood up. He stood a head taller than Richard and was fully aware of the intimidating effect his greater height had on the other man. He was not disappointed. Although Richard's expression did not change, he took an unconscious step backward.

"I'm afraid you have the situation reversed, Langley," he said. "*I* am allowing you and your uncle to remain at Summerhill and work for *me*." He paused, then added meaningfully, "For now."

The color drained from Richard's face before returning in a rush. "Go to hell," he muttered.

Adam raised dark eyebrows in barely concealed amusement. "In good time. Today, however, we need to take inventory of the warehouses. In the morning, we'll ride out and survey the property."

Richard's jaw knotted as he struggled to get his temper under control. The calm he had displayed earlier in his uncle's study was gone, and he felt like a spring that had been wound too tightly. "You won't get away with this, Burke," he ground out between clenched teeth. "I'll get Summerhill back if it's the last thing I do."

Adam eyed Richard evenly, allowing nothing of what he was thinking to show in his expression. He extended a hand toward the door. "The inventory?"

His nostrils flaring, Richard marched to the bookshelves and snatched up one of the leather-bound volumes. "Let's get on with it then," he said curtly. He went to the door and yanked it open, then abruptly stopped. He swore aloud.

Curious, Adam peered out the window.

A portly priest, the sunlight glinting off his nearly bald pate, was marching toward the building at a determined pace with an obviously reluctant young lady in tow, although at the moment the word "lady" wasn't what came to mind. There was a look of outright rebellion on her face that was evident even from a distance.

"Who is she?" Adam asked.

"My sister," Richard bit out. "God only knows what Regina has done this time." He stepped outside and descended the steps. "Father Tidewell, what brings you here?"

So this is Langley's younger sister, Adam thought, studying the girl with renewed interest as the priest brought her to an abrupt halt before her brother. She was not pretty, not by conventional standards. Her cheekbones were too high and her mouth too full to be considered fashionable, but with her black hair tumbling around her shoulders and her dark eyes smoldering with anger, she was attractive in a sultry, exotic way seldom seen outside the foreign quarter of London. There was a definite family resemblance between the two. Adam could not help wondering if Regina Langley's reputation suffered as much in Virginia as her brother's did in England.

Father Tidewell fought to catch his breath. "I regret to inform you, sir, that I caught Miss Regina tormenting the prisoner you have chained to the auction block."

Richard stared at her in disbelief. "You were doing *what?*"

"Richard, why are you here? I thought you were at the house with Uncle—"

"Answer me!"

"We didn't mean any harm. It was only a jest."

"A jest!" Father Tidewell fairly shrieked the words, causing Regina to wince. "I must say, Mr. Langley, your coming home is an answer to my prayers. There is no telling what might have become of this poor child had you stayed away much longer. The good Lord knows your uncle has done his best, but he has proven himself far too lax in matters of discipline. Your sister's morals have suffered terribly during your absence. I pray to God it's not too late to turn the girl around and set her on the path to salvation. It won't be easy, I assure you, but she is young yet, and her soul is malleable."

Regina could not stop the retort that rose to her lips. "Last week you said women didn't have souls," she muttered resentfully.

Father Tidewell stiffened, and for a second Regina thought she might have gone too far. Although she neither liked nor respected the priest, he wielded a great deal of power in the parish, and she knew it would be foolish to offend him.

Richard hurried to smooth over Regina's blunder. "Thank you for coming to me with this matter, Father. I will deal with my sister accordingly."

At the window, Adam felt a reluctant smile tug at the corners of his mouth. The girl had a quick tongue and an even quicker temper. He did not doubt that she gave her family a great deal of trouble. He also suspected that Regina Langley was accustomed to getting what she wanted, no matter who she hurt in the process. If so, it would be a trait she shared with her elder brother.

A smug look passed over the priest's face. "You should also know, sir, that Miss Regina has been seeing far too much of young Mr. Fitzhugh, a deplorable situation under any circumstances, but especially so in this instance considering the gentleman in question is betrothed to another. During this morning's mass, the two of them were flirting outrageously. 'Tis a miracle the young man has not yet gotten her with child."

Regina jerked her arm out of the priest's grasp. "Why, you . . . you—"

"Reggie, don't say it," Richard cautioned sharply.

Father Tidewell folded his hands on top of his broad stomach. "I hope, my child, you will have seen the error of your ways before next Sunday's service and will have the good grace to repent. Otherwise, you leave me no choice but to reprimand you before the entire parish."

Regina's eyes narrowed dangerously. "Hypocrytical old goat!" she finished.

Shock registered on the priest's face. He took a sudden step backward.

"Regina, that will be enough!"

Regina glared at her brother. With an angry toss of her head, she pivoted and started to walk away, but Richard caught her arm, foiling her escape. "Father Tidewell, I apologize for my sister. I promise you, her behavior will not go unpunished."

"Richard, let go of me!"

Giving neither his sister nor the priest a chance to say another word, Richard hauled Regina up the stairs and into the office, slamming the door after them. He spun her around to face him. "What in the hell was that all about?"

Regina shook off Richard's hand and tried to smooth the wrinkles from her dress with several angry swipes. "There's no need for you to get so lathered up, Richard. Father Tidewell merely jumped to conclusions."

"Why were you taunting McLean?"

"I wasn't doing anything—"

"Answer me, damn it!"

"We were just pretending to want to buy his term. We didn't do anything wrong, and we certainly didn't hurt anyone."

Richard's brows lifted questioningly. "We?"

For a fleeting second, Regina considered revealing the identity of her accomplices so she wouldn't have to bear the penalty alone, then decided against it since telling wasn't likely to result in a lessening of her own punishment.

"I-I mean . . . I. I just wanted a closer look at him."

"What has gotten into you? Reggie, he is a convicted murderer!"

"I-I didn't know—"

"Where is your head? Damn it, the man is not in irons because he filched a loaf of bread!" A look of disgust passed over Richard's face. "What am I going to do with you? I'm beginning to believe that everything Father Tidewell said about the way you behaved while I was away is true."

Regina clenched her fists. "Don't you dare start preaching to me, Richard Langley! You are both fine ones to talk, you with your escapades in London and Father Tidewell spending his Saturday nights in the upstairs room at the Boar's Head with John Towson's wife!"

Richard faltered as curiosity momentarily distracted him from his anger. "How would you know about that?"

Regina rolled her eyes in disgust. She plunked her fists on her hips. " 'Cause Saturday's me night off, mate, so for a couple o' pence I lets the good Father and his doxy use me bed o'er the public room."

"Regina!"

At her brother's shocked expression, she sighed and continued wearily, "Oh, Richard, don't be such a ninny. You've been gone two years. I haven't. I know everything there is to know about everyone in this county. I know who's bedding whom, who's about to have a child that might not be her husband's, who lost money on last year's tobacco crop, and who beats his wife. And if you'd stayed home instead of running off to London to trifle away my dowry, you might know those things, too."

The sudden stiffening of Richard's shoulders told Adam that the girl had struck a nerve. He also knew that sooner or later Richard was going to have to tell her—tell all his relatives—that he had "trifled away" far more than his sister's marriage portion. While he had no sympathy for Richard Langley, he could not deny that the man was in an unenviable position. He cleared his throat. "If you'll pardon me, I'll leave you two to discuss this matter in private."

Regina gasped and her gaze riveted on him. Horror and embarrassment consumed her face in a bright surge of color. Until now, she hadn't the faintest idea that anyone else was in the room. He was standing only a few feet away, yet she had been so caught up in defending herself against Richard's accusations that she hadn't even noticed him. Why hadn't Richard warned her? Why hadn't *he* spoken up sooner instead of standing there listening to the heated exchange between Richard and herself? She gaped at him, unable to move, as he crossed the room toward them.

He was probably the handsomest man she had ever seen. His features were cleanly chiseled and nicely balanced, and there was an air of authority and restrained power evident in his self-assured stride and in the confident set of his wide shoulders that made Regina's knees suddenly feel as if they might give out on her. His dark coffee-colored jacket and pale fawn breeches hugged his tall, well-proportioned figure without a wrinkle, attesting to both the skill and costliness of his tailor. Like her brother, he eschewed the curled wig that was rapidly gaining in popularity among the colony's landed gentry and wore his dark hair long and unpowdered and tied back from his face.

He also was regarding her with a blatantly appraising look that made her feel as if she were ten years old.

If it were possible for her face to turn an even deeper shade of red, it did.

She snapped her mouth shut.

Adam took the inventory book from Richard before turning his hazel eyes on her. He studied her for a moment, his compelling gaze dropping to linger on the mark on her neck for several seconds before returning to capture hers in a piercing look that sliced right through her defenses.

A knowing, almost insolent smile, touched his

lips. He inclined his head. "Miss Langley," he said, his deep, utterly masculine voice as seductively addicting as Aunt Caroline's apple brandy. He turned and left the office without looking back, and Regina winced as the door closed behind him with a definitive *click*.

For several seconds, Regina couldn't move. She couldn't even breathe. She'd only had that feeling once before, when she was twelve and had fallen out of the grand old oak tree in front of the house and landed on her back. The fall had knocked the wind out of her and left her feeling stunned and disoriented.

He had hazel eyes.

She groaned inwardly. Of all the stupid, idiotic things she could have done! Why hadn't she made certain they were alone before she opened fire on Richard with her angry words? Between her lack of discretion and Father Tidewell's castigating tirade there was no telling what was going through the stranger's mind. On second thought, she could guess all too well what was going through his mind. The suggestive look he had given her spoke volumes.

She suddenly felt as if she might be ill.

Richard dragged his fingers through his hair and resumed his agitated pacing. "So that's what this is about," he muttered. "Your blasted dowry."

"I-I don't know. I hadn't really given it much thought until now. Maybe it is about my *blasted* dowry. Or rather, my lack of one. Thanks to you, Richard Langley, Uncle William is making me receive Charles Toliver's attentions."

Hazel. A dark, rich mahogany shot through with flecks of gold.

"Charles Toliver!" Richard had stopped pacing, and now he was staring at her in undisguised disbelief. "Good God! What must William be thinking? Charles Toliver?" He started to laugh.

Annoyed that her brother found her predicament amusing, Regina glowered at him. "I won't marry him. I'll run away first."

"Don't be ridiculous."

"I mean it, Richard. If Uncle William says I have to marry him, I'll—"

"Enough said, Reggie. I'll speak to Uncle William."

Caught off guard by his unexpected compliance, she eyed him warily. "You will?"

"I will. I promise. On one condition: I want you to stay away from James Fitzhugh."

Regina expelled her breath in a sigh of annoyance and started to turn away, but Richard caught her arm and yanked her against him.

"Ow! Richard, you're . . . hurting . . ." The words died in her throat.

The light in his eyes had turned hard and unrelenting, and for the first time in her life, Regina realized that there was a side to her brother that she had never seen before. A dark, dangerous side that made her uneasy. His hand tightened on her arm, and when he spoke, his voice held a threat. "I'm not playing games, Reggie. Keep away from James."

Regina drew a shaky breath, but she refused to be cowed. "And if I don't?" she asked defiantly.

Richard's eyes narrowed until they were dark slits in his tanned face. "Don't test me, Regina. I have enough problems right now without you causing me more. If you disobey me, I swear I will give you cause to regret it."

Beatrice and Izzy pounced on Regina the instant she emerged from the warehouse. "Are you all right?" Izzy asked. "We could heard Richard shouting at you. He sounded furious."

Regina flashed her a resentful look. "No thanks to you two. Fine friends you are, abandoning me like that."

"I tried to warn you that Father Tidewell was coming, but I couldn't get your attention until it was too late," Beatrice said. She hesitated, then asked in a small voice, "Did you tell Richard we were involved?"

"Don't worry," Regina retorted, her pride still smarting. "Richard thinks you're as sweet and innocent as a baby." *If he thinks of you at all*, she added silently. She wondered how Beatrice would take to the news that her beloved Richard was not as wonderful as she seemed to think he was. Her brother, Regina decided, was downright boorish. "Come on. Let's go back to the house."

"Who was that man we saw coming out of your uncle's office?" Izzy asked as they started toward the sandy trail that led up the embankment. "I've never seen him around here before."

Remembering the insinuating look he had given her, Regina felt her face color with embarrassment. "I don't know. He's not a local."

"He's so handsome," Izzy said. "I wouldn't mind letting someone like *that* make love to me. Next to him, James looks like a skinny little boy."

Regina flashed her a sharp look. The unnerving thing about Izzy's observation was that it coincided with a disconcertingly similar one that was coursing through her own thoughts. While the stranger did not have the same massive appearance as the prisoner down on the docks, he nonetheless cut a powerful, athletic figure that his tailored clothes did little to disguise. Izzy was right: In comparison, James looked positively frail.

"I doubt that Reggie even paid him much notice," Beatrice said. "James is the only man she has eyes—" Suddenly, she stopped. "I don't have anything to wear to dinner tonight, and I can't wear *this*! It has grass stains on it!"

Dear God, was he coming to dinner?

He couldn't be, Regina thought frantically. It had never occurred to her that he might be among the guests Richard had invited to Summerhill. How was she going to face him after what had happened this afternoon? She had certainly made a memorable first impression. A memorably *horrible* first impression. How could she even bear to be in the same room with him, knowing what he must be thinking about her?

He has hazel eyes. Beautiful, gold-flecked hazel eyes.

"Reggie, you're not listening to me! I don't have anything to wear!"

"Don't worry. When one of the servants goes to tell your mothers where you'll be, he can bring back something for you to wear." She was beginning to wish she hadn't invited her friends to dinner. With them there, *she* couldn't very well back out. Besides, she might need both Beatrice and Izzy to vouch for her whereabouts later tonight, when she sneaked out to meet James.

After what had happened today, Richard would probably welcome her absence, which was all the more reason for her to put in an appearance at dinner, if only to spite him. Besides, if she feigned a headache and retired early, Aunt Caroline was likely to look in on her later, something she absolutely could not allow to happen.

"I think I'll put up my hair," Izzy said, out of breath from climbing the embankment. She lifted her hair with one hand and piled it on top of her head. "It makes me look older, don't you think? I have to look perfect, in case *he* is at your house for dinner tonight. King George's codpiece! I think I might faint if he notices me!"

Regina eyed her warily. "If you do, I'll never invite you to another dinner party."

"Reggie, may I borrow your pearl ear bobs?" Beatrice asked.

Regina looked from one girl to the other and shook her head in exaggerated incredulity. "I don't believe you two! A person would think you'd never seen a man before, with the way you're both behaving."

"No worse than you behave when you're with James," Beatrice reminded her, and batted her eyelashes.

"She's right," Izzy said. "You were that way with Robert Beauchamp and Harry Lee, too. Now it's our turn to act silly and addlepated." She blushed, and for the first time Regina realized that, as long as she wasn't swearing, Izzy was quite pretty in a dainty, feminine way that made men want to jump to her aid like besotted knights rescuing a fair damsel. Izzy sighed wistfully. "I wonder what color eyes he has?" she mused aloud.

Hazel, Regina thought, and she felt an unfamiliar twinge of jealousy.

Chapter 4

The big red brick house at Summerhill contained three full floors and an attic. The reception and sitting rooms, the formal dining room, and Uncle William's study were on the main floor. Bedchambers for the adults and guests were upstairs, while the children and servants slept on the lower, ground-floor level. The kitchen and laundry were located away from the main house, a necessary precaution since the kitchen had already burned down twice in the eighteen years since the house was built.

During the raw coastal winters, Regina would give anything to have one of the upstairs rooms with a fireplace, but in the warmer months, the ground-floor bedchambers with their two-foot thick walls and stone slab floors were the coolest rooms in the house.

Sleeping downstairs also made it easier for her to sneak out at night since she didn't have to contend with loose floorboards or squeaky stairs. It was exactly thirty-two steps from her bedroom to the side door that led out to the kitchen.

She'd counted them.

The girls were in Regina's bedroom. The dresses

and stockings and chemises they had worn earlier in the day lay scattered about the room—on the bed, draped across a chair, on the floor—wherever the girls happened to drop them. Izzy, who was waiting for her gown to be ironed, was sitting in her shift in the middle of the bed, rummaging through a small wooden jewel chest, and Regina was helping Beatrice pin up her hair.

"You don't have to do anything," Regina said as she pushed the last hairpin into her friend's up-swept tresses. "I'll stuff a quilt under the covers so it will appear as if I'm asleep." She stood back to survey her handiwork. Brushed up off her neck and coiled around her head, Beatrice's hair gleamed like a copper crown. The pale peach of her gown reflected in her cheeks, making them glow with delicate color.

"But what if you get caught?" Beatrice asked.

Instead of deterring her, the possibility of getting caught made sneaking out to see James all the more exciting. Regina wondered if he would try to touch her under her clothes, just as he had at the Randolphs's party. In the dream she wove and embroidered in her thoughts, she saw him kissing her, touching her, and a delicious warmth surged through her limbs. She envisioned herself, breathless from his kisses, lifting her gaze to his—

The face before her shifted and changed, and suddenly it wasn't James's clear blue eyes she was staring into, but dark, gold-flecked hazel ones that silently mocked her.

Startled, she shoved the image out of her mind. "I haven't gotten caught yet," she said, an unintended edge to her voice. "I just don't want to take any chances."

Beatrice eyed Regina wistfully in the looking glass on the dressing table. "I'm so jealous. I wish there was someone waiting for *me* down at the mill."

Izzy glanced up from the jewel box. "It wouldn't do you any good. You'd be too scared to sneak out to meet him."

"I would not!" Beatrice frowned. "Well, maybe a little."

"All you two have to do is say that I never left the house," Regina continued. "And that's only if someone questions you about it."

"Just be certain you're back before morning," Izzy warned. "I don't want to have to explain to your aunt why you're not in your bed."

"Don't worry. I'll only be gone a few hours." Regina tugged impatiently on the bodice of her pale yellow gown and turned sideways to get a better look in the mirror. She frowned. The dress just didn't look quite right. She didn't know why she suddenly disliked it; it had always been one of her favorite gowns. Muttering an oath under her breath, she reached behind her and began undoing the buttons.

Beatrice turned around to stare at her in dismay. "Are you changing *again?*"

"I don't like the way this one looks," Regina said.

"It looks *fine.*"

"I want to look special."

Beatrice batted her lashes. "For James?"

"Of course, for James." Regina turned her back to Beatrice. "Help me with these buttons."

Beatrice sighed. "I don't know why you're going to all this trouble," she said, undoing the last six buttons. "By the time you see him, it's going to be dark. He won't even be able to see what you're wearing."

Regina pulled the dress off over her head.

Izzy snorted. "He won't even *care* what she's wearing. All James is concerned with is how easily it comes off."

"Very funny," Regina said dryly.

Beatrice choked on a giggle.

Tossing the dress across the bed, Regina took another gown from the deep chest, shook it out, and held it up in front of her. It was pale blue, not a particularly flattering color for her, but James liked it because of the way it hugged her body, making her waist look tiny and her bosom generous.

Expelling her breath in annoyance, she refolded the gown and laid it aside.

"What, pray tell, is wrong with *that* one?" Izzy asked.

"It's blue," Regina said. "I can't wear blue. *Your* gown is blue."

Izzy rolled her eyes and flopped onto her back on the bed. "King George's codpiece," she muttered.

Suddenly Regina froze.

The red silk.

Her hand trembled as she touched a tentative finger to a whisper-soft crimson fold.

It had only been finished the week before. She was supposed to save it for the dance Uncle William was going to be hosting after the tobacco harvest. If she wore it now, she wouldn't have a new gown to wear to the party.

Taking the gown from the chest, she crossed the

room to stand before the mirror. She held the gown in front of her.

Her pulse quickened.

It was the most grown-up gown she had ever owned. There was nothing the least bit demure or childish about it. It was red. It was unabashedly sensuous. It was provocative.

It was perfect.

Her gaze met Beatrice's in the mirror. She lifted her brows in a mute question.

Beatrice's eyes widened. "It's beautiful!"

Izzy rolled onto her side and propped her head on her hand. "I've never seen you wear that one before."

"I haven't." Regina began to put on the gown. "Did you see anything in the jewel box you want to borrow?" she asked as she pulled the gown over her head. The voluminous skirt muffled her voice.

"I get to wear your pearl ear bobs," Beatrice reminded her.

Izzy stared at the red gown with envy. "I don't know . . . maybe the ivory comb. You still have to help me put up my hair—oh, Reggie, I wonder if that man is going to be there. Do you think he'll notice me?"

Regina's head emerged from the red silk. "If he doesn't notice you, he's a fool," she said grudgingly. She didn't know why it should disturb her that Izzy had taken an interest in the handsome stranger. It wasn't as if she held any claim on the man herself. After all, she had James.

And tonight she was going to sneak out to meet him.

The bedroom door swung open and a tall, white-haired black woman entered the room, carrying a cornflower-blue dress edged with froths of white lace neatly draped over one arm. Her dark brown skin was flushed from the heat, and perspiration had beaded across her upper lip. She stopped short just inside the door, and her eyes narrowed in disapproval. "Just what do you think you're doing, child? Miss Caroline's going to have a hissy fit when she sees you in that gown!"

"Bertie, thank goodness you're here. I need you to go get my red kid slippers back from Jethro. He can put the new soles on them another time."

The old woman looked appalled. "I most certainly will not! Now you get yourself out of that dress 'fore you muss it up."

Izzy scrambled off the bed and took the freshly ironed blue dress Bertie held out to her.

"I'm not going to ruin the gown," Regina protested. "I'm only going to wear it to dinner."

"You're going to take it off, is what you're going to do. That dress is for the harvest party, and well you know it."

"Bertie!"

Bertie plunked her hands on her hips. "You take that dress off right this minute, or I'm going to go fetch me a willow switch, and then we'll see just how fast you can move."

Regina expelled her breath in a sigh of frustration. It just wasn't fair. The red silk was the prettiest gown she had. If she couldn't wear it tonight, she might as well go to dinner naked. Nothing else she owned was even remotely suitable.

She reluctantly took off the gown and handed it over to Bertie.

Bertie shook her head in annoyance. "I don't know what I'm going to do with you, child," she said as she returned the gown to the trunk. "I swear, you're more stubborn than your daddy ever was." She closed the trunk lid. The brass hinges squeaked. She retrieved the yellow dress from the bed where Regina had tossed it.

Regina grimaced.

"I'm not going to stand for no nonsense, so you can just wipe that look off your face. Now be a good girl and put this on. Miss Caroline's got enough to worry about right now without you makin' trouble for her."

Something in Bertie's voice caught Regina's attention. "What's wrong with Aunt Caroline?"

Bertie pressed the yellow gown into Regina's hands. "Don't you fret none about Miss Caroline. There's nothing wrong with your aunt that seven months and a little more help from you won't cure."

Seven months? Was Aunt Caroline with child again?

Bertie picked some of the clothes that had been left lying on the floor. "You girls had better get a move-on if you don't want to miss dinner," she said on her way out of the room.

Regina fought back an overwhelming urge to run after Bertie. She didn't know why, but she felt a sudden need to hold on to the old woman, to hold on to all that was familiar and safe and dear to her.

"Hurry up, Reggie," Izzy said, dressing quickly. The blue gown settled gracefully about her slender hips. "Get dressed or we're going to be late."

Regina snapped out of her daze. Forget the red slippers, she thought. Her black ones would do nicely. Flinging the yellow gown across the bed, she marched to the trunk and opened it. She took out the red silk.

Izzy frowned. "What are you doing?"

"Getting dressed."

By the time the girls went upstairs, the rest of the guests had already gathered in the large oak-paneled reception room. Regina saw Uncle William carry tankards of ale to Captain Morrison of the *Lady Anne* and Captain Bebe of the *Triumph*. Aunt Caroline, seated in a wing-backed chair and fanning herself with a delicate fan of carved ivory, was engaged in conversation with Leticia Sandhurst and Nancy Lee, wives of two of the local planters. Aunt Caroline didn't look the least bit ill, Regina thought. A little tired, perhaps, but not ill. Regina wondered again if her aunt was all right.

Seeing her, Caroline Langley smiled and inclined her head in Regina's direction, and Regina breathed a little easier. Either Aunt Caroline hadn't noticed that she was wearing the new red gown, or she had no objections.

Suddenly, Izzy grabbed her arm and whispered in her ear, "There he is!"

Regina's heart missed a beat.

He was standing beside the fireplace, one elbow propped casually on the mantel and a glass of port in his hand, his brow furrowed as he listened to an exchange between Roger Washington and John Sandhurst. He had changed into an elegant, impeccably cut garnet-colored jacket, white shirt, white cravat, white brocade waistcoat, and close-fitting white breeches that flattered his athletic build. His dark hair was drawn back from his lean, tanned face, and his long fingers cradled the wine glass seductively.

Elation at seeing him again, then anger at the insolent way he had looked at her earlier, surged through Regina in rapid succession, only to be followed immediately by an intense longing as the image of those strong hands untying the laces of her corset flickered through her mind.

It hurt to breathe. Regina stared at him, unable to move, every nerve in her body tingling as she imagined him loosening her corset and brushing his hands against her skin—

"He's so *handsome*," Izzy whispered, startling her out of her reverie.

Shaken, Regina shoved the provocative image aside. Good Lord, what was wrong with her? She was in love with James, for crying out loud!

"I don't see Richard anywhere," Beatrice said.

Regina scanned the room. "Don't worry. He'll be here. Richard's not one to miss . . . a . . . meal." She broke off and choked back an oath as she spotted Charles Toliver by the window with Edward Lee, Thomas Parke, and a man she didn't recognize. Clad in a full-skirted coat of teal green velvet and matching velvet breeches, Charles was more appropriately attired for a Christmas ball than a summer dinner. Framed by the cascading curls of his long white wig, his face was flushed from the heat.

Regina pivoted around, turning her back toward him. "Charles is here," she whispered frantically.

Beatrice strained her neck. "Where?"

"Bea, don't stare! He'll see you."

Beatrice ducked. "He already saw me," she groaned.

"He's coming this way," Izzy said. "What's he

doing here? Did your uncle invite him?"

"Probably," Regina muttered. *Damn, damn, damn!* Richard had promised he would speak to Uncle William. *He'd promised!*

"Here he is," Beatrice whispered.

Regina turned and feigned surprise. "Charles! I didn't expect to see you tonight."

Charles extended his hand toward her. "Did you think I would miss an opportunity to spend an evening in such lovely company?"

Swearing silently, Regina pasted a smile on her face and clasped her hands demurely in front of her, deftly avoiding taking Charles's outstretched hand. "You must stop flattering me, Charles, or I shall get a swelled head."

"Nonsense. A beautiful woman deserves to be flattered. And pampered. And spoiled." He grasped her elbow and led her toward the window. "Come. Let me introduce you to everyone."

"Charles, please. This really isn't necessary."

"Of course it is. I want to show you off."

Through sheer dint of will, Regina managed not to shudder. She glanced over her shoulder to see if Beatrice and Izzy were following only to see them giggle and wave to her as if sending her off to her fate. She shot them both scathing looks.

"Regina, I believe you already know Lee and Parke."

Regina turned her head back to the front.

"It's good to see you again, Reggie," Edward Lee said, his tone and the look in his eyes as he regarded her reminding her that he had never quite forgiven her for snubbing her in favor of his younger brother. "Harry sends his regards."

Regina pretended not to notice the resentment in

Edward's voice. "Tell Harry I'm looking forward to seeing him at the harvest dance." *Damn Bea and Izzy for abandoning me again!*

"If Harry thinks to keep you to himself this year, he'd best think again," Thomas Parke said. "You must save at least one dance for me."

"I don't think you'll have to worry about Harry," Edward said dryly. "Reggie has her eye on Fitzhugh these days."

Battling a revealing blush, Regina smiled sweetly. "Of course I'll save a dance for you, Tom. I promise."

"This is Miles Jordan," Charles said. "He's newly arrived from London to survey some property for Adam Burke. Mr. Jordan, Regina Langley."

Adam Burke? The name sounded familiar, but Regina couldn't remember where she had heard it before. Extricating her elbow from Charles's possessive hold, she extended her hand toward the small, wiry man. "I'm pleased to meet you, sir."

The man had sharp critical eyes with which he sized her up much as one would assess a piece of land. He shook her hand. "I must say, the pleasure is mine, Miss Langley."

Regina's brow furrowed. "I don't recall ever meeting your Mr. Burke. Is he from around here?"

"London," Miles Jordan said. "And yes, you have met him. This afternoon, down at the waterfront. He's over there, talking with your friends."

Regina felt a twinge of panic as she wondered just how much Miles Jordan knew about this afternoon's escapade and whether he had told anyone else. She followed his gaze toward the fireplace just in time to see the handsome stranger bow and lift Izzy's outstretched hand to his lips, and it was all she could do to keep her envy from showing on her face. *He* was Adam Burke?

Izzy, you've let him hover over your hand long enough!

She forced herself to think rationally. She should be glad that Izzy had captured Adam Burke's attention. If he was preoccupied with Izzy, then he would be less likely to dwell upon their unfortunate encounter in Uncle William's office. And Izzy seemed to be enjoying herself, so why should she begrudge her friend a little fun?

Besides, inasmuch as she hated to admit it, Izzy's criticism of her this afternoon had hurt. It wasn't the observation that men fawned over her that troubled her as much as the insinuation that she *encouraged* their fawning. While she couldn't deny that she enjoyed the attention, it made her uncomfortable to be accused, however subtly, of soliciting it.

Summoning every ounce of self-control she had, she tore her gaze away from Adam and Izzy and turned back to Miles Jordan. "You're partially right," she said with feigned detachment. "I did see Mr. Burke this afternoon, but I'm afraid we weren't formally introduced."

"Why were you at the docks?" Charles asked.

"I always go there," Regina said. She glanced nervously at Miles Jordan, but his expression revealed nothing.

"I know you do," Charles said, a note of disapproval in his voice. "But I wish you wouldn't. It's not a particularly safe place for a woman."

"Charles, you're being preposterous. It's as safe a place as any other on Summerhill. Besides, Richard was there. No harm would have come to me."

"Toliver's right," Thomas Parke said. "Ever since that slave uprising down in Hampton, none of our women are safe."

Thomas's mention of the slave uprising caught Regina's attention, but she was careful to keep her expression unreadable. It wasn't often that the men discussed anything important in front of her, and she had learned from previous experience that the least show of interest on her part was enough to make them change the subject. "It's not a topic for delicate ears," Uncle William had an annoying habit of saying.

You're too young to understand, was what she suspected he meant.

Just then, Bertie appeared in the doorway and announced dinner. Bertie started to leave, then stopped, her eyes narrowing when she saw Regina. She pursed her lips in disapproval and shook her head.

Charles crooked his elbow toward her. "Shall we?"

Regina's eyes darted around the room while her mind scrambled for some excuse not to accompany Charles to dinner, but she couldn't think of one. She saw Adam Burke escorting Izzy and Beatrice toward the doorway. Swearing silently, she fought for composure. The only thing she would accomplish by creating a scene would be to make herself look foolish. She had no choice but to accompany Charles to dinner—and endure his attentions. Swallowing her frustration, she placed her hand on his arm.

"None of us is truly safe," Edward Lee said, continuing the conversation as they made their way toward the dining room. "Although, if the truth be known, I think we have less to fear from our slaves than from the Scots. If we don't watch our backs, the troublesome bastards will stab us in our sleep."

"More arrived yesterday," Charles said. "I hope Langley has the foresight to send them on to Barbados and not let them remain here." He stepped aside and allowed Regina to pass before him through the doorway.

The dining room was the largest and most elegant room in the house. Paintings of the Langley ancestors adorned cream-colored paneled walls, while tall mirrors in gilded frames at both ends of the room reflected the light from the wall sconces and from the polished brass chandelier suspended from the middle of the deep-cove ceiling. Over the mantel was an elaborate carving of the Langley crest—a stag and a crown. Several tables had been pushed together to form one long table, and were covered with white damask cloths and set with Sevres porcelain. French doors thrown open to the stone terrace that stretched across the back of the house admitted cooling breezes from the river.

Charles pulled out a chair for Regina. Several places down, on the opposite side of the table, Adam Burke did the same for Izzy.

"As it stands, there are already far too many foreigners in the Northern Neck," Lee said, continuing the conversation as the diners helped themselves to a first course that consisted of roasted and boiled West Indian green turtle, corner dishes of turtle in a variety of rich sauces, and turtle soup laced with Madeira. "Unfortunately the laws don't allow us to send them back to Scotland when their terms of indenture are ended. We must either give them land and set them free or find them guilty of enough transgressions that we can prolong their terms indefinitely. Personally, I'd like to deport them all."

Regina immediately thought of the prisoner chained to the auction block. Something her brother had said tugged at her memory. She frowned, trying to remember what it was.

Suddenly it struck her. McLean. Richard had called him McLean. So he too was a Scot. She wasn't surprised. In the past two years, more Scottish than English convicts had been transported to Virginia.

She remembered the look of hatred in his eyes and involuntarily shuddered.

Against her better judgment, Regina succumbed to temptation and looked at Adam Burke only to find his amber-flecked eyes fixed on her. Her heart missed a beat. How long had he been watching her? He lifted his glass toward her in a silent toast, then, his gaze never leaving hers, he brought the glass to his lips and took a swallow of wine.

"Would you care for more soup?" Charles asked.

Startled, Regina jumped and tore her gaze away from Adam. She shook her head. "No, thank you. I'm fine."

Charles allowed his gaze to travel where Regina's had just been. "It would appear that Miss Fitzhugh has found herself an admirer."

Her heart beating unnaturally fast, Regina cast Adam and Izzy a glance from beneath her lashes. Adam had turned back to Izzy and was smiling over something she had just said. "I think you might be right," Regina said to Charles, her voice strained. Unaccountably agitated, she took a large swallow of wine.

One of the slaves removed Regina's soup bowl, but she barely noticed the girl. The wine she was consuming did little to ease the churning in her stomach. This was going to be a painfully long evening. She couldn't wait to escape.

From where he sat, Adam could discreetly observe Regina while appearing to be lavishing attention on her friend. While Isabel Fitzhugh was a pleasant-enough dinner companion, he felt no attraction to her. It was Regina Langley who piqued his interest.

She was wearing her hair up, which mildly surprised him, since he had assumed she would want to hide the mark her lover had left on her neck. On the other hand, he was quickly reaching the conclusion that Regina Langley was the type of woman who would flaunt her sexual conquests much as another woman might flaunt a trinket.

Elise had been one of those women.

Annoyed by the unwelcome intrusion, Adam shoved the memory from his thoughts and concentrated on Regina. He looked at the two wigged men seated on either side of her. One man appeared to be taking great pains to ignore her, while the other one—the one who resembled a peacock in full spread—could not take his eyes off her. *Two lovers?* Adam mused. *One jilted and one hopeful?*

He allowed his gaze to travel slowly downward to rest on the mark that marred her slender throat, then farther, over her shapely shoulders and the seductive curve of her breast. He wondered how difficult it would be to get her into his bed.

Without warning, she turned her head and looked straight at him. The look in her eyes was openly challenging. Defiant.

Edward Lee's voice abruptly intruded on Adam's thoughts. "You're a landowner now, Mr. Burke. Where do you stand?"

Adam put down his glass. He had been half-listening to the discussion as he observed Regina, and had hoped to avoid voicing his opinion; he knew it was not likely to be a popular one. He had learned a long time ago that people who indulged in such discussions were usually defensive and unyielding in their views. They weren't interested in weighing all sides of an argument, merely in forcing their opinions upon others. "I don't see it as an issue."

Edward snorted. "Nonsense. Sooner or later, you're going to have to decide whether to invest in slaves or hire indentured servants. You must have given the matter some consideration."

Adam did not miss the note of antagonism in the other man's voice, and he knew Lee was trying to goad him into a fight. "Personally," he said steadily, fixing Lee in his sights, "I believe that any form of human bondage for profit is unethical."

As Adam spoke, the other diners fell silent and there was a stir of uneasiness that ran the length of the table.

From the head of the table, Richard erupted into a drunken laugh, a hard laugh, accompanied by a thin smile that did not extend to his eyes. "Mr. Burke is new to the colony. He'll soon learn that the entertainment of lofty ideals is a luxury best left to schoolboys and dreamers."

Regina could tell from Richard's reddened face, and the look of meanness in his eyes, that he had probably spent the last several hours down at the Boar's Head getting drunk. She glanced from him to Adam. Had she been mistaken in assuming they were friends? This afternoon at the warehouse, she had been too angry to even ask what business Adam had been conducting with her brother.

And what of Miles Jordan? What role did he play in all this? She looked down the table at him, but his expression revealed nothing.

At the far end of the table, Uncle William was moody and withdrawn. Aunt Caroline placed a comforting hand over his and smiled reassuringly, and Regina wondered if something had happened. Perhaps they were worried about the baby—if there was a baby. Aunt Caroline was no longer young, and she had not been able to carry a child to term since she had given birth to Timmy.

"I'm not so enamored of slavery myself," John Sandhurst said, oblivious to the Negro girl who was clearing away his dishes, "but for reasons that have nothing to do with ethics. For one thing, it's damned expensive. A slave owner is condemned to feeding the lazy bastards from cradle to grave."

Leticia Sandhurst giggled nervously. "John chafes at the expense of feeding his own family," she joked, and laughter rippled around the table.

Charles leaned toward Regina. "I've spoken with your uncle. He's granted me leave to call on you."

Regina pulled away, trying to hear what Richard was saying. "What do you intend to do, Burke? Free all the slaves?" Richard was glowering hard at Adam, and she had the uneasy feeling that she had missed something.

"I'm already obligated for this Sunday," Charles said in a low voice. "But I'm free the next. We'll go riding."

"Fine," Regina muttered. She wished Charles would be quiet.

"I'm curious about something," Captain Bebe said. "I always thought the prospect of owning land was a powerful incentive toward working off one's term of indenture. Does the system not work the way it was intended?"

"It works all too well," Edward Lee retorted. "Give me a good English indenture, and I'll be satisfied. But, for chrissake, keep those bloody Scots off our land before they destroy what we've built here."

Richard scowled at Adam. "Tell Burke that. He's the one who wants to change the way we've always done things."

Caroline Langley abruptly stood up. "Excuse me," she muttered, and hurried from the room. Uneasy, Regina watched her aunt leave. She placed her napkin on the table and pushed back her chair, then hesitated when she saw Uncle William rise and follow his wife.

Charles covered Regina's hand with his. "Is your aunt ill?" he whispered.

Regina extracted her hand. "I don't know."

"Correct me if I'm mistaken," Captain Bebe said. "I thought most Virginians were Royalists who supported the Jacobite cause."

"He's right," Beatrice said, glancing shyly at Richard. "St. John's Parish was founded by Sco—"

"Yes, we supported the Jacobite cause," Richard snapped, cutting Beatrice short. "And as soon as Charles took the throne, he promptly forgot just who his supporters were."

Regina slipped away from the table. She followed her aunt and uncle upstairs. The door to their bedchamber was closed, but she could hear their voices. Stepping carefully so as not to make a sound, she crossed the hall and pressed her ear to the door.

"Oh, William, surely there is something we can do," Caroline said. Her voice sounded agitated.

"There's nothing. Richard is fully within his rights."

"But what of Regina? What is going to become of her?"

"I've given Charles Toliver my blessings. I'm praying Regina will come to her senses and accept his offer. He can give her a secure future, which is more than I can say of the other young man she's seen fit to set her heart on."

Regina's stomach knotted. How could Uncle William do this to her, knowing how she felt about Charles? She would not marry him. She absolutely would not!

Too angry to listen to another word, Regina tiptoed downstairs.

She returned to the dining room, but did not go in. She stood in the doorway and stared at Charles, battling the urge to scream. The man repulsed her. She couldn't imagine spending the rest of her life with him. Why couldn't he be James? Or even Harry Lee? Or . . .

She looked at Adam. He was leaning toward Izzy, and the two were laughing as if over a shared secret. They looked so perfect together—Adam strong and sophisticated, and Izzy delicate and pretty—that Regina was gripped with envy.

Swallowing the knot that had lodged in her throat, she turned and fled.

Chapter 5

The night air, warm and damp, was made heavier by the sound of cicadas and the groan of the water wheel. Lightning flickered through the trees, followed by the distant rumble of thunder. Regina leaned against the cool stone wall of the mill and scratched absently at the bug bites she had gotten in the crook of her elbow when she had sprawled on the grass that afternoon with Beatrice and Izzy.

Where was James? She had been waiting for hours, ever since she left the dinner. She was beginning to wonder if he was going to meet her as he'd promised.

Damn him! Damn Charles Toliver! Damn Uncle William! Damn Richard! Damn all men!

Damn that Adam Burke! An image of Adam and Izzy kept repeating itself in her mind, fueling her jealousy and her hurt. Adam Burke had appeared to be genuinely interested in Izzy. She should have been glad, but she wasn't. No matter how hard she tried, she could not make herself feel genuinely happy for Izzy.

The wine she had drunk at dinner was giving her a headache. She pulled the restraining pins from her hair and rubbed her temples with her fingers.

She fidgeted. She was beginning to doubt the wisdom of coming here. It was not the first time she'd met James here at the stone mill late at night. But tonight was different somehow. There was a charge in the air, although whether it was from the impending thunderstorm or from something else, she didn't know. Through the canopy of leaves she saw lightning flicker again, closer this time.

Impatience gave way to mounting unease. Could something have happened to James? Her mind raced. She thought of her uncle's "talk" with him at the church. She wished she knew what Uncle William had said to him. She thought of the rumor James had supposedly told everyone at the Boar's Head.

She couldn't believe James would brag that he'd bedded her. He wouldn't do such a thing, she tried to convince herself. Uncle William was obviously attempting to discourage her from seeing him.

She remembered the conversation she had overheard between her aunt and uncle, and her anger gelled into an overwheming sense of helplessness. Why couldn't Uncle William let her choose her own husband? She was beginning to feel as if her life was controlled and manipulated by Uncle William and Richard and Charles Toliver.

And she was beginning to hate them all for it.

Somewhere in the night a twig snapped, jolting Regina out of her thoughts. She flattened her back to the stone wall and listened. Her heart pounded. She was tempted to call out James's name, but held back. Suppose it wasn't him? What if someone else was out there in the darkness? There had been no Indians in the area since she was a child. She thought of the slave rebellion down in Hampton, but she couldn't imagine anything like that happening in St. John's Parish. Then she thought of the prisoner down on the docks. She shuddered. If *he* were to escape, they would all be in danger.

Blast you, James Fitzhugh! Where are you?

Suddenly a face emerged from the darkness. Regina barely choked back a scream. "James!"

James took her in his arms and kissed her. His mouth was hot on hers, and his breath smelled like ale. Regina pulled her face away, angry that James had been out drinking while she was waiting for him. "Where have you been?" she demanded.

"The Carlisles came to dinner." James's words were slurred slightly. "I spent the evening trying to avoid Lucy's doting."

"You were at the Boar's Head."

"Reggie, I couldn't get away sooner, I swear. Everyone would have been suspicious."

"Don't lie. You reek of ale and tobacco smoke."

"All right, all right," James conceded, his tone cajoling. "I went to the Boar's Head. I didn't stay long. Forgive me?" He lowered his head to hers.

Regina squirmed out of James's arms. She marched several paces away, then rounded on him. "Uncle William told me you've been telling everyone at the Boar's Head that you've lain with me."

"I have not!"

"Then what have you been telling everyone about us?"

"Nothing."

"I don't believe you."

James was starting to get annoyed. "Regina, I love you. Why would I say anything to hurt you?"

Regina had no answer for that. All she knew was that she was hurt and angry and didn't know who to believe.

Going to her, James took her by the arms and pulled her toward him. Still angry, she started to pull away, but he refused to release her. "I want to marry you."

Regina stopped struggling in his arms. This was the first time James had mentioned getting married. She eyed him warily. "You do?"

"I want you to be my wife."

Regina shook her head. "But what of Lucy? And your father? We can't get married here. I know Richard won't allow it, and without his approval, Father Tidewell certainly won't perform the ceremony."

James eased her gown off her shoulders. He kissed her shoulders. "Then we'll go somewhere else."

"Where?" The feel of James's lips on her skin distracted her, making it hard to think.

"We'll go to Philadelphia. I have relations there. We can stay with them until I can get us a place of our own."

"Philadelphia! But that's so far away. It will take weeks to get there!"

James eased her to the ground. The grass was wet with dew. "I'll take care of it."

Regina gazed up at his face, not knowing what to say, or even what to think. Above him, lightning illuminated the night sky. Everything was happening so fast. "We'll need money."

James lowered his body atop hers and took her in his arms. "Don't worry. I said I'll take care of it." He kissed her neck, and the soft swells of her breasts above her bodice.

"James, we can't just run away. We need to make plans."

He covered her mouth with his, silencing her protest.

Usually, Regina would have welcomed his kiss, and would gladly have lost herself in it, but tonight was different. Even this newfound knowledge that James wanted to marry her paled in comparison to the realization that he had offered her a way out of marrying Charles. She did not want to take the chance that the opportunity would slip through her fingers. Finally she shoved James away and sat up. "We need to make plans," she repeated, the urgency she felt unmistakable in her voice. "There's no time to waste. Uncle William has given Charles Toliver leave to call on me."

James raked his fingers through his hair in frustration. "I don't want to talk about your family, and I certainly don't want to talk about Toliver."

"Nor do I! But Uncle William is—"

"I want to make love to you."

Regina suddenly felt uneasy. Although she wanted desperately to lie with James, she couldn't shake the nagging fear that once she relented, he might not go through with the marriage. She didn't question his love for her, only her ability to hold onto him. "James, I-I can't," she stammered. "You promised you'd wait . . ."

Angry, James surged to his feet. "Damn it, I'm tired of playing these cat-and-mouse games with you. I'm going home."

Regina jumped up. "James, wait!"

He hesitated.

"James, I'm not playing games, I swear. I just want to wait until after we are married."

"Why? We've done everything else short of consummation. You're hardly an innocent, Regina."

James's harsh words stung. "I'm still a virgin," she said defensively.

"I'm beginning to wonder," James retorted. "It has occurred to me that the real reason you are holding out is so I won't learn the truth until it is too late."

Anger exploded in Regina's chest. "Fine. As far as I'm concerned, you just go right ahead and marry that cow, Lucy Carlisle, and live under her father's thumb for the rest of your life. See if I care. I hope you grow old and gray and miserable and . . . and . . . *fat!*"

So angry she could hardly see where she was going, she whirled around and started to storm away, but James caught up with her. He grabbed her arm. "Regina, wait. I'm sorry. I didn't mean to say those things. Please forgive me."

Regina fumed but said nothing.

James wrapped his arms around her from behind, and gently nuzzled her ear. "I am truly sorry, Reggie. I don't know what has gotten into me. I want you so much, I can't think clearly. Sometimes I feel as if I am going insane with longing for you."

Regina felt her anger start to wane. "I want you

too," she whispered. "But you promised me we would wait."

He moved his hand up over her breast. "I know. I won't force you. I swear. Please, just let me hold you."

In spite of her determination not to give in, her body began to ache with longing. If he kept touching her like that, she didn't know how much longer she could keep resisting him.

James eased her sleeves farther off her shoulders and slipped his hand beneath the silk.

A shudder rippled through Regina. She lay her head back on his shoulder and closed her eyes.

Regina ran across the yard toward the house. She had stayed out later than she had planned; it would soon be dawn. Her dress was rumpled and damp, and her hair tangled. Her mind ran rampant with the promises that James had made, and with their plans for the future. She and James were to be married! She was so excited, she felt as if she would burst. She wanted to tell somebody, anybody—Beatrice especially—about her good news, but she couldn't tell anyone. The elopement must be kept absolutely secret.

She had come dangerously close tonight to giving in to James's demands. If it hadn't started to rain, forcing them to seek shelter in the deep-set doorway of the mill house, they might have gone too far. Now that they were to be married, it was becoming more and more tempting to cast caution aside. The storm had passed, but not the gnawing ache Regina felt inside.

Glancing around to make sure no one else was

up and about, she hurried around to the back of the house and came up hard against a broad wall of muscle and silk.

Strong hands caught her by the shoulders, stopping her from reeling backward. A scream rose in her throat, then faded into a strangled gasp as the face in the darkness assumed a recognizable form.

Adam Burke!

Regina struggled to catch her breath. Adam had removed his coat and waistcoat, and his white shirt stood out in startling contrast against the dark brick wall of the house. "You frightened the wits out of me!" she admonished in a fierce whisper. "What are you doing here?"

"I went for a walk."

"In the middle of the *night?*"

Unable to rest, Adam had been thinking of her, and now his blood was running hot. He wanted her. He wanted her in his bed. He wanted to feel her naked beneath him. He knew how she would be, daring and dangerous and unprincipled, like an expensive whore. A mistress of whom he would never tire.

And he was not willing to share her.

Yet from her disheveled appearance, it was apparent that she had been with another man. His desire turned to annoyance. She might be without morals, but he refused to believe that she could throw herself away on the beruffled peacock who had hovered over her at dinner. *If not Toliver, then who?* The mysterious Mr. Fitzhugh to whom the parish priest had referred? He had a sudden irrational urge to hunt down this Mr. Fitzhugh and break every bone in his body. "I couldn't sleep," he said tersely. "Obviously, neither could you."

Anger and embarrassment welled up inside Regina. She did not need to see Adam's face clearly in the darkness to know what he was thinking. She could *feel* the tension that emanated from his body like shimmering waves of heat.

"Good night, Mr. Burke," she said icily, hoping to make it clear by her tone that she had no desire to continue this conversation. She tried to go around him, but he caught her arm, stopping her.

"Ouch! What do you think you're—"

"I'm curious about something, Miss Langley." His hushed words hovered in the cool air between them. "I've met your Mr. Toliver. Please forgive me, but I cannot fathom you going out of your way to spend time with *him*."

"Let go of me!"

"Who were you with?"

Regina tried to pull free, but his fingers tightened on her arm. His face was only inches from hers, and she could feel his gaze drilling into her. "I-I don't know what you are talking about," she stammered, suddenly feeling very small and vulnerable.

"I think you do," Adam said slowly, pulling a grass stem from her hair with his free hand. His gaze captured hers. "Let me guess. Would he perchance be this Mr. Fitzhugh whom your parish priest is worried will be your moral downfall?"

The determination in Adam's voice and the steady pressure he was exerting on her arm were undermining what remained of her confidence.

She had never met anyone quite like Adam, and she didn't know how to respond to him. She nervously moistened her lips. "Mr. Burke, I don't know who you are or why you're here, but you are overstepping the bounds of propriety."

A deep chuckle sounded in his throat. "From what I've witnessed of your behavior, Miss Langley, I'll avow you don't even know the meaning of the word."

There was something unnerving about Adam Burke that sent warning bells pealing in her head. Something dangerous. "Let go of me, or I'll scream."

Adam drew her toward him. "Does your brother know you sneak out at night to meet your lover?"

Alarm surged through her. If he were to tell Richard, would her brother believe his word or hers? Like Uncle William, Richard was prone to jumping to conclusions. Neither of them were likely to believe that she had not lain with James. If they even suspected she had lost her virginity, they were likely to force her into marriage just to prevent a scandal.

Determined not to let Adam intimidate her, she masked her fear with defiance. "As far as you or my brother or anyone else is concerned, I spent the entire night in my bed. I have two witnesses who will swear that I never left the house. Now if you will please let go—"

"*Two* witnesses?" Adam's voice was suddenly silky smooth and seductive. His breath was like a whisper on her face.

"Yes, *two*. Now unless you want me to report you for accosting me, I suggest you let go of me!"

Adam slipped an arm around her waist. "Accost

you? Ah, but who will believe such an accusation? You have *two witnesses* to the contrary. Remember?"

Regina grew fearful. Adam Burke was no callow youth she could wrap around her finger, and she was beginning to get a pretty good idea what his intentions were toward her. She tried in vain to push him away.

"Since you never left the house," he said huskily, ignoring her efforts to free herself, "you have no proof that I ever saw you. Nor do you have proof that I did this . . ."

He lowered his head to hers.

Her body went rigid with shock.

His mouth was hard and hot and demanding. Regina tried desperately to squirm out of Adam's grasp, but he refused to yield his hold on her. He coaxed her lips apart and kissed her deeply, until her head swam and her knees threatened to buckle beneath her. She could no longer think clearly. A small flame sprang to life inside her and spread until her entire body felt as if it were on fire. His hands moved down her back, pressing her tighter against him. Through her gown, she could feel the hardness of his arousal against her stomach.

The erotic invasion of her mouth, the feel of his hands on her backside, all filled her with a dizzy, intoxicated feeling that eroded her resistance. His hard-muscled thigh pressed between her legs, against that part of her that had begun to throb with a painful, unquenchable ache. She leaned deeper into his embrace, her body instinctively seeking release from the fire that felt as if it would consume her.

He moved his hands down over her hips to cup her bottom and Regina shuddered, reveling in the wonderful sensations he was arousing in her. Not even the way James touched her had ever made her feel the way she did now.

James!

The abrupt awareness of what she was doing jolted her back to reality. Summoning every ounce of strength she had, she shoved Adam away.

He released her, and she staggered backward, dazed and out of breath. Adam's face blurred before her eyes. Sputtering an oath, she drew back her hand and slapped him hard across the cheek, then turned and ran into the house.

She ran to her bedroom, not stopping until the door was safely closed behind her.

Dear God, what have I done? she silently screamed, horrified that she had let Adam touch her so intimately. How could she have betrayed James? James just revealed that he wanted to marry her, and she had nearly destroyed that chance by allowing herself to be seduced by a *stranger*.

Her hands trembling, she undressed in the dark and put on her white cotton nightgown. She could not stop shaking. She could not believe she had been so wanton as to allow a man she had not even formally met make such outrageous advances toward her. What was she trying to do? Throw away her future?

Goose bumps raised on her skin and she shivered, remembering the way Adam had touched her. His touch was skilled and purposeful, making James's caresses seem like the fumblings of an inexperienced schoolboy. Another moment of such exquisite torture, and she would have gladly surrendered her virginity to him.

And she didn't even know him!

She groaned inwardly. *Forget Adam!* she chastised herself. *Forget he ever existed. Forget him!*

She poured water from the pitcher into the basin and tried to wash away the memory of his touch, but to no avail. His kiss and the feel of his hands on her skin were burned indelibly into her memory.

Still shaking, she climbed into the bed with Beatrice and Izzy. Beatrice stirred and mumbled something unintelligible. "Move over," Regina whispered, and she did.

She lay down on the edge of the bed and pulled the sheet up to her chin. She couldn't relax. She couldn't sleep. She couldn't get Adam out of her mind.

Without question, he had the upper hand. She couldn't tell anyone what he had done to her without getting into trouble for sneaking out to see James. Both Richard and her uncle would demand an explanation as to why she left the house in the first place. Being unable to sleep and going for a walk in the middle of the night would not only sound silly, but guilty as well. She would be lucky if she got off with nothing more than a severe scolding. For now, Adam's secret—and hers—was safe.

Whenever she closed her eyes, his face loomed before her. She couldn't explain exactly what it was about him that intrigued her so. He was incredibly handsome; that she couldn't deny. But then, so was James. Yet James didn't arouse the same erotic, confusing feelings in her that Adam did. By concentrating hard, she tried to replace the image that danced before her eyes with one of James, but within seconds the wheat-blond hair darkened and blue eyes turned hazel.

She squeezed her eyes shut. *Go away!* she pleaded.

She was still wide awake when the sun came up.

Chapter 6

Adam was sitting behind the desk in William Langley's former office in the warehouse, trying to decipher the terms of a tobacco order, when the door opened, and two armed guards escorted the prisoner into the building. The chains fastened to the man's wrists and ankles clanked when he moved. Adam arranged the papers he had been going through into a neat stack on top of the desk, then he stood up. He nodded a dismissal to the guards who exchanged wary glances before leaving the room.

Adam turned his attention to the prisoner.

The prisoner's name was Duncan McLean. Unlike the other indentures, McLean had not been arrested for participating in the Jacobite rebellion, but had been transported to Virginia to serve a nine-year term of indenture for the murder of an English dragoon. He had also stirred up trouble on the Atlantic crossing by assaulting one of the crew of the *Lady Anne* a mere two days out of port. The act put him in chains for the remainder of the voyage. With a little discreet questioning, Adam had learned that the seaman Duncan had attacked had made sexual advances toward another indenture, a boy of fourteen, and refused to take *no* for an answer. Duncan McLean had been protecting the boy. The seaman was not particularly well-liked, and the assault might not have raised a brow had it not been accompanied by an unreasoning rage that left the rest of the crew members fearing for their lives. Still, the fact that McLean had risked punishment to help someone incapable of protecting himself spoke well for him in Adam's eyes.

He had bathed and shaved and was dressed in dark breeches and a shirt of coarse linen that fit him poorly, but were at least an improvement over the vermin-ridden rags he had been wearing. Yet even cleaned up, he was a formidable presence.

Duncan McLean was several inches taller than he, broader through the shoulders, and with hands the size of dinner plates. He was big, but there wasn't an ounce of fat to be seen on him. While Adam prided himself on his excellent physical condition, he knew he would be hard-pressed to win a fight with this one.

Yet, in spite of his uncommon size, there was no mistaking the intelligence in the man's blue eyes.

Eyes filled with an unforgiving, soul-chilling hatred.

Adam looked Duncan straight in the eyes. "The court records claim you murdered one Captain Lawrence Berry in cold blood. Did you?"

The man's jaw tightened. "If the law says I did, then I did." His Highland accent was thick, but not unpleasant.

"I don't want to hear what the law has to say. I want to hear what you have to say. Did you kill the man?"

Duncan was silent for several noticeable seconds before answering. "Aye," he said slowly, measuring his words, "and I'd do it again, too."

"Why?"

"That's between me and Berry."

"It's between you and me now, McLean. I'm familiar enough with the courts to know they aren't always just. I'm giving you a chance to set the record straight. As far as I'm concerned, you are merely one of a group of indentures whose terms I've purchased. You have no past; your slate is wiped clean. This is a new land, with grand possibilities for all who choose to take advantage of them. I'm not one of those landowners who extends indefinitely a man's term of indenture until he is virtually a slave. If you treat me fairly, I'll treat you fairly. Once you serve your time, you'll be a free man, with land to your name. If it should come to pass that we are unable to work together, I'll sell the balance of your term to another, giving you an opportunity for another start."

Adam could tell from the suspicion in the man's eyes that he didn't believe a word he was saying, an understandable reaction in light of the way the English were inclined to treat the Scots. Nor did he expect McLean to believe him. He merely wanted to plant the idea so it could take root and grow. In time, the Scot would trust him. He also knew that he was going to have to decide just how much he was willing to trust the indentured man. "Why did you kill Captain Berry?" he repeated.

Still McLean did not answer. Blue eyes met hazel in silent combat, in a battle Adam knew neither of them could win. He could stare at the prisoner until the day one of them died, and still not get a concession out of the man. In truth, he preferred it that way. Considering the danger inherent in the role he intended McLean to fill, he did not want someone who was easily cowed working for him.

After several minutes of pregnant silence, Adam reached a decision. He opened the desk drawer and removed a ring of keys. Going around to the front of the desk, he approached the prisoner. "I acquired Summerhill legally and by honest means. However, there are those here who do not—and will not—see it that way. I cannot be everywhere at all times." Adam knelt and unlocked the fetters around the man's ankles. "Therefore, I'm going to need someone to oversee the estate, to protect what is mine."

The chains fell away, landing on the wooden floor with a dull *thud*. Adam stood and went behind the man to unlock the manacles that bound his wrists.

He removed the manacles and took them to his desk. "The first order of business will be to get you some clothes that fit. I'm going to put you in charge of making certain the other indentures are suitably clothed. You men are going to be clearing land and building your living quarters. You'll need clothing that will withstand hard labor, and sturdy boots that will protect against snake bites. This isn't England, or Scotland for that matter. What you encounter here is likely to have venom in its bite." Adam turned to Duncan. "Do you have any family in Scotland whom you would want to join you here in the colonies?"

Surprise flickered in the Scot's eyes. He shook his head.

"As I said before," Adam continued, "you treat me fairly and I'll do the same. Give me an honest day's work, and you'll be suitably compensated. Do we understand each other?"

McLean rubbed his chafed wrists. His eyes narrowed as he regarded his employer. "Aye," he said. "That we do."

Hoping he had not misjudged Duncan McLean, Adam went to the door and opened it. He gave orders to the guards, then stood aside to allow McLean to leave. "You work for me now, McLean. Remember that. If anyone gives you any trouble, come to me."

McLean started out the door, then stopped. For several minutes, he stood there, gripping the door frame so tightly, his knuckles whitened. Finally, he squared his shoulders and took a ragged breath. "My sister was alone in the house the day the soldiers came," he said in a low, hollow voice. "Captain Berry and his men raped her. They took turns with her, doing things to her no man should ever do to a woman. When I found her, she was barely alive. Her body healed, but no' her mind. She couldna live with the shame. She hung herself."

Duncan turned his head toward Adam. The hatred in his eyes was still there, but was now tempered with sorrow. "If I could do it over, I'd still kill the man, but I'd take my time doing it. I'd make him suffer the way he made my Jenny suffer."

Adam did not speak immediately. He could not condemn the prisoner. Given the opportunity, he would have killed Lawrence Berry himself. And the nature of Berry's crime explained Duncan's violent reaction the day the seaman forced himself upon the young boy. In his mind, Duncan McLean had been reliving his sister's horror.

Had McLean been English, the case against him might never have gone to court. As it was, the principle of a man protecting his family paled beside what to many was the greater crime of a Scot killing an Englishman.

"I believe you were unfairly convicted," Adam said. "I will do everything within my power to have your sentence repealed or shortened. I can't make any promises, only that I will try."

McLean regarded Adam warily. "Why?"

Why, indeed, Adam wondered. To prove to himself that he was still—despite a brief lapse of common sense when he had allowed himself to be led by his heart instead of his head—a good judge of character? *To assuage an overwhelming need to be able to trust again?* His expression was closed. "I have my reasons."

McLean's icy gaze seemed to look right through him. "Aye, I suppose you do," he said with deliberate slowness. He paused, then added quietly, "Thank you."

After McLean had gone, Adam pulled off his neck cloth and unbuttoned the neck of his white shirt. *Damn, it's hot here!* he thought. He had already removed his coat, but the summer air was so damp and oppressive that it was like trying to breathe with one's head under water. He couldn't understand why the Virginia gentry insisted upon wearing wigs and heavy velvets and other attire more suited for London than for America. He didn't know whom they were trying to impress.

Personally, he thought they were insane.

It was one thing to dress for dinner, but he decided right then and there that for all other occasions he was going to make comfort a priority.

He was rolling up his shirtsleeves when the door opened and Miles Jordan entered the office. Closing the door behind himself, Miles addressed Adam, "I thought you were going to send the Scot on to Barbados. What made you decide to keep him?"

"It was a business decision."

Miles eyed him knowingly. "It wouldn't have anything to do with last night's dinner conversation, would it?"

"No, it would not." Adam circled his desk and draped his neck cloth across the back of his chair. "What were you able to find out?"

Miles pulled another chair up to the desk and sat down. "She's seventeen. Her mother died when she was born; her father passed away two years ago. That's when Richard inherited the plantation and a modest fortune."

Adam sat down. Placing his elbows on the desk, he steepled his fingertips and rested them against his chin. "Go on."

"She's had numerous suitors, and several offers of marriage, but none that her uncle approved of. Until now."

One dark eyebrow angled quizzically.

"Charles Toliver is actively pursuing Miss Langley's hand," Miles continued. "From what I was able to determine, the man comes from one of Virginia's founding families. He's wealthy, and he adores her. She, on the other hand, despises him."

"I see."

"William Langley is determined to see his niece betrothed to Toliver before he leaves Summerhill," Miles continued. "With no dowry, the family's fortune squandered, and Miss Langley's penchant for scandal, her chances of receiving any other suitable offers are exceedingly slim."

"Anything on Toliver?"

Miles smiled wryly. "Where shall I begin? Charles Toliver has an insatiable carnal appetite, and he's hardly discriminating about whom he takes to his bed: slaves, servants—male and female—other men's wives. He has been conducting an affair with Marion Randolph for the past two years. Apparently, the lady's husband knows nothing of the liaison. Except for an occasional dinner party getting out of hand, the Randolphs have a reputation for being respectable to a fault. Arthur Randolph is an influential member of the vestry."

Adam leaned back in his chair. That bit of intelligence could prove useful. He thought of Beatrice Randolph, with her flaming hair and freckles, and her unsuccessful attempts to attract Richard Langley's attention at dinner last night, and wondered if she knew anything of her mother's indiscretion, then decided it wasn't likely. Beatrice didn't strike him as a particularly observant young lady.

Whereas Regina, he speculated, probably allowed very little to escape her notice.

"Anything else?"

"Just one more thing," Miles said. "The Carlisle-Fitzhugh nuptials are being moved up. It would

appear that it's only a matter of weeks before Miss
Lucy's delicate condition will be apparent to all."

"Lordy, child, look what you've done to your
gown! What in heaven's name were you doing?
You've got grass stains all over it!"

Regina pulled the covers over her head to drown
out the sound of Bertie's voice, but the old woman
yanked the sheet away. "Miss Regina, you get your
bones out of that bed right this minute."

Regina's temples throbbed. She pressed her
hands over her ears and squeezed her eyes shut.
"Go away!"

Ignoring her, Bertie handed the red gown to one
of the servant girls with orders to take it out to the
kitchen. She retrieved a pale pink summer gown
from the wardrobe. "Miss Beatrice and Miss Isabel
have been up for hours, and here you are, still in
your nightdress lying abed—"

Bertie broke off suddenly and frowned. She
grabbed one of Regina's ankles and lifted her foot
so she could see it better. "Child, your feet are
filthy! I can't believe you put them dirty things in
your bed!"

"Bertie!" Regina pulled her foot free and struggled to a sitting position. She winced at the bright
sunlight that streamed in through the open window. "I went for a walk," she mumbled. "It started
raining. I took off my shoes so they wouldn't get
ruined."

Bertie snorted. "That's a likely story. You try telling that one to Miss Caroline and see if she believes
it. C'mon, now, get up so I can strip the bed and
put the sheets out to air. I swear, you're the laziest

body I know. Even Mister Richard don't sleep as late as you."

Regina groaned. She opened one eye as Beatrice and Izzy came bouncing through the doorway. They were both already dressed. To Regina's chagrin, they were *smiling*.

"You're up!" Beatrice said. "We thought you were going to sleep all day."

Regina glowered at her. "I couldn't sleep last night. You snore."

"I do not!"

Bertie shooed Regina off the bed.

Regina managed to get to her feet, but she was too tired to move. She stood in the middle of the room in her nightdress, her hair tangled and matted.

Bertie handed her the pink gown, then began removing the sheets from the bed. She gathered them up into a ball. "Get dressed and go get you some breakfast before the dishes are taken away. And wash them feet!"

The instant Bertie was gone, Beatrice pounced. "Well? Did you see James last night? What did he do?"

Regina tossed the dress across the foot of the bed and flopped down on the mattress. She grinned and stretched. Her bare feet poked out from beneath her nightdress. She wriggled her toes. "He kissed me."

Beatrice sat down on the edge of the bed. "Is that all?"

Regina regarded her through one eye. "Not exactly."

Izzy sucked in her breath. "Did he make love to you?"

"He wanted to."

"Reggie!"

Regina sat up and shoved her hair away from her face. "I didn't let him!" She paused, then added impishly, "But I wanted to."

"You'd better not!" Beatrice admonished. "Reggie, what if he gets you with child?"

"If that happens," Izzy said, "Father Tidewell will chastise you in front of the entire parish like he does Betsy Staunton."

Beatrice gaped at Izzy. "He would not! The only reason he does it to Betsy is because her father is poor. He wouldn't dare chastise Reggie in public. Richard won't stand for it."

"He didn't have any qualms about scolding her yesterday," Izzy reminded her.

Regina didn't hear them. She was no longer even thinking of James, but of Adam. The way he'd kissed her. The way he'd touched her. The way his touching her made her feel.

A delicious warmth spread through her limbs, and she felt her face grow hot.

Uneasy with the disquieting feelings that Adam aroused in her, she bounded off the bed and went over to the wash basin. She picked up her hairbrush and started working the tangles out of her hair. "Tell me what happened after I left the dining room," she said, changing the subject. "Did the men keep arguing?"

"They finally gave up when the main course was served," Beatrice said. "Where did you go? Everyone noticed when you left so suddenly. Did Charles say something to upset you?"

"Of course not. He just slobbered down my neck

all evening. I went to see if Aunt Caroline was all right."

"I think Captain Bebe is sweet on Bea," Izzy said. "He's going to take her to see the *Triumph*."

Beatrice grimaced. "He offered to show *all* of us the ship. Besides, you're a fine one to talk, with the way you hung on Adam Burke's arm all evening."

Regina held her breath. "Well, was he as wonderful as you hoped he'd be?"

"Oh, Reggie, he is so handsome, and he's intelligent. I can't believe Richard never told you about him. Your family has been doing business with him for several years."

Regina frowned as something long forgotten stirred in the far reaches of her memory. Richard had only been in control of Summerhill's business concerns for the past two years, ever since her father's death, and he had been in England most of that time. She couldn't remember him mentioning Adam's name.

So why did it sound so familiar?

"Edward tried to provoke him into an argument," Izzy continued, "but Adam refused to take the bait. It made Edward so angry, he sulked through most of dinner."

Regina found herself gritting her teeth. In her mind, she could see Adam and Izzy together, whispering intimately, enjoying each other's company. She didn't know why the thought of them together annoyed her so much. After all, she had no claim on Adam. She didn't even *like* him. He was the rudest, most arrogant man she had ever met.

And the way he'd touched her had made her body feel as if it were on fire.

"James asked me to marry him."

Regina didn't even realize she had spoken until her friends' startled "*What?*" jolted her back to reality.

Her gaze darted from one to the other. "He wants to run away and get married."

Beatrice and Izzy stared at her in disbelief. Suddenly Beatrice jumped up off the bed and squealed. "That's wonderful!"

"Shhh!" Regina glanced nervously at the door.

Beatrice's voice dropped to a whisper. "When?"

"I don't know!" Regina gripped the hairbrush with both hands. "We really didn't make plans. Soon, though. I told James we had to do something quick because Uncle William won't let go of the notion that I should marry Charles."

Izzy was eyeing her oddly. "Do you really think you should elope?"

Suddenly Regina wished she had not said anything. She didn't even know why she had blurted out her secret. If Beatrice or Izzy told *anyone*, her plans would be ruined. She nervously moistened her lips. "I can't think of any other way. Uncle William is utterly against me even seeing James, and you know how Richard feels about him. You would think Richard would have forgotten their little feud, but he hasn't."

"A little feud! Reggie, they fought a duel!"

"Over Leticia Sandhurst, for crying out loud! Good heaven's, Izzy. I can't think of anyone *less* worth getting killed over."

"Father Tidewell will have a fit of apoplexy," Beatrice said. "He might even try to have you excommunicated!"

"Oh, Bea, don't be ridiculous. Uncle William is a member of the vestry. He won't allow it."

"He'll have to pay the Church a handsome sum," Izzy said.

Regina resumed brushing her hair. "Don't worry, he will. He paid the fine for Richard's duel, didn't he?"

"Yes, but this is different."

"How?"

"I don't know," Izzy said, frustration in her voice. "It just is. Richard is . . . is . . . *a man.*"

In her heart, Regina knew Izzy was right. Uncle William might not show her the same tolerance he had for Richard. Somehow men seemed to hold women more accountable for their foibles than they did other men. Still, it was a chance she had to take. Anything was better than marrying Charles. "I'll just have to risk it," she said, "and hope for the best."

Adam crossed the yard at a leisurely pace, taking in the stark beauty of the tall brick house, its front portico shaded by a huge oak tree. Immaculately kept, the lawn was a deep emerald green and was bordered by brick walks and perennial beds. It was a solid house, built with skilled hands, and showed a quality of craftsmanship that came only at a dear price.

It would be a good place to raise a family.

William and Caroline Langley were good people, and he regretted that his purchase of Summerhill would result in their departure from the place they called home, but he felt no sympathy for William's nephew. Had he not bought the property from Richard Langley, someone else would have. Richard would not have been able to hold on to it much longer. Not with his addiction to gambling and his fondness for living beyond his means.

With its warehouses and mills and a deepwater port on the Potomac, Summerhill had the potential for being virtually self-supporting, something that would never happen as long as the plantation remained solely dependent on the cultivation of tobacco for its income.

It was no secret that tobacco wore out the land, rendering it useless in a few short years, yet he had seen no evidence of any attempts to conserve the fertility of the soil. The Langleys practiced neither crop rotation nor crop diversity. From the books that William Langley kept, it was evident that Summerhill, as with many of the large plantations along the river, did not produce enough wheat and sorghum to feed its people, but purchased most of its grain from smaller farms inland. He wanted to change that. He wanted to reduce the amount of acreage planted to tobacco and increase the production of grain and hemp and sheep and cattle.

He wanted to expand Summerhill's dockside repair facilities into a full-fledged shipbuilding operation that would produce not only ships, but ships' fittings, ropes, hardware, and other necessities.

As for the tobacco trade itself, there was much to be done to lessen the animosity between the planter who seldom felt he was being given a fair price for his crop and the merchant who complained of receiving an inferior product. He had walked in the merchant's shoes for a good twelve years. Now he would feel the pinch of the planter's.

As he neared the portico, his thoughts turned to Regina. He could not forget the way she had looked last night when she returned to the house from her rendezvous with her lover, her clothes rumpled, her hair damp and tangled. There was a wildness about her that begged to be tamed, a willfulness that challenged his sensibilities and awakened something in him that he thought had died years ago.

She reminded him of Elise.

He had been twenty-two at the time, and Elise was seventeen, the same age as Regina. Like Regina, Elise Haverly had been blessed with exotic good looks that contrasted sharply with the pale blond English definition of beauty, and which had made her stand out in a crowd. Like Regina, she had been bold and daring. Like Regina, she had refused to fit into society's mold.

He had loved her with a passion that bordered upon desperation.

And she had betrayed him.

For as long as he lived, he would never forget the night he'd found her in bed with one of the grooms.

He had sworn then that he would never again allow himself to fall in love.

He wanted Regina, but he was not in love with her. Still, when he was near her he felt alive in a way he had not felt since he had broken off his engagement to Elise.

He wondered where she would go when her aunt and uncle left Summerhill.

In the house, Adam found Richard Langley seated at the dining-room table, unshaven and uncombed, his eyes bloodshot, nursing a tankard of ale.

Casting Richard a cursory glance, he went to the

sideboard and poured himself a cup of coffee. A hearty breakfast was laid out on the sideboard for those who chose to partake of it. As with dinner the previous night, the selection was enormous. There was crispy bacon, link sausages, and paper-thin slices of ham. There was a choice of biscuits or cornbread. There were boiled eggs and baked yams and sausage gravy and grits. There was fresh butter in a blue clay crock that stayed cool to the touch no matter how hot the weather. There were jars of molasses and honey and an assortment of preserved fruits. To Adam, it was becoming apparent that, in the Langley household, appearances were everything, and the appearance of abundance was valued above all.

Forgoing breakfast, Adam took his coffee to the table and sat down.

Richard eyed him resentfully over the rim of his tankard. "I saw your man with his surveying equipment."

Adam said nothing. He looked at Richard Langley with his unkempt appearance and the self-pity that he wore like a badge of honor, and he felt only disgust. He was beginning to regret his agreement to allow Langley to remain at Summerhill.

"If you're thinking of breaking up the plantation and selling off parts of it, I'll fight you," Richard bit out. "I'll turn every planter in the colony against you. You'll never be able to make a living here. I'll ruin you; I swear I will."

Adam's eyes narrowed as he regarded the other man. "Actually, selling part of the plantation might not be a bad idea. There is plenty of land upriver that has yet to be cleared and improved. I'm certain we can reach some sort of agreement."

Richard's face turned livid. He gripped the edge of the table and half rose from his chair. "God damn you."

"It would be a way for you to regain a part of what you lost. I'm willing to negotiate."

Silence, thick and unfriendly, hung between the two men as they stared at each other across the table.

Richard slowly sat down. Uncertainty and fear flickered behind the anger in his eyes. "You are determined to humiliate me, aren't you? To make me beg for what is rightfully mine."

"I'm offering you a chance to buy back part of Summerhill."

"With what? You've taken everything I own! My land. My house. My ships. Good God, Burke! You've taken away my livelihood!"

Adam had no patience for Richard's histrionics. "You have your health and two hands," he said sharply. "You can do as others do and *work* for a living."

Richard's face darkened.

Adam took a drink of his coffee. "You are well-known and liked in the Northern Neck, Langley. You have an intimate knowledge of both tobacco production and of Westmoreland County's social structure. And, upon occasion, I've seen you make an astute business decision. With a little self-discipline, you might make something of yourself. You can either stay here and work for me, and take advantage of the opportunity to earn back a portion of Summerhill. Or you can leave at the end of the month with the rest of your family. The choice is yours."

The veins in the side of Richard's neck bulged.

He jumped to his feet so abruptly, his chair toppled over, but before he could speak, there was a loud knock at the front door. He muttered an oath under his breath, then bellowed, "Bertie, get the damn door!"

Richard glowered at Adam. He struggled to keep his temper under control. "We'll continue this discussion later, Burke."

Adam stood up. "There is nothing to discuss. I've made my offer. You can either accept my conditions or get off my land. You have until the end of the month to decide."

Men's voices coming from the foyer suddenly grew louder. Father Tidewell pushed his way past Bertie and marched into the dining room, with several prominent members of the vestry close on his heels. Father Tidewell puffed out his chest. "We wish to speak with your sister. Please summon her."

Richard frowned. "Why? What has she done now?"

From the back of the group, one of the other men said loudly, "We'll look for her ourselves!"

"You'll do no such thing," Richard retorted. "State your business or get out of my house."

Arthur Randolph moved toward the front of the group. "Where is my daughter? She spent the night here. I want to see her."

"What in the hell is this all about?" Richard demanded, trying to take control of the situation. He looked from Arthur Randolph to John Carlisle to the other men in the group.

"Someone set fire to the parsonage last night," Arthur Randolph said. "Fortunately that sudden downpour we got kept the damage to a minimum."

Richard looked incredulous. "Surely you don't think my sister had anything to do with it?"

"I do, indeed," Father Tidewell said.

"Why do you suspect Miss Langley?" Adam asked, speaking for the first time.

Arthur Randolph stiffened. "This is none of your concern."

Adam mentally sized up the man. He knew that Richard and his uncle did business with the Randolphs, and he wondered if Arthur Randolph would turn out to be a decent businessman or a thorn in his side. He also wondered if Randolph had any inkling of his wife's liaison with Charles Toliver. "Unfounded accusations have a way of turning into witch hunts," he said. "I'm sure none of you want to see that happen."

"I have every reason to suspect Miss Langley," Father Tidewell said. "I believe the fire may have been set in retaliation for the scolding I was forced to give her yesterday."

William Langley entered the room. "What scolding? What did Regina do?"

The other men parted to let William pass.

"It's not important," Richard said. "Reggie was up to her usual mischief. I've already spoken to her about it. She's promised to conduct herself more appropriately in the future."

"I would hardly call setting fire to the parsonage appropriate behavior," Father Tidewell retorted.

William gaped at him. "What?"

"Regina did not set fire to the parsonage," Richard said. "You have my word on that."

William held up his hand. "Wait just a minute.

If anyone in this room is going to accuse my niece of any crime, she deserves to be present to defend herself. Richard, go get your sister."

"Get my daughter too," Arthur Randolph said. "I'm taking her home where she belongs."

Affronted at being ordered about like one of the servants, a disgruntled look passed across Richard's face. Going to the door of the dining room, he bellowed, "Bertie! Go get Regina!"

Chapter 7

Regina knew the moment she heard Richard yell for Bertie to find her that she was in trouble. It wasn't until she and Beatrice and Izzy reached the dining room that she realized how much.

William Langley met her at the door. "Regina, these men have some questions to ask you. I want you to answer them truthfully."

Normally Uncle William's serious tone would have had little effect on her, since he tended to take everything too seriously, but the protective arm he placed around her shoulders as he led her into the room gave her cause for alarm.

She looked around the room. There were at least fifteen men present, most of them members of the vestry. She saw Adam, and hot color flooded her face. His white shirt was open at the neck, and his shirtsleeves were rolled up, exposing his tanned, muscular forearms. She remembered the way those arms had felt around her, the way he'd touched her, and a sharp, almost painful, tingling shot through her body as if she'd just been struck by lightning.

"Father, what are you doing here?" Beatrice blurted out.

"We have some questions to ask of Miss Langley," Arthur Randolph said curtly.

Feeling a little unsteady on her feet, Regina tore her gaze away from Adam and glanced at Beatrice. Bea's eyes conveyed her confusion, and concern. Regina shrugged her shoulders in an effort to express to Beatrice she had no idea what the men wanted.

She found out soon enough.

"Someone set fire to the parsonage," Father Tidewell said in a clipped, impatient tone. "What do you know of it?"

Regina nearly sighed in relief. They weren't going to question her about anything she'd done after all. They were merely looking for information about something else. She shook her head. "I didn't know anything about it. When did it happen? Was there a lot of damage?"

"Where were you last night?" Arthur Randolph demanded.

The relief Regina had felt vanished as she realized they weren't merely questioning her about the fire; *they suspected her of setting it.*

Her gaze riveted on Adam.

His expression was unreadable, but his dark hazel eyes were boring into hers with an intensity that made her squirm inwardly. *Dear God!* What had he told them about her? Did they know he had seen her sneaking back into the house in the middle of the night?

"I asked you a question," Arthur Randolph snapped. "Please answer it. Where were you last night?"

Regina jerked her gaze toward Beatrice's father. "I-I was here . . . with Bea . . . and Izzy." It wasn't entirely a lie. She had spent part of the night with them.

"All night?" Randolph asked.

Regina's heart was pounding so loudly she was certain everyone in the room could hear it. "Yes."

She held her breath, almost expecting Adam to betray her. Instead, it was Beatrice who spoke. "Father, Reggie was with Izzy and m-me all night," she said shakily.

"It's true," Izzy piped up. "We told ghost stories during the thunderstorm. I got so spooked I couldn't sleep." She cast Adam a shy glance from beneath her lashes and blushed.

"Miss Langley, you left dinner early," John Sandhurst said from the back of the room. "Where did you go?"

"I went to see if my aunt was all right," she said, glancing at Uncle William in time to see the look of surprise that crossed his face. "Surely you don't think *I* had anything to do with the fire?"

"We don't know what to think," Randolph said. "That's why we need to know where you were last night."

Beatrice sucked in her breath. "Father, I told you—"

"Where *I* was last night?" Regina interrupted. "What about *you*? Where were all of *you*?"

"Regina, watch your temper," William ordered.

"Uncle William, it's not fair! Why aren't they questioning anyone else? What about Beatrice and Izzy? Why doesn't anyone ask where *they* were?"

"Reggie!" Beatrice and Izzy cried out in unison, shock and indignation in their voices.

"How can you even suggest such a thing?" Beatrice added in a hurt whisper.

"I'm not suggesting anything. I just want to know why I'm the only one being questioned."

"We have no reason to believe that your friends would commit such a crime," Father Tidewell said.

"And what reason do you have to believe that *I* would?"

"Regina . . ." William cautioned.

Father Tidewell clasped his hands behind his back. "Need I remind you, young lady, of your shameful behavior on the docks yesterday?"

William frowned. "Exactly what did you do yesterday?"

Beatrice sucked in her breath. She cast her father a fearful glance.

"I told you, it was nothing," Richard quickly interjected. "Just a bit of childish exuberance that got out of hand. I've already taken care of it."

"Damn you, Richard, I won't be put off!" William snapped. "I want an answer, and I want it now. What did Regina do?"

"She was tormenting one of the prisoners," Father Tidewell said. "I was forced to chastise her, which I'm certain has caused her a great deal of resentment. She was quite vexed with me yesterday."

"I wasn't the only one you humiliated yesterday," Regina retorted, angry at being singled out. "What of the Stauntons? The way you dragged poor Betsy's name through the mud in church—"

"Regina, that will be enough," Richard barked, cutting her off. "Father Tidewell, my sister was here last night. We had guests. I doubt that she could have left the house without one of them taking notice. Now, if you gentlemen are finished hounding Regina, I must ask you to leave. I wish to finish my breakfast.''

"I'm satisfied that Regina didn't set the fire," Arthur Randolph said, his tone begrudging. "Although I am concerned, William, at the example she is setting for my daughter. I think these girls have been seeing far too much of each other. I intend to keep a tighter rein on Bea, and I expect you to do the same with your niece.''

William's face was dark beneath his white wig. "Believe me, Arthur, Regina's freedom will be drastically curtailed in the future.''

"Good. I'm relieved to hear it. Beatrice, get your belongings. You too, Miss Fitzhugh. I'm taking both of you home.''

"But, Father!''

"Now!''

"Bea, don't go.'' Regina cast Mr. Randolph a pleading look. "Sir, Beatrice didn't do anything wrong—''

"I'm sure she didn't, Miss Langley," Randolph said stiffly. "But I'm holding fast in my decision to limit her contact with you. I should have put my foot down after your scandalous behavior with Mr. Fitzhugh at our home last week.''

"But Mr. Randolph—''

"I have nothing more to say to you, Miss Langley. Beatrice, I'll see you and Miss Fitzhugh outside.'' Arthur Randolph pivoted and marched from the room.

William followed him. "Randolph, wait!''

Father Tidewell fixed Regina with a stern look. "I'm not so sure I agree with Mr. Randolph in regards to your innocence. You are on the road to destruction, young lady. I implore you to attend to your salvation before it's too late."

Father Tidewell left the room, followed by the men who had arrived with him.

A heavy silence hung over the dining room.

Beatrice shifted uneasily. "We'd better go. Father doesn't like to be kept waiting."

Still angry and hurt at being singled out, Regina started to follow her friends. "I'll help you get your things together."

Richard caught her arm, stopping her. His expression was menacing. "I stuck my neck out for you," he said after her friends were out of earshot. "If I find out you were lying . . ." He left the sentence unfinished, but the implied threat was clear enough.

Regina recoiled from the smell of ale that emanated from her brother. The tears she had been trying to hold back clogged her throat. "I told you the truth," she choked. "I had nothing to do with the fire at the parsonage. I almost wish I *had* set it. It simply never occurred to me."

Richard's eyes narrowed and his free hand tightened into a fist, and Regina unconsciously braced herself against the anticipated blow. Then, without warning, Richard flung her arm away from him. He turned on his heel and strode angrily from the room.

Regina slowly released her breath and rubbed her arm where Richard had grasped it. She felt as if she would be sick. She didn't know what had happened to Richard during his absence, but he wasn't the brother she remembered. In fact, during the two years he had been away, he had become downright cruel.

From where he stood near the sideboard, Adam saw Regina's slender shoulders sag, and in that instant she seemed so utterly alone that he felt a twinge of sadness for her. He cleared his throat. "A cup of coffee, Miss Langley? You look as if you could use one."

Startled, Regina jumped. She whirled around to face him, and the uncertainty that had clouded her eyes disappeared so fast that Adam almost doubted his own observations. He picked up the silver coffeepot and arched one brow quizzically.

Regina thrust out her chin and regarded him with an air of haughty disdain. "You think I'm guilty, don't you."

Her skin was pale and drawn this morning, and dark shadows ringed her eyes, attesting to a sleepless night. His gaze settled on her mouth, as soft and full and tempting as ever, and his body responded immediately to the remembered feel of her lips beneath his.

Turning back to the sideboard, he took his time refilling his own cup as he regained control of his body's reactions. "I think you're guilty of a great many things, Miss Langley," he said, his voice deceptively calm. "Setting fire to the parsonage is not one of them."

Regina's brows dipped in puzzlement. She eyed him warily. She folded her arms across her chest, not realizing how defensive the gesture seemed. "You could have told them I left the house last night, Mr. Burke. But you didn't. Why?"

Adam returned the coffeepot to its place on the matching silver tray on the sideboard. "I could ask you the same thing. I wasn't in my bed last night either, and I have even less of an alibi than you."

Uncomfortably aware that he wasn't referring to either Beatrice or Izzy, Regina fidgeted. In her family's eyes, being with James Fitzhugh was nearly as unforgivable a crime as putting a torch to Father Tidewell's living quarters. Inasmuch as she hated to admit it, Adam had done her a favor.

She lifted her chin, hiding her unease behind a mask of arrogance. "That's partially true," she quipped, giving her shoulders a quick shrug of indifference. "You *weren't* in your bed last night. But as for not having an alibi, I disagree. I'd be more than willing to tell everyone that you couldn't possibly have set the fire because when I looked out my bedchamber window, I saw you standing near the house. Or I could say I saw you strolling through the garden. No, better yet, I could say I saw you standing beneath the oak tree in the front yard, lost in thought, obviously pining away for your beloved England."

Adam chuckled and took a drink of his coffee. "You could do that," he said, regarding her with amusement. "However, I could just as easily dispel all doubts by informing everyone concerned that *you* couldn't possibly have set the fire last night since you were with me."

Regina's body went ramrod straight. It took every ounce of self-control she could summon not to lunge at him and slash his arrogant face to ribbons. She clenched her fists so tightly her nails dug into her palms. Her dark, expressive eyes snapped with anger. "I don't know who you are, Mr. Burke, or what you are doing here, but if you know what's good for you, you'll be on the first ship back to England."

She whirled around to leave, only to find her uncle standing in the doorway, regarding her with a look of displeasure. She started to go around him, but he extended his arm across the doorway, blocking her exit. "Not so fast, young lady. You have some explaining to do."

"Uncle William, I didn't do it! I wasn't anywhere near the parsonage last night. You have to believe me."

William folded his arms across his chest. "Where did you go last night when you left the dinner table?"

"I told you, I went upstairs to see if Aunt Caroline was all right. But you two were talking privately, so I didn't go in the room. I went back downstairs."

William eyed her sternly for several agonizingly long seconds before expelling his breath in a resigned sigh. "If I find out you are lying . . ."

He left the warning unfinished.

Acutely aware of Adam's gaze boring into her back, Regina fidgeted. That her uncle would question her word in front of a virtual stranger cut to the quick. "Would you like for me to repeat what you and Aunt Caroline talked about?" she retorted. "I'm not lying, but I *am* guilty of eavesdropping."

William's eyes narrowed dangerously. "That won't be necessary." He stepped aside. "You're dismissed. And one more thing: You are not to leave this house."

"Uncle William!"

William pointed to the door. "Out."

Regina took two steps, then stopped and glowered at her uncle. Tears stung her eyes. "I wish that just once you would listen to me, instead of always taking someone else's word—"

"*Out!*"

Regina snapped her mouth shut. Her head held high and her shoulders rigid, she marched from the room.

Adam's tall frame shook with silent mirth. Damn, the girl was an entertaining piece of work. He was never quite certain what to expect from her. That she lacked a conscience was not lost on him. With autumn looming on the horizon, he wouldn't mind having her to chase the chill from his bed.

It was a shame she would be leaving Summerhill soon with the rest of her family.

If Regina saw little of either her brother or her uncle during the days that followed, she saw even less of Adam Burke. He didn't join the rest of the family at dinner, although Miles Jordan was often present to entertain them with stories of his travels.

"I like that man," Aunt Caroline said one morning after a particularly enjoyable evening. "He's easy to talk to, and he doesn't put on airs."

"Unlike his employer," Regina retorted. She placed the newly polished soup tureen in the oversized cupboard, built into one wall of the dining room, and wiped her hands on her apron.

Caroline marked her place in the household ledger with one finger and glanced up. "You're not being fair, Regina," she scolded gently. "You cannot very well sit in judgment of a man with whom you're barely acquainted."

Regina wasn't inclined to be so forgiving toward Adam Burke—not after the insolent way he had touched her. "I know all I need to know. He's arrogant and overbearing and—"

"He's aloof. That doesn't make him arrogant. How many cones of sugar do we have left?"

Regina looked in the cupboard. "One white and five brown, and I still say he's arrogant."

Caroline frowned. "That won't be enough sugar to get us through the winter. I wish Richard hadn't forgotten to fill the order." She entered the number in the ledger and sprinkled sand on the page to dry the ink.

Regina had to bite her tongue to keep from reminding her aunt that forgetting to purchase sugar while he was in London was probably the least of Richard's crimes. "Aunt Caroline, exactly why is Adam Burke here?"

Caroline closed the ledger and stood up. "He's here on business. There were some . . . problems . . . with the shipping company that he is . . . correcting."

It was Caroline's hesitation as she spoke, rather than what she said, that aroused Regina's suspicions. "What kind of problems?"

"That's not a topic a young lady should be concerning herself with. Leave the dry details to the men."

"Aunt Caroline, you're hedging."

Caroline smiled. "You're right." Going to the cupboard, she returned the ledger to its place on the middle shelf, closed the door, and turned the heavy brass key in the lock. It was a ritual with which Regina was intimately familiar and which had been impressed upon her from an early age. Everything of value that the Langleys possessed was in that cupboard—the family silver, medicines, rare spices.

Regina cast her aunt a sidelong glance. "Why is

everyone being so closed-mouthed about Mr.
Burke? You won't talk about him. Uncle William
won't talk about him. And Richard simply won't
talk to anyone."

"Then perhaps you should take the hint and not
pry."

"I'm not prying; I'm merely curious."

"There's a fine line between curiosity, Regina,
and interfering in matters that don't concern you.
Now, it's a lovely day outside and not the least bit
stifling. Why don't you go sit on the terrace and
enjoy this pleasant weather while it lasts. You've
been moping around here ever since that debacle
over the fire at the parsonage."

"Uncle William forbade me to leave the house."

"I'm sure he wouldn't object to you sitting on
the terrace. Go. Enjoy yourself."

Aunt Caroline was right; the day was glorious,
and there was not a trace of the suffocating humidity that was common this time of the year. Regina
stood on the stone terrace at the back of the house,
looking out toward the Potomac. Slaves and indentures were at work clearing away the pine and ma-
ple saplings that impeded the view of the river. At
one time, all the trees had been cleared away, but
over the past few years, the woods had gradually
encroached upon the broad expanse of lawn, and
now she could barely catch a glimpse of the water
through the thick brush.

Regina frowned pensively. Uncle William had always been too busy to do anything about improv-
ing Summerhill's grounds. Nor was it a task that
Richard was likely to initiate. She couldn't help
wondering what had prompted the sudden effort

to return the plantation to its original state.

At the south edge of the lawn, where the land sloped slightly upward, Regina could see Miles Jordan, setting up his surveying equipment. Her frown deepened. Mr. Jordan was supposed to be surveying some land for Adam Burke. What was he doing on Summerhill?

Unable to contain her curiosity, Regina cast a hasty glance back at the house to be certain no one was watching, then started across the yard at a brisk walk.

Miles Jordan looked up from the telescope he was mountng on the tripod. As she neared, an enigmatic smile touched his mouth. "Good morning, Miss Langley. What brings you out here this fine day?"

Regina clasped her hands behind her back and tried to see through Miles's closed expression. She smiled back. "I could ask you the same thing, Mr. Jordan. I thought you were working for Mr. Burke. I wasn't aware that you also had been tasked with surveying Summerhill's lands."

If anything, Miles Jordan's expression became even more unreadable, a half-smile of regret complicated by a twinkle of amusement in his eyes. "I'm afraid, Miss Langley, that I'm not at liberty to discuss that matter."

Damn! How was she supposed to find out anything about Adam Burke if everyone was going to be so secretive? Then another thought occurred to her. She gave Miles a calculating look from beneath her lashes. "I suppose that also means you're not at liberty to discuss your employer either?"

"It depends upon what you want to know. And why."

Regina fought to keep her expression indifferent. She didn't want to appear to be showing too much interest in Adam Burke. "Well ... at the dinner party last week, he talked for hours to my friend, Iz—I mean, Isabel—and she was curious about him ... about who he is. What he's like." Behind her back, Regina crossed her fingers. "And, being Isabel's friend, I'm naturally concerned for her. I, too, would like to know more about this ... stranger."

"Are we, perchance, playing at matchmaking, Miss Langley?"

"Not at all. I'm merely trying to make certain that my friend doesn't set her sights on a man who might not be suitable for her."

"I see."

Something in Miles Jordan's voice set Regina's teeth on edge. She had the uncomfortable feeling that he didn't believe a word she'd said. She smiled sweetly. "Of course, if talking about him makes you feel that you're being disloyal, then I would certainly understand your reluctance to do so."

"In truth, if you were going to ask anyone about Adam, I would probably be the best person to ask. After all, I know him better than anyone. We grew up together."

Regina held her breath, wondering if he would say more.

Miles was thoughtful for a moment before continuing. "Adam had a difficult childhood. He was orphaned at an early age, and sent to live with an uncle who treated him worse than you people would dare treat your slaves. The man brutalized him ... starved him ... until he finally ran away.

By the time my father found him, he was little more than skin and bones."

"Your father *found* him?" Regina asked, surprised.

"Caught him would be a more accurate choice of words. He was stealing cabbages from our kitchen garden. My parents took him in. Adam and I have been pretty much inseparable ever since."

Regina didn't know what to say. Somehow, the picture of Adam Burke as a starving waif refused to be reconciled with the robust, self-confident man he had become. "It sounds as if Adam was very lucky to have found your family."

Miles shook his head. "No, *we* were the lucky ones."

Before Regina could ask what he meant by that, Miles changed the subject. "There seems to be a great deal of animosity here between the English and the Scots, far more than I would have thought, considering that the Virginia colonists have a long history of Royalist affiliation, even supporting the Stuart kings against Cromwell."

Regina snickered inelegantly. "What your tutor obviously failed to tell you, Mr. Jordan, is that our support of the Stuarts was rewarded by a slap in the face when Charles II regained the throne. He tried to take the entire Northern Neck away from us and give it to his friends."

One corner of Miles's mouth twitched in a barely controlled smile. "*Us*, Miss Langley? You speak as if the incident happened yesterday instead of fifty years ago."

When put that way, it did seem a bit ridiculous, but Regina didn't know how else to explain why the English colonists disliked the Scottish indentures so much, except to remind him of what everyone already knew: that the Scots were treacherous, back-stabbing thieves, just like the Irish. She gave him a sheepish grin. "We Virginians have long memories."

The tavern keeper carried two tankards of ale across the room and set them on the table. "Anything else I can get for you gentlemen?"

Adam tossed him a coin. "Not yet."

After the man left, Adam leaned back against the wall and let his gaze travel around the room. From his seat in the corner, he had a good view of the entire common room and the door. The only other patrons in the Boar's Head were two men who were rolling dice at a table across the room. It was early still, and Charles Toliver had yet to arrive. Adam wondered if the man would even respond to his request for a meeting.

"You have doubts about her innocence, don't you?" Miles Jordon asked.

Adam glanced across the table at him. "Regina lied about being at home all night," he said, his brows drawn. "But I'm not so certain she was involved in this. I think the fire was merely an unfortunate coincidence."

"Apparently, there was a similar fire less than a month ago. Someone torched Edward Lee's tobacco barn. No one has ever been arrested for the crime. If the good citizens of St. John's Parish know the identity of the culprit, they're not talking."

Adam's frown deepened as he remembered the tension that hung between Lee and Regina last night at dinner. Perhaps the thinly veiled hostility Lee had displayed toward Regina had nothing to do with being jilted after all. Still, he did not want to believe that Regina was capable of arson. He took a long drink of his ale. "I have to give you credit, Miles. You have an uncanny ability to wheedle information from the local gentry. Give us a full month here, and you'll know the sordid details of *everyone's* life."

"The gentry isn't talking, Adam, but their servants are. There's an undercurrent of discontent in this parish that rivals that in Barbados a few years ago."

"Summerhill?"

"Summerhill doesn't seem to have quite the problems the other plantations do. Of all the planters in the county, the Lees seem to have experienced the most aggravation from their servants."

"Still thinking of bringing your wife here?"

"I don't know yet. Give me a few months. I don't want to take Mary away from her family unless I'm certain she'll like it here."

The conversation lapsed for several moments, each man lost in his own thoughts. Miles was the first to break the silence. "Miss Langley asked about you today."

Adam stopped with his tankard halfway to his mouth. "What did she say?"

"She said her friend had taken a liking to you, and she wanted to be certain you were suitable."

Why, the conniving little liar, Adam thought. After the way he had kissed her, he couldn't imagine Regina doing anything but warning her friends away from him. No, it was her own curiosity she was trying to satisfy, and she wasn't being very subtle in her methods. "So what did you tell her?" he asked.

Miles chuckled. "That you were an ogre who ate naughty little girls for breakfast."

Adam gave him a pained look. "Surely you could have come up with something better than that?"

The front door to the Boar's Head opened and a half-dozen men filed into the tavern. The men were a ragtag lot, poorly dressed, with a hungry-for-a-fight look about them. The two men who were rolling dice paused in their game and watched with guarded expressions as the men crossed the room and sat down at a nearby table.

Suddenly alert, Jordan nodded toward the group. "They're Scots. The tall one with the leather jerkin is indentured to Randolph. His name's McGrath. I hear he's a troublemaker. Encourages the others to revolt against their masters. He came to Virginia on a nine-year indenture, and has been here fifteen years. His term has been extended four times."

"Were you able to find out why?"

Jordan shook his head. "Nothing specific. Only vague accusations of insubordination."

Adam studied the man closely, as well as his companions. While he chose to make his own assessment of the men, and draw his own conclusions, he had no wish to be caught by surprise.

A movement at the door caught his eye. "He's here."

Both men got to their feet as Charles Toliver approached the table. While not as colorfully clad as he had been last night at dinner, Charles was still overdressed for the climate in a heavy jacket of black brocade, tight black breeches, and an abundance of starched white lace. Sweat trickled from beneath his wig. He crossed the room and extended his hand toward Adam. His smooth smile did not extend to his eyes. "It's good to see you again, Mr. Burke. You too, Mr. Jordan."

After the men shook hands, Miles Jordan excused himself. Adam and Charles sat down. Adam motioned to the tavern keeper.

"I didn't get much of an opportunity to speak with you at dinner last night," Charles said. "I understand you're surveying some property here in Virginia."

"You understand correctly."

The tavern keeper brought two more tankards of ale to the table.

"Speculation, or do you plan to settle here?"

"I intend to stay."

"This colony is wide open for settlement," Charles said. "There is still plenty of good, fertile acreage to the north. Unfortunately, it's not well-suited for tobacco."

"I'll remember that."

A look of annoyance flickered across Charles's face. He took a hefty drink of his ale. "How long have you known the Langleys?"

Adam sensed that his short, unrevealing responses made Toliver nervous. "I've done business with them for several years."

"William's never mentioned you to me."

"He's never mentioned you either."

"I would hardly expect my name to come up in a business discussion. My association with the Langleys is purely social."

Adam did not miss the note of pique in the other man's voice. "Social connections can be invaluable," he said. He paused, then added meaningfully, "Or they can be a thorn in one's side."

Charles's pupils contracted. "I'm curious as to why you called this meeting," he said, abruptly changing the subject. "I should inform you that I'm a very busy man. I hope you don't intend to waste my time."

"I don't think you'll find what I have to say a waste of your time, Sir. Indeed, I'm certain that once you've heard me out, you will agree with me that it is in your best interests to give my proposition serious consideration."

Charles looked puzzled. "Go on."

"Does the name Arthur Randolph strike a familiar chord? Or perhaps you are better acquainted with Marion Randolph?"

Charles's face flushed a dark, angry red. "I don't know what you're talking about."

"Of course you do, Mr. Toliver. You're not a stupid man. I'm sure you are well aware of what is likely to transpire should Arthur Randolph learn that you are bedding his wife."

Charles's eyes narrowed ominously. His fist clenched and unclenched around the handle of his tankard. "What do you want from me?"

Chapter 8

"**I** love this gown," Regina said, holding the sapphire blue silk beneath her chin and twirling around in a circle.

"I do too," Caroline Langley said. "'Tis a pity I won't be able to wear it again until next summer." Taking the gown from Regina, she carefully folded it, placing sprigs of dried lavender between the layers to discourage pests, and laid it in the bottom of the leather-and-brass-bound trunk.

Regina selected another gown from the pile on the bed and started to pass it to her aunt. Without warning, Caroline clamped one hand over her mouth and bolted for the washbasin.

Regina tossed the dress aside. Her stomach rebelled in sympathetic reaction, and it was all she could do to keep her own breakfast down.

Caroline finally pulled herself upright and drew a trembling hand across her mouth. "I-I'm sorry," she said weakly.

Regina took her aunt's arm and helped her to the bed. "Are you all right? You're awfully pale."

"I'll be fine. I just need to lie down."

"I'll go get Bertie."

"No, no, please don't trouble Bertie."

"But Aunt Caroline—"

"I'll be *fine*," Caroline repeated. She lay down on the bed and closed her eyes. Her face was devoid of color, and sweat beaded across her brow.

Not knowing what else to do, Regina set the porcelain wash basin on the floor outside the door, then fetched a clean towel. Dampening one corner of the towel with water from the pitcher, she pressed the cool wet towel against Caroline's forehead.

"That feels good. Thank you." Caroline took the towel from her and blotted her face.

Regina sat down on the edge of the bed. She nervously chewed on her bottom lip. She had never seen Aunt Caroline like this. "Are you sure you don't want me to go get Bertie?"

"No, it'll pass. I'm not ill. Breakfast simply didn't agree with me."

"It didn't agree with you yesterday either," Regina pointed out. "Nor the day before."

Caroline smiled weakly. "Now, who told you that?"

"Bertie. She also said that there was nothing wrong with you that seven months wouldn't cure." Regina left out the part about her aunt possibly needing a little more help from her.

"Bertie fusses too much. I'm fine. Really."

"Aunt Caroline, are you pregnant?"

An uncomfortable silence fell over the room for several seconds. Caroline blushed. "Yes."

"Then why are you taking this trip to Williamsburg? Is it safe for you to travel in your condition?"

Caroline took Regina's hand. "There is something I need to tell you. Your uncle and I have decided to stay in Williamsburg until the baby is born. Dr. Morrow is there, and I shall feel better knowing that he will be nearby."

Regina's brows knitted. "Why? What's wrong? Are you ill? Is there something wrong with the baby?"

"Of course not. I'm in excellent health, and I see no reason that the baby should not be healthy as well. But I cannot ignore the fact that I am no longer young, and there could be unpredictable complications."

"But what of Robert and Timmy? What will they—"

"They will come with us. William cannot find a suitable tutor for them. At least in Williamsburg they will be able to go to school."

Regina's breath caught in her throat. She regarded her aunt with a mixture of hope and trepidation. "What of me?"

"Well . . . we discussed it with your brother," Caroline said haltingly, "and it was decided that . . . for now . . . it would be best for you to remain here."

Regina's mind raced. With Uncle William and Aunt Caroline gone, she would be able to see James any time she wanted, as long as she was careful to steer clear of Richard.

She was mentally planning her next liaison with James when she suddenly realized that she had come to think of her aunt and uncle and cousins as her immediate family. She had never questioned what life would be like without them nearby. Richard was not the most entertaining company. Her throat constricted. "I'm going to miss you," she blurted out. "The house will be lonely without you here."

Caroline gave her a tired smile. "I'm going to miss you, too. And I can't help being concerned for you. William and I know that Richard is your legal guardian, but after the disastrous way he managed your inheritance, we don't want to risk leaving you without any other means of support. I hate to say this about my own nephew, but I don't trust Richard to look out for your well-being."

"You don't need to worry. I can take care of myself. And I'll have Bertie here, watching over me like a mother hen."

"I'm glad for that. But I would rest easier, Regina, if I knew that you were properly settled before we leave. I do wish you would give serious consideration to Charles's proposal."

Regina groaned. "I *hate* Charles."

"Hate is an awfully strong word for someone who has done you no harm. He's a good man, Regina. Give him time. I'm sure you will find, as your uncle and I have, that Charles has some very admirable qualities."

"I know. Uncle William has already pointed them out. He's wealthy, and he's just demented enough to think that he's in love with me."

"Don't be so cynical," Caroline chided gently. "If you give the matter some objective thought, you might realize that Charles's affections can work in your favor. If given a choice between marrying a man I loved and one who loved me, I would much prefer the latter."

James loves me, Regina thought. She plucked nervously at the bedcover and said nothing.

Caroline covered Regina's hand with her own, stilling it. "Regina, why are you so opposed to marrying Charles? *Has* he done something to you that your uncle and I are not aware of?"

Regina caught her bottom lip between her teeth and looked away as she wondered uncomfortably just how much she should tell her aunt about Charles. Aunt Caroline was a good person who always tried to see the good in others, sometimes to the point of being naive. "I just don't want to marry him. Do I need a reason?"

"It would help me understand your reluctance better."

"I don't want to upset you. It's not good for the baby."

"Let *me* worry about the baby. Now, tell me, what is it about Charles that upsets you so?"

Regina avoided her aunt's gaze. "He . . . he's intimate . . . with his slaves."

"Oh, Regina, that's hardly reason to—"

"Even the boys!"

A moment of taut silence filled the room. "I see," Caroline said at last.

Regina's gaze riveted on her aunt. Caroline's voice was so resigned, and the look on her face so calm, that a sickening feeling gripped Regina's stomach. "You knew," she whispered painfully.

Caroline smiled sadly and squeezed Regina's hand. "Regina, there are other factors one must take into consideration when choosing a husband—his ability to support you, his standing in the community—"

"Aunt Caroline!" Regina jerked her hand free of her aunt's and stood up. "I can't believe you know what Charles is like, and yet you still expect me to marry him!"

"I understand your concerns, but Charles is

hardly the only man in the parish who . . . avails himself . . . of his servants. As unpleasant as you and I might find it, it's a fact of life that we must learn to live with."

A disquieting thought coursed through Regina's mind: *Surely Uncle William isn't like that?* And what of her own father? Had he too been unfaithful to her mother? She wrapped her arms defensively in front of herself and shook her head. "I can't do it. I can't marry a man who beds his slaves—or anyone else for that matter. I want a husband who is going to be faithful to *me*. Surely that's not too much to ask?"

"Of course it's not. But it might be too much to expect."

Regina crossed the room to stare glumly out the window. "It's not fair," she said in a low voice. "Father Tidewell turns a blind eye to the sins committed by the men in his parish, yet he holds the women responsible for the least little trespass. Everyone in the Northern Neck knows that it was Kyle Jamison who got Betsy Staunton with child, but does Father Tidewell say or do anything to Kyle? No. He simply humiliates poor Betsy, week after week after week."

"Regina . . ." Caroline said wearily.

Regina saw Adam crossing the yard toward the kitchen, and she wondered if he, too, was one of those infuriating men who would expect his wife to remain faithful while he sowed his seed in every fertile field he encountered.

Probably.

But then, maybe not.

She turned away from the window. "I'm going downstairs to see if Bertie is finished with the ironing. I'll bring the rest of your things up here so we can finish packing them."

"You're angry with me, aren't you?"

"I'm not angry with *you*, Aunt Caroline. I just feel a little . . . betrayed."

"I know. I felt the same way when my parents told me I had to marry your uncle."

Regina's eyes widened. "But you and Uncle William seem so—"

"I'm content with my lot. But it took me a while to accept it. These matters take time."

Regina grimaced. "I'll never learn to love Charles the way you love Uncle William. I *can't*."

"Of course you can. Just think about the good things Charles can provide for you, and try not to dwell on the other."

Regina opened her mouth to say that she would never, for as long as she lived, learn to love Charles Toliver, then closed it again. She didn't want to risk upsetting her aunt.

"Go see about the ironing," Caroline said gently. "My stomach is beginning to settle. By the time you return, I'll be ready to continue with the packing."

"Will you be all right?"

"I'll be fine. Now, go."

Regina hesitated a moment, unable to believe that Aunt Caroline *knew* about Charles, and still expected her to marry him. She had thought that Aunt Caroline, of all people, would have stood by her.

Glad for any excuse not to have to discuss Charles Toliver any longer, Regina turned and bolted down the back stairs and out the door. As she neared the kitchen, she slowed her footsteps and fought to catch her breath. It briefly occurred to her that for someone who was in love with James Fitzhugh, she was showing an inordinate amount of interest in Adam Burke. She shoved the unwelcome thought out of her mind. *I'm not interested in Adam Burke*, she rationalized. *I'm merely curious.*

And curious she was. Ever since Miles Jordan had told her about Adam's childhood, she had become obsessed with seeing him again. She thought of what he had endured as a boy, and her heart went out to him. She thought of the way he had kissed her, and she longed to strangle him. Somewhere, in the jumble of confused feelings, lay the truth about Adam Burke. One way or another, she intended to find out just who he was and what he was doing here.

The outbuilding contained two downstairs rooms—a kitchen and a laundry—separated by a massive central fireplace. An upstairs loft was used for storage. The kitchen door was propped open to allow a cooling breeze to pass through. Regina stepped inside.

No one was in the kitchen. The room was uncomfortably hot, and the smell of freshly baked bread filled the air. A dozen golden-brown loaves lined the long table beneath the tall windows, and another dozen, in various stages of rising, swelled beneath clean, white linen towels.

Voices came from the laundry area on the far side of the building. "You put your shirt back on," Regina heard Bertie say. "I'll finish hemming this and sew on the buttons, and you'll be able to wear it tomorrow. Good Lord, if you aren't the biggest man I've ever seen."

Regina choked back a giggle. Adam Burke the biggest man Bertie had ever seen? What was she trying to do? Fill his head with flattery? She heard Bertie's footsteps on the wooden stairs that led up to the loft.

Regina went to the narrow doorway beside the fireplace and peered through the door. Her view into the room was blocked by undergarments draped over a folding rack that stood in front of the fireplace. She slipped quietly into the room, just far enough to see around the clothes rack.

He was standing with his back to her, buttoning his shirt. Regina's breath caught in her throat. Bertie was right; he was *big*. His shoulders strained against his homespun work shirt, and his muscular calves bulged below his knee-length breeches.

Then she realized that his breeches were patched and the fabric worn. He was tall, too tall. And his hair was too dark. Adam's hair was dark, dark brown, with a whisper of red. This man's hair was the deep blue-black of obsidian.

Suddenly he turned around. His fingers froze on the buttons he had been fastening, and he snared Regina's wide-eyed gaze with his startling blue eyes.

Regina gasped. It was the prisoner she had seen down on the docks. The one Father Tidewell was never going to let her forget she had teased. Only now he was no longer safely chained.

Determined not to let him see her fear, she stepped around the clothes rack and plunked her hands on her hips. "What are *you* doing here?" she demanded.

He calmly resumed buttoning his shirt. "I work

here." His voice was heavily accented.

Regina could not quite grasp what she was hearing. Surely there was some mistake. How could Richard have retained *that man* after telling her he was a murderer? Had Richard lost his mind? Her eyes narrowed in suspicion. "Are you trying to tell me that my brother purchased your term of indenture?"

"No, I did," came a voice from behind her.

Regina whirled around to find Adam standing so close that her skirt brushed against his legs. His nearness startled her, and she took an involuntary step backward. *"You?"*

Adam ignored her. "You may go now, Mr. Mc-Lean. The others are waiting for you down by the springhouse."

Duncan tucked his shirt into his breeches. As he did so, he fixed Regina with an inscrutable gaze that made her squirm inwardly. Without a word, he left through the side door.

Still in shock, Regina followed him to the door and stared in disbelief as he walked away. No shackles. No guards. For all practical purposes, he was a free man. Furthermore, there was a confidence in his stride and in the proud set of his shoulders that set Regina's teeth on edge. For a criminal, the man was insufferably arrogant. She rounded on Adam. "What is the meaning of this, Mr. Burke? Are you insane? That man is a murderer!"

"That man, Miss Langley, works for me. You are going to be seeing a great deal of him around here. I suggest you get used to the idea."

Regina's mouth fell open. "I beg your pardon!"

"I see no need to offer it."

Anger flashed in Regina's eyes. "Perhaps you are willing to endanger your own life by letting that man walk free, but I cannot stand by and allow you to put the rest of us at risk. Unless you want me—"

"You are not at risk. Duncan McLean's presence here is endangering no one."

"Of course not," Regina retorted. "The man is merely a convicted felon. A perfectly respectable member of society."

"A human being."

"Who has no business walking about freely! You have overstepped the bounds of propriety, Mr. Burke. A man who is a guest in someone's home does not offend his host's sensibilities by exposing his family to dangerous criminals. I'm telling my brother about this. I suggest you leave before he throws you out."

"Richard knows I purchased Duncan McLean's term of indenture."

Regina gaped at him. "He *knows*? And he did nothing to stop you?"

"He had no say in the matter. Now, if you will excuse me, Miss Langley, I have work to do." Adam looked at Bertie who had quietly come down from the loft, and was standing at the bottom of the stairs with a folded stack of mending in her arms. "Thank you for sewing the new clothes the men need. I'm indebted to you."

"You're sure welcome, Mister Adam."

You're sure welcome, Mister Adam, Regina mimicked silently, not quite certain why she felt so resentful. Before she could recompose her expression, Adam glanced in her direction and witnessed the tail end of her show of disrespect, and a look of annoyance passed across his face. "Good day, Miss Langley," he said curtly and left the building.

As soon as he was gone, Regina rounded on Bertie. "What did he mean about Richard having no say in the matter?"

Bertie carried the stack of clothes across the room to the chair near the open window. She sat down. "You'll have to ask Mister Richard about that."

"Bertie, you know something, don't you?"

The old woman pursed her lips and declined to answer.

"Bertie!"

Still no response. Bertie's refusal to divulge anything made Regina uneasy. She didn't know what was going on here, and she had an uncomfortable feeling that she wasn't going to like the truth. Frustrated by her inability to get any answers to her questions, she returned to the house. She took the stairs two at a time. "Aunt Caroline!"

Caroline was sitting at her dressing table, hurriedly blotting her eyes when Regina entered the room. The skin around her eyes was red and blotchy.

Her anger momentarily forgotten, Regina went to her. "Are you all right? Did you hurt yourself?"

Caroline shook her head. "No, no. I'm fine."

"Then why are you crying?"

"I was just thinking about how much I'm going to miss you." Caroline smiled sadly through her tears. "You've been like a daughter to me. I hope this baby is a girl. I want a little girl to remind me of you."

Regina's brows knitted in bewilderment. Her aunt was talking as if they were never going to see each other again. "Aunt Caroline, what is going on here? Everyone is behaving strangely. Bertie knows something and she's not talking. You know something, too. I can see it in your eyes."

"Regina, please—"

"Tell me!"

"I can't. Your uncle and I promised Richard we would let him break the news to you. I'm sorry."

"What news? You can tell me. Richard doesn't have to know."

"Regina, please don't ask me to break a promise. Besides, it would be best if you heard it from your brother. He's your legal guardian."

Panic surged through Regina. "He told Charles I'd marry him, didn't he?"

Caroline shook her head. "Of course not. This has nothing to do with Charles."

Regina's relief was so sudden she felt as if she might faint. *Anything but that,* she thought. Yet if it wasn't that, then what was it? "Aunt Caroline—"

"Talk to Richard," Caroline said firmly.

Richard wasn't to be found in the house or in any of the outbuildings. Nor was he at the mill. His horse was still in the stables, so she knew he couldn't have gone far. He *had* to be down at the waterfront. If he wasn't there, she didn't know where he could be.

By the time she reached the river, Regina was out of breath. She scanned the waterfront, but there was no sign of Richard. The *Triumph* was still anchored offshore, but the *Lady Anne* had already set sail for the port of Belhaven farther upriver. The air was hot and humid, and there was little activity on the docks during the midday heat. Even the river seemed to move with an uncharacteristic laziness.

Regina went to Uncle William's warehouse office. No one was there, but the sight that greeted her when she opened the door stopped her in her tracks.

The office had been stripped of its furnishings. The bookshelves that had once lined the wall behind Uncle William's desk had been torn down, and a doorway cut through the wall to the adjoining warehouse and was roughly framed with new lumber. Thin wooden lath, like the kind used to prepare walls for plastering, was stacked in neat piles along one side of the room. The outline of a fireplace had been drawn with chalk on the far wall.

She fidgeted. This didn't make sense. Surely Uncle William hadn't ordered this construction work on the office, not when he was preparing to leave for Williamsburg. He would want to oversee the work, to be certain he was getting what he had paid for. And Richard simply wasn't that industrious.

And what about the fireplace? Even Richard, who was accustomed to getting what he wanted, knew better than to indulge in such an extravagance. Brick was costly, and the kilns had fallen into disuse years ago.

Feeling decidedly ill-at-ease in the once familiar

room, Regina pulled the door shut and hurried away from the building.

She approached a group of men sitting in the shade beneath one of the docks. She recognized one of them. He had come to Virginia as a servant indentured to her father and had earned his freedom after four years of service. He now worked as a laborer on the docks. "Mr. Marley, have you seen Richard?" she called out as she neared the men.

Jeb Marley got to his feet and stepped out into the sunlight. His red-blond hair was thinning on top, showing the freckles on his scalp. "Last time I saw him, he was at the Boar's Head, burying his sorrows in a bottle of rum. I'd keep my distance if I was you. He looked like he was wantin' to chew up anybody who crossed him."

Wonderful, Regina thought sourly. Richard was already drunk, and it was only midday.

"You can ask Captain Bebe over there." Jeb glanced past Regina and nodded. "He was with him."

Regina turned around. Captain Bebe raised his arm and waved.

"Thank you," Regina said. "I'll do that."

But when she asked the captain of the *Triumph* about Richard, his answer was even less encouraging than Jeb Marley's. "I'd leave him be for now, Miss Langley. He'll get over it in time. Losing Summerhill to Burke hit him hard. But he's young yet. He'll rebuild his fortune."

Regina felt as if Captain Bebe had punched her in the stomach. *Richard lost Summerhill to Adam Burke?*

"Miss Langley, are you all right?"

Regina jerked her gaze up to Captain Bebe's face. "Y-yes."

He eyed her skeptically. "You didn't know, did you?"

Regina started to shake her head. She barely stopped herself. She forced a smile. "I-I knew. It's unsettling for all of us."

"I'm glad you knew. When I discussed the matter with Beatrice earlier today, I feared I might have overstepped my bounds."

Beatrice knows? Regina felt as if she would be ill. She nervously moistened her lips. "Richard doesn't like . . . discussing it. We still don't know how it happened."

"Faro. What else? Your brother is addicted to it."

They started to walk slowly, aimlessly, along the river bank. "I was afraid of that." Regina struggled to keep her voice from trembling. "Richard has always had a weakness for gambling. I just can't believe he would gamble away Summerhill."

"He didn't. But the men he lost to were thirsty for blood. If Adam hadn't stepped in and paid his debt, he'd have likely found himself in an alley with a knife in his back."

Regina stopped walking and turned to face the captain. She lifted her chin and looked him squarely in the eyes. "Captain Bebe, exactly how much did Richard . . . lose . . . to Mr. Burke?"

"From what I heard, he lost everything. The house. The plantation. The warehouses. The shipping business."

"The shipping business? Does that mean you now work for Adam Burke instead . . . of . . ." Regina's voice faltered.

Captain Bebe issued a shrug of resignation. "It was a cruel lesson. I hope your brother learned it well. To repeat the same mistake would destroy him."

Chapter 9

The conversation at dinner was strained. Aunt Caroline tried her best to keep the mood light, but her efforts were for naught. Uncle William was civil to Adam, but little more. And Richard never showed up. Only Robert and Timmy seemed oblivious to the tension. Never having been away from Summerhill, they talked excitedly about the upcoming trip to Williamsburg, their conversation punctuated with repeated reminders from Aunt Caroline not to talk with their mouths full.

Regina's stomach was so tied in knots, she could barely eat. The thought that Adam now owned Summerhill made her physically ill. He owned *everything*. The house. The food they were eating. The slaves and servants who waited on them. The clothes they wore. He even owned the beds in which they slept.

And it was Adam, she suspected, who had ordered the construction work started on Uncle William's warehouse office.

Well, it used to be Uncle William's office.

Uncle William and Aunt Caroline were lucky; they still had a home in Williamsburg. But what of her and Richard? What was going to become of them?

What was going to become of *her*?

She could always marry Charles. She shuddered. She would rather die than marry Charles. Aunt Caroline kept insisting that Charles was a good man, in spite of what she knew about him; but Aunt Caroline just didn't understand how much she hated him. And *hate* was the mildest word she could think of.

There was only one person she hated more.

She glanced up at Adam to find him staring at her, and annoyance surged through her. She thrust out her chin and glowered at him. He was so confident, so smooth, so smug: she had a boiling desire to lash out at him.

He lifted his wine glass toward her in a silent salute.

Anger surged through her. Unable to bear being in the same room with him a second longer, she dropped her fork and shoved her chair away from the table. "Excuse me," she muttered, and bolted away from the table.

Richard slammed the front door and staggered into Uncle William's study. The house was dark. Even the slaves had long since retired for the night. Fumbling around in the dark, he poured himself a glass of port. He set down the flint decanter too close to the edge of the table. The decanter toppled over and landed on the floor with a loud *crack,* and port splashed over his shoes. He swore aloud.

Regina stood in the doorway, her stomach rebelling as she watched her brother's display of drunken clumsiness. "Haven't you had enough?"

Richard turned to face her. She was clad in only a nightdress. Her feet were bare and her hair hung down her back. Richard couldn't see her face in the darkness, but he could hear the disapproval in her voice. "Go back to bed."

"How could you sell Summerhill to Adam Burke?" Regina blurted out.

Richard swayed on his feet. "So you know."

"Yes, I know. So does everyone else in the parish by now, I'm sure. How could you do it, Richard? How could you be so irresponsible?"

"I had no choice."

"Don't tell me you had no choice! You could have found a way to pay your creditors without selling our home out from under us!"

Richard downed his port in a single gulp and flung the glass aside. It struck the wall and shattered. "I had no choice, Regina," he repeated, spitting out the words as if they left a bitter taste in his mouth. He started toward her. "They were going to kill me if I didn't come up with the money right away."

"You could have borrowed it!"

"From whom, Regina? The house was already mortgaged. The Crown had placed a lien on Summerhill for back taxes. I couldn't have borrowed enough to buy breakfast."

Richard started to move around her, but Regina stepped in his path, blocking his exit from the room. His face was a shadow in the darkness. "I'm not finished talking to you."

"Get out of my way."

"Damn you, Richard! Wasn't it enough for you to gamble away my dowry? Did you have to lose Summerhill, too?"

Richard siezed Regina's arms and shoved her up against the doorframe. "I don't ever want to hear you mention it again. Do you understand me? It's over. It's done."

When she didn't answer, he shook her hard, causing her to smack the back of her head on the doorframe. "Answer me!"

Regina's eyes watered from the blow on the back of her head, and the stale smells of sweat and spirits that clung to Richard made her stomach roil. Before she could speak, Adam Burke's voice pierced the darkness. "Let go of her."

"She's my sister. I'll do what I—"

Adam grabbed Richard by the back of the collar and swung him around. "I said, let go of her."

Richard growled low in his throat and lunged. He crashed into Adam with enough force to send them both reeling across the foyer.

Regina screamed.

Adam quickly regained his footing. Grabbing the front of Richard's shirt, he hauled the other man upright and slugged Richard in the jaw. Richard crumpled to the floor.

Regina ran to him and dropped to her knees beside him. "Richard? Richard, answer me!"

Adam placed a hand on her shoulder. "He'll be all right."

Regina recoiled as if his touch had scorched her. She scrambled to her feet and rounded on him. "Damn you! Look at what you've done!"

"He's not hurt, Regina. Only unconscious. He'll be fine once he's slept it off."

Uncle William appeared at the top of the stairs in his nightshirt, with a candle in his hand. "Who's there?"

The candle cast a thin flickering light into the foyer, and for the first time, Regina realized that Adam was wearing only his breeches, and his muscular chest and arms glistened like polished oak. His hair was not tied back, but hung loose around his face. The candlelight emphasized the angles and planes of his finely chiseled face, and reflected in his amber-flecked eyes. For several long silence-filled seconds, he stared at Regina, his expression inscrutable.

Regina stood motionless, unbreathing, acutely aware of a fluttering warmth uncurling in the pit of her stomach. Below her stomach. Deep, deep inside her. She clenched her hands. "You had no right to do that. Richard never hurt you."

William held the candle up over his head. "What's wrong?"

Bending down, Adam picked up Richard as if he weighed no more than a sack of flour and slung him over his shoulder. He turned and started up the stairs. "Your nephew came home drunk," he said. "He won't trouble anyone the rest of the night."

"Regina, are you down there?" William called out.

"Sir?"

"Go back to bed."

"Yes, sir." Regina did not return to her bedchamber, but stood in the doorway to Uncle William's study, listening to the noises coming from upstairs, and wrestling with her tumultuous emotions. *Damn him!* He had no right to hurt Richard. No right at all.

And yet he had stopped Richard from hurting her. With her fingertips, she gingerly felt the tender

lump on the back of her head. If Adam hadn't in-
terfered, there was no telling what her brother
might have done. As drunk as Richard was, she
doubted that he would even remember any of this.

She heard footsteps leading into Richard's bedchamber, followed by the creak of the ropes on Richard's bed. She heard Adam and her uncle
talking, but their voices were so low, she couldn't
make out what they were saying.

She wished Adam would leave. She wished that
this was nothing more than a bad dream and she
would wake up in the morning and everything
would be as it was before. Before Richard returned
from England. Before Uncle William gave Charles
Toliver permission to call on her.

Before life became so bloody complicated.

The sound of footsteps on the stairs jolted her
back to the present. Alarmed, she slipped inside
Uncle William's study and pressed her back to the
wall. She didn't know if it was Adam coming down
the stairs, or Uncle William, but she had no wish
to speak to either one of them. She hoped that whoever it was would think she had already gone back
to bed and would leave.

Adam entered the study. His bare feet made no
sound on the wood floor. Crossing the room, he
picked up the decanter from the floor and placed
it on the table.

While Adam's back was toward her, Regina
slipped out the door and tiptoed toward the stairs.

"You can't keep running away," Adam said quietly.

She froze. Her heart pounded. Every nerve in her
body shrieked at her to get away, to escape while
she still had a chance. Still, the challenge in his

voice was too great to resist. Turning, she went back into the study. Not wanting Uncle William to find out that she had disobeyed him by not going straight to her room, she quietly closed the door and leaned her back against it.

Adam was standing near the window with his feet apart and his hands on his hips. His face was hidden in darkness, making him appear seductively mysterious. Her pulse quickened. Shutting the door was the stupidest thing she could have done, and she knew it. "Running away from what?"

"From what you're feeling."

From what she was feeling? God forgive her, but she couldn't help what she was feeling! She was trying her best to think rationally. Instead, all she could think about was Adam's state of near undress. Of his maleness. Of an overwhelming longing to feel his arms around her, to lose herself in his kiss. "I-I don't know what you're talking about."

Adam closed the distance between them. He buried his fingers in her hair and tilted her face up toward his, and Regina winced as his fingers touched the bruise on the back of her head. "I think you do," he said huskily.

Regina gasped as his lips claimed hers. Desire, hot and liquid, washed over her. Forgetting everything she had ever been taught about right and wrong, she returned his kiss with a hunger that came from deep within her soul. Never in her life had she experienced a longing so intense that she feared she might die if that longing were not satisfied. Her body felt as if it were on fire. Adam pulled her against him, and she leaned into his arms and kissed him fiercely, passionately. She glided her hands over his back, reveling in the silken hardness of his muscles beneath her fingertips. She pressed her body against his, starving for his touch. She couldn't get enough of him.

Adam wrapped his arms around her and lifted her off the floor. His lips still locked with hers, he carried her across the room and sat her on the edge of the big oak desk.

He pushed her nightdress up over her knees, then slipped his hands beneath her and pulled her toward him, moving her bottom closer to the edge of the desk. He slid his hand over the nest of silky curls at the juncture of her thighs.

No longer in control of her actions, she instinctively opened her legs wider and pressed against his hand.

Gently parting her honeyed flesh, he buried his fingers inside her and Regina cried out in surprise.

She clung to him, digging her fingernails into his back as he repeatedly withdrew his fingers and drove them into her. With his free hand, he loosened the ribbon at her neck and eased her nightdress off her shoulders. He kissed her neck, her shoulders. He cupped her breast, teasing the sensitive peak until she thought she would go insane. Then, just when she thought she could stand no more, he closed his lips around her nipple and drew it into his mouth.

She groaned and clutched his head to her breast, unable to get enough of the intoxicating sensations he was arousing in her. Her body ached with a sweetness that was pure torture.

Again and again, Adam plunged his fingers into her, until he felt the beginning of the telltale contractions that signaled the imminence of her release. He touched his thumb, wet with her dew, to the taut little bud that guarded the entrance of her womanhood, and the tension that had been building inside her shattered.

Smothering her cries with his mouth, he held her tightly against him until her shuddering began to subside, then slowly withdrew his hand.

Dazed, Regina lifted her gaze to his. In the pale gray light that filled the room, his eyes smoldered with a haunting, hungry look, and his face was taut with the effort of holding back his own unmet passions.

Still in awe over what had just happened, she reached up to touch his face, then jerked her hand away. Dear God, what had she done? She loved James! So why had she let Adam touch her in a way that she had never allowed James to touch her? While denying James her virginity, she had come dangerously close to giving it away to Adam.

Mortified, she scooted off the edge of the desk. She yanked her nightdress up over her shoulders and clutched it together at her neck. Adam reached for her, and she darted out of his reach. "Please . . . excuse me." She choked on her words.

"Regina, wait."

"I shouldn't have let you do that. I don't love you, Mr. Burke. I don't even like you!"

Puzzled, Adam watched her go. "Liar," he muttered.

Regina Langley might have fooled her family into thinking she was an innocent, but he knew better. He could see the truth in her eyes and feel it in the way she responded to his touch. Regina wanted him just as much as he wanted her.

He wondered just how much longer he was going to be able to restrain himself.

Regina sat on the edge of Aunt Caroline's bed, helping her aunt fold the last of the clothes to be packed in the small traveling trunk. Caroline and William planned to leave in the morning to pay a final visit to friends before departing for Williamsburg.

The month had passed so quickly. It had been nearly a week since that night in the study, but she could not stop thinking about it. Never in her life had she been so angry with herself. She should have stopped Adam. She should have said something to let him know that she didn't want him touching her that way. But the truth was, she had enjoyed it. Even now, just thinking about it was enough to ignite that peculiar warmth deep in her core. She clutched Uncle William's shirt against her stomach, wrinkling the freshly ironed fabric. "God, I hate him!" she blurted out.

Caroline glanced at her in dismay. "Regina, I wish you would stop talking about Charles that way. He hasn't done anything to—"

"I'm not talking about Charles. I'm talking about Adam Burke. I hate what he's done to our family. I wish he would go back to England."

"Sometimes I wish that, too. But to be honest, Adam hasn't done anything wrong. He merely took advantage of a lucrative business opportunity. Given the chance, William would have done the same."

"No, he wouldn't. Uncle William might purchase a piece of property, but he would never force the occupants out of their home."

Caroline's brows drew together in bewilderment. "Adam isn't forcing us out."

"But I thought—"

"Goodness, no! Adam told us we could stay as long as we wanted. He even proposed building another house so we could remain in this one."

It was Regina's turn to look confused. "Then why are you leaving?"

Caroline sighed. "William and your brother quarrelled shortly after Richard returned home. In a fit of anger, William announced we would be out of the house by the end of the month, and Richard is holding him to that promise. I swear, those two men are so stubborn. Once the angry words were spoken, neither of them was willing to forgive the other."

Regina didn't want to think that Adam had *any* redeeming qualities. Still, the entire situation puzzled her. "Is Mr. Burke letting Richard and me stay?"

"For now. Although to be truthful, I have my misgivings. You know how hotheaded your brother can be. I wanted you to come to Williamsburg with us, but Richard won't allow it." Caroline hesitated. "Regina, I'm sorry I didn't tell you all this before. I was trying to spare you."

Regina handed a stack of folded shirts to her aunt. "I would have found out soon enough. Captain Bebe told Beatrice, and I'm sure she's already told Izzy. It won't be long before the entire parish knows we've been reduced in our circumstances."

Caroline smiled sadly. "You're probably right."

Regina got up off the bed and began pacing. "I can't believe Richard was so stupid as to lose *everything*. My God! What will people think of us?"

"If all people care about is our material wealth, Regina, then they are only fair-weather friends, and we're better off without their company. If it's any consolation, Charles has known about it for several days. It matters not to him. He still wants to marry—"

"*I don't want to marry him!* Why doesn't anyone ever listen to me? Doesn't anyone care what *I* want?"

Caroline placed the stack of shirts in the bottom of the trunk. She straightened and dragged the back of her hand across her forehead. "Do you know what I'm craving?" she said, abruptly changing the subject. "Apple cider. I think there's still a jug or two left from last winter. Will you go look?"

Stung at being so abruptly dismissed, she shrugged. "I suppose."

"I think I'm going to lie down for awhile. I'm feeling a little tired."

Regina eyed her aunt closely. "Is the baby—"

"The baby is *fine*. Now, go. I need to rest."

A refreshing draft brushed against Regina's face as she descended the steps into the thick-walled, stone springhouse. No matter how oppressive the heat, the inside of the springhouse was always cool and damp. The blocks of ice that had been cut during the winter and packed in hay had long since melted. They were seldom able to keep ice through the entire summer. Usually the weather was too hot.

There was only one jug of cider left from last year's batch. Moving the jug nearer the door so she wouldn't forget it, Regina retrieved an apple from the bushel basket in the far corner of the dark room, and sat down on the bottom step to think.

Everything was happening too quickly. In the month that had passed sinced Richard returned home from England, her entire life had been turned upside down. Everything that she had thought secure, inviolate, was now gone. Uncle William still had the house in Williamsburg, but she and Richard had nothing. They were penniless.

They were paupers.

It wasn't fair! She couldn't bear the thought that it was only due to Adam Burke's generosity that she and Richard still had a roof over their heads. To be indebted to that man for anything was intolerable.

She took a bite of the apple. That it had lost its crispness was inconsequential; she barely tasted it.

Against her will, the memories of what had happened in Uncle William's study returned to haunt her. She swore inwardly. *Damn you, Adam Burke! Why did you have to come here? Why couldn't you have just stayed in England and appointed someone to come to Virginia in your stead?*

Why did his handsome face keep invading her thoughts?

"Reggie?"

Startled out of her reverie, Regina jumped to her feet, dropping the apple. It rolled across the floor. "James! What are you doing here? How did you know where to find me?"

James descended the stone steps. "One of the slaves saw you come in here."

"What if Uncle William catches you here?"

"He won't. He and Richard are down at the waterfront." James took her in his arms and kissed her.

Regina pulled away. "James, if we get caught—"

"I had to see you, Reggie. It can't wait. My father and Mr. Carlisle have decided that the wedding will be next week."

"Next week!"

"This Sunday, meet me by the mill after church."

"James, I'm not going to church this week. Aunt Caroline and Uncle William will be away, and I have no intention of sitting on that hard pew, listening to Father Tidewell tell the whole world that I'm headed straight for hell."

James stared at her for several seconds before remembering his voice. "Reggie, that's perfect! By the time anyone realizes you're even missing, we'll be married."

"Married?"

"Bring a change of clothing, but nothing more. We'll have to travel light. I'll buy you more clothes when we get to Philadelphia."

Regina stared at him in disbelief. "Do you really mean it? Are we really going to be married? You're not teasing me, are you?"

"I've never been more serious in my life."

"But what about your father? What will he do when he finds out we've eloped? And what about Lucy? What is she going to think when you just disappear and leave her—"

"I don't care what Lucy thinks. Or my father, for that matter. You're the one I want to marry."

Regina couldn't believe that what she had wanted for so long was finally coming to pass. She and James were to be married! She couldn't wait to get away from Summerhill and from Richard. Most of all, she wanted to get away from Adam Burke. She didn't want to risk another encounter like the one she had with him last week.

Still, a nagging misgiving cast a shadow over her happiness. No matter how glad she was to be marrying James, the necessity for sneaking around seemed to diminish what should have been the most important day of her life. Nor could she shake the disquieting suspicion that James's eagerness to marry her was less an indication of his love for her than of his reluctance to marry Lucy.

He kissed her quickly and climbed the stairs. "I need to go before anyone discovers I'm here. Remember: this Sunday. At the mill."

"After church?"

"I can't get away before then, and we'll need to make as much progress as possible before nightfall."

Suddenly remembering the last time she had agreed to meet him at the mill, when he was so late she feared he had forgotten her, she grabbed his arm. "James, wait. What if you can't be there? How will I know—"

"If I can't be there, I'll get word to you. At church."

"I told you, I'm not going—"

"And I'm sure as hell not going to risk my neck by coming here. The last thing I need is to cross paths with your brother." James grinned. "He might challenge me to a duel."

Regina grimaced. "We can't have that now, can we?" she said, trying unsuccessfully to mask her misgivings with sarcasm. She hesitated before finally giving in. "All right. I'll go to church this Sunday, just in case you need to get word to me. But if you do break our appointment, you had better have a good reason, or I'll never forgive you."

"Don't worry. I won't stand you up." James stuck his head out the door and glanced around to make sure no one was about before slipping out into the bright sunlight.

So excited she could barely stand still, Regina waited until James was safely away from Summerhill before picking up the jug of cider and heading back to the main house. She had not taken more than a few steps when she saw Duncan McLean leave the kitchen, wearing the new shirt Bertie had made for him.

She stopped. She wasn't certain if she was beginning to accept his presence at Summerhill or if her excitement over marrying James made her a little more accommodating than usual, but Duncan McLean didn't seem as menacing as he had in the past. She had seen him several times since that day in the kitchen, and she couldn't help noticing that he held himself apart from the other indentures, seldom talking with them, never quite becoming one of them. At one time, she would have interpreted his standoffishness as the arrogance of a man who thought himself above his station, but now he just seemed lonely.

She remembered the way she had taunted him down at the docks, and a feeling of shame crept up her neck and made her face feel hot. She was not very proud of herself. What she had done that day was despicable.

Seeing her, the Scot inclined his head toward her, then continued on his way.

Regina squirmed inwardly. She couldn't repair the damage she had done that day, but she could run away from it.

Duncan McLean was just one more reason to put Summerhill as far behind her as possible.

From the dining room window, Adam watched James Fitzhugh sneak away from the springhouse and sprint across the lawn toward the woods. A few minutes later, Regina emerged from the springhouse carrying an earthenware jug and strolled casually toward the main house. Adam's gut tightened. He could no longer ignore the fierce possessiveness he felt toward Regina or the irritation he felt at the thought of her being with another man.

He dropped the curtain and turned away from the window. It was time, he thought with grim determination, to do something about James Fitzhugh.

Chapter 10

Never had Sunday service seemed to drag on so long. Regina could not believe she was putting herself through this torture. Richard was at home, sleeping off the effects of last night's excesses. Left to her own devices, that was where she'd rather be, but she couldn't risk missing James's message—if there was one.

She fidgeted. Two days prior, immediately after Uncle William and Aunt Caroline and her cousins had departed to visit Aunt Caroline's stepsister, she had tied a change of clothing and some toiletries into a small bundle, which she had stashed beneath the bushes at the top of the cliff overlooking the docks. As soon as church services ended, she planned to retrieve the bundle and meet James by the mill.

She twisted around and looked behind her in hopes of getting a glimpse of James, but he wasn't in the Fitzhugh pew. Neither was Izzy. She looked at Beatrice who cast her a covert glance from beneath her copper tipped lashes, then hastily lowered her gaze.

She was just turning back to the front when she

caught sight of Charles, sitting with his back rigid, staring straight ahead.

Panic surged through her. She had forgotten all about promising to meet Charles after church to go riding. *Damn, damn, damn.* She hoped he didn't detain her. She didn't want to be late meeting James.

"Unfortunately," Father Tidewell said, "the culprit who set the fire has yet to be apprehended. However, sinners know who they are."

Regina turned back around and saw Father Tidewell staring straight at her as he spoke, and she felt a stab of resentment. When was he going to get it through his thick skull that she had nothing to do with the fire?

She took a deep breath and silently coaxed herself into remaining calm. It wouldn't be long now before she was with James. There was nothing to be gained by letting Father Tidewell ruin her day.

After what seemed an eternity, the service ended, and the parishioners began filing out of the church. Regina started toward Beatrice, but Arthur Randolph whisked his family away from her before she could get within ten feet of them.

Outside, Regina stopped a few yards away from the church and squinted into the bright sunlight. There was still no sign of James. Across the yard, the shingles on the parsonage roof gleamed pale and new. In time they would weather to a dark, silver-gray, but for now, they were a glaring reminder that an arsonist still walked about freely. Regina wondered uncomfortably if the person who had set the fire would ever be identified, or would everyone continue to think that she was the guilty one.

She was still trying to determine the best way to

slip away unnoticed when she saw Charles coming toward her. She swore inwardly. There had to be some reasonable, thoroughly plausible, excuse she could come up with to avoid riding with him, but for the life of her, she couldn't think of one. By the time he reached her, she had managed to force a smile. "Good morning, Charles."

"Good morning, Regina," he said stiffly. "If you will forgive me, I won't be able to take you riding today. Some other time, perhaps."

Taken aback, Regina stared at him. She had been fighting off his attentions for so long, that she didn't know how to respond to this uncharacteristic abruptness. "Of c-course," she stammered. "Some other time."

His gaze, hard and unforgiving, focused on a point just beyond and above Regina's shoulder. Then, without another word, he stalked past her. Curious, Regina looked around, and was startled to see Adam right behind her. She didn't even know he was at church. Somehow, she didn't perceive him as being the devout kind.

Still, she could not forget the antagonistic look Charles had given him. She eyed Adam suspiciously, wondering just what was going on between them.

"It would appear that your suitor has lost interest," Adam said offhandedly.

Regina didn't know whether to be relieved or alarmed. She shrugged. "Thank God. Charles Toliver is the only person in the parish whom I dislike as much as I dislike you."

Adam chuckled. "Odd, but I got the impression that you rather enjoyed my company."

Regina glanced around nervously before shooting him a venomous look. "Would you keep your voice down!" she whispered angrily. "There are already enough people in this parish who harbor a questionable opinion of me without you adding fuel to their fire."

Amusement tugged at the corners of Adam's mouth. "Unless my memory has failed me, which I seriously doubt, it was your fire I was stoking the other night. A rather hot one, I might add."

Regina blushed furiously. "Don't flatter yourself, Mr. Burke. I've already told you that I'm in love with someone else, and that's not likely to change just because you tried to seduce me."

Adam took a step toward her, and it was all Regina could do not to cringe from the heat of his gaze. "Seduction is a two-way street, Regina," he said in a low, carefully controlled voice. "Do you think I haven't noticed the way you look at me, your beautiful eyes issuing a challenge and an invitation at the same time? Do you think I didn't see your jealousy when I was talking with your friend at your uncle's dinner party? Do you think I don't feel your body's response when I kiss you? When I touch you? Do you think I don't see your rebellion against the attempts of your family and society to mold you into a dull, passionless, obedient shadow, rather than allow you to be the vibrant, incredibly attractive woman you are?"

The husky, intoxicating tone of his voice and the smoldering look in his eyes scorched through Regina's defenses, leaving her feeling vulnerable and exposed. The rest of the world around her seemed to have dropped away, colors dimmed, voices hushed to a distant hum, until she was aware only of him, of the golden light in his hazel eyes, of the way his presence surrounded her, engulfed her, threatened to swallow her.

What frightened her most was that she *wanted* to be swallowed up. She wanted to disappear. She wanted to forget, if only for a moment, that she was Regina Langley of Westmoreland County, who was expected to marry some pompous man her family chose for her, run his household, and bear him a child every year until she died, old and tired and never knowing how it felt to be truly alive.

And loved, unequivocally and unconditionally.

She took a shaky breath. "Mr. Burke, please forgive me for being so bold as to say so, but I fear the weeks you spent at sea have affected your mind. You are quite clearly suffering from a severe bout of dementia. Now, if you will excuse me, I have things to do. Good day, sir." She pivoted and marched away, not looking back until she had put a respectable distance between them.

She could no longer see Adam, but at least he had not followed her. She saw Beatrice with her family, and her throat constricted when she realized that she might never see her friend again. As if it mattered, she thought peevishly, remembering Mr. Randolph's coldness toward her. Even if she weren't leaving Summerhill, she still might not get to see Bea as much as she wanted. Mr. Randolph would see to that.

She stared long and hard at the gathering on the church lawn, the people who had been her friends and neighbors for as long as she could remembered. "Good-bye," she whispered hoarsely.

She turned away and broke into a run.

By the time she retrieved her bundle of clothes from its hiding place and reached the mill, she was out of breath from running. She didn't see James anywhere. She felt a moment of uncertainty. Had she misunderstood him? *Of course not*, she chided herself. He had distinctly said Sunday, after church.

He'll be here, she reassured herself. If he couldn't make it, he would have gotten word to her at church. He was simply late. Perhaps he had trouble getting the horses. Perhaps—

"He isn't coming."

Regina whirled around at the sound of the voice. "Izzy! What are you doing here?"

Izzy came toward her. Her eyes were red and puffy from crying and her hands were knotted into fists. "Damn you, Reggie! How could you? I thought you were my friend!"

Regina gaped at her. "What are you talking about? Of course I'm your friend! What's wrong? Why are you crying?"

Fresh tears streamed down Izzy's tear-blotched face. "You knew I liked Adam, and you had to throw yourself at him anyway, just like you throw yourself at every man who looks your way. Isn't it enough that every other man in the parish pants after you as if you were a bitch in heat? Must you also steal the only man I've ever wanted?"

Regina recoiled from her friend's verbal assault. "Izzy, I don't know what you're talking about. I don't even like Mr. Burke. I swear it!"

"Stop lying! I know the truth about you, about how you couldn't wait for your aunt and uncle to leave so you could take Adam into your bed."

Regina vehemently shook her head. "That's not true! I've never lain with Mr. Burke! Who told you such a horrible thing?"

"James did, you idiot. You broke his heart. He wanted to marry you, and you betrayed him."

"I did not! Izzy, I love James. I would never—"

"You don't know how to love anyone but yourself, Regina Langley. You're spoiled and selfish and you don't care who you hurt, as long as you get what you want. You're just what everyone says you are. A whore!"

Izzy started to walk away, but Regina went after her and grabbed her arm. "Izzy, wait."

Izzy jerked her arm out of Regina's grasp. "Don't you ever put your filthy, whoring hands on me again. I hate you. I hate the sight of you. Just get away from me!"

Regina wrapped her arms around her stomach and watched in numb horror as Izzy walked away. She felt as if she was going to be sick. She couldn't believe any of this was happening. Why had James said those awful things about her and Adam Burke? James knew she loved *him*. She had agreed to run away and marry him, for God's sake!

Then she remembered something else. Something Uncle William had told her, about James telling everyone at the Boar's Head that he had had his way with her. She hadn't wanted to believe Uncle William, and when James had denied the accusation, she had willingly put it out of her mind.

But now she could no longer ignore it. James had told everyone that he had bedded her, and now he was telling Izzy that she had lain with Adam Burke. *Why?* Why was James lying about her?

Tears stung her eyes and a lump so big it hurt to swallow wedged in her throat. Beatrice wasn't allowed to be with her. Izzy hated her, and so did

James. Even Charles Toliver, whom she despised, now behaved toward her as if she disgusted him. Was she really that awful a person? Did everyone, as Izzy said, really believe she was a whore?

She burst into tears.

Adam was sitting at the big oak desk in what used to be William Langley's study, making a list of items he intended to order from London, when he heard one of the downstairs doors slam with a force that reverberated throughout the house. He returned the quill to its holder, put the stopper back on the bottle of ink, then went to investigate.

He descended the stairs to the lower level of the house, where he heard muffled weeping. The sound grew louder as he neared Regina's bedchamber.

He knocked on the closed door. "Regina? Are you all right?"

She didn't answer.

Adam opened the door.

She was curled into a ball in the middle of the bed, with her back toward him, crying as if her heart was broken. Bitter sobs racked her entire body. He had a pretty good idea what had happened, and he didn't know whether to feel guilty or relieved. James Fitzhugh must have told her that he couldn't see her any more. It was part of the agreement he had made with him.

He closed the door quietly behind him and went to the bed. He put his hand on her shoulder. "Regina."

"Go away!" She cried harder.

Sitting down beside her, he grasped her shoulder and rolled her over so that she faced him.

She flung herself away from him and sat up. Her dark hair rioted wildly around her face and over her shoulders, and rage burned through the tears that flooded her eyes. "I told you to go away! I don't want you here. I don't want you anywhere near me!" She clamped one hand over her mouth and squeezed her eyes shut as uncontrollable sobs wracked her body.

Adam touched her hair. "Regina . . ."

She slapped his hand away. "Don't touch me!"

Adam withdrew his hand and watched uncomfortably as she sat, hunched over in the middle of the bed, bitter sobs wrenching her slender shoulders. Women's tears had always had a disquieting effect on him, and his first instinct was to put as much distance between Regina and himself as possible. Instead, he sat without moving, denying himself the luxury of escape.

Damn, if he didn't feel guilty as hell. If he hadn't been so determined to claim Regina for his own, she wouldn't be sitting here now, crying her heart out. Instead, she would be throwing herself away on some cowardly youth who had already impregnated the girl he was betrothed to marry. He knew that in the end Regina would be better off without Fitzhugh. So why did he feel like such an unprincipled bastard?

After what seemed an eternity, her tears began to subside.

Adam waited until she had managed to regain some of her composure, then said quietly, "Tell me what happened."

She hiccuped. "*Y-you* . . . are w-what happened," she bit out. "Ever since you came here, you've done nothing but interfere in our lives. Because of you, James hates m-me. Izzy hates me. You've ruined everything! I wish you'd go back to England where you came from. I wish I'd never laid eyes on you! *I hate you!*"

His stomach knotted. She wasn't the only one who hated him. He was beginning to dislike himself. "I'm sorry. I never meant to hurt you."

"Of course you didn't," she retorted. "You simply pawed at me every chance you got, and you made lewd remarks. It wouldn't surprise me if *you* were the one who has been spreading falsehoods about me."

Adam's brows knitted. "What are you talking about?"

"I'm talking about the rumors that I've lain with you!"

Adam suddenly felt as if he had lost control of the situation. There was something else going on here, something beyond the agreement he had with Fitzhugh. He had never told anyone—nor even remotely implied—that the conduct between Regina and himself had ever been anything but chaste. Yet, apparently, someone was spreading tales to the contrary.

Tales that bore an uneasy resemblance to the truth.

"I-I went to the mill to meet James," Regina continued, the anger in her voice giving way to a poignant ache. She nervously twisted her finger in the folds of her skirt. "We were going to run away and get married. But he wasn't there. Izzy said James thought I had betrayed him by lying with you. I tried to tell her it wasn't true, but she didn't believe me. She said I threw myself at you, and that . . . everyone thought . . ." Her voice broke and her shoulders began to jerk with renewed sobs. "I loved him . . . so much . . ."

Adam swore inwardly. He took Regina's arm and drew her toward him. "Come here."

She tried to pull away, but he wrapped his arms around her and held her tightly. He threaded his fingers through her hair and held her head against his chest. "Go ahead and cry," he murmured hoarsely, gently rocking her. "Get it out."

Gradually, Regina quit fighting him and wept freely, soaking his neck and the front of his shirt with scalding tears that seemed to have no end. As she cried, she closed her fingers around a fistful of his shirt and clung to it with a desperation that awakened a protective instinct in Adam that he had long thought to be dead.

He understood her. He understood what she was feeling. And that was dangerous, because understanding destroyed the emotional distance he needed to maintain to keep from falling in love with her. Elise had hurt him as James Fitzhugh had hurt Regina. If he lived to be a hundred, he never wanted to experience that kind of pain again.

And yet he was guilty of inflicting it upon Regina. Not only had he succeeded in putting an end to her romance with Fitzhugh, he had destroyed her friendship with Isabel—something he had not anticipated. He didn't know how he was going to compensate for her loss. He didn't even know if it was possible; the kind of pain that he had inadvertently caused her was the kind that left deep scars that never completely healed.

Growing increasingly uncomfortable in the awkward position in which he was sitting, he shifted his weight, holding Regina securely against his chest as he lowered her to the bed and lay down next to her. That she didn't resist spoke volumes; Adam knew all too well how the need to be held could overwhelm one's instincts for self-preservation. He'd been there himself.

After a while her sobbing subsided, until all that remained was an occasional muffled hiccup against his chest. He looked down at the top of her head, at the shiny mass of soft black curls, and he felt an overwhelming urge to bury his hands in them. "Feeling better?" he asked softly.

Regina nodded. "Thank y-you," she hiccupped. She made no effort to pull away, but lay there in his arms, trailing her fingertips over his shirtfront. The feel of his arms around her made her feel safe and protected in a way that James had never made her feel. With James, she had always felt on edge, as if she might do or say something to anger him.

But with Adam it was different. Even after the unkind words she had said to him, he had not abandoned her like the others but had held her while she cried. Right now, he was her only friend in the world.

Slowly, she became aware, not just of his closeness, but of the feathery warmth of his breath against her hair, of the beat of his heart beneath her fingertips, of the strength in the arms that held her.

Of her own growing desire.

Pulling away slightly, she tilted her head back and gazed up into his face, and just as she had the very first time she saw him, she was rendered breathless by his handsomeness. She was mesmerized as she watched his expression soften, and the light in his eyes turn to longing, infusing her with a golden warmth. Suddenly nothing else mattered except being with him.

She tentatively touched a trembling hand to his strong, chiseled jaw. Her gaze dropped to his lips. "Please . . ." she whispered. "Kiss me."

Adam's eyes darkened. Raising himself up on one elbow, he lowered his head to hers and kissed her eyelids, soothing the tender trail of her tears. His lips moved over the petal-soft curve of her cheek and down her temple to tease the corner of her mouth. His hair fell forward, surrounding her like a veil as it brushed softly against her skin. She rolled onto her back and lifted her face to his, her lips slightly parted in invitation, but when his mouth fully claimed hers, the assault to her senses stunned her.

She groaned into his mouth and wrapped her arms around his neck, pulling him to her. Her tongue fenced with his, boldly returning his dueling thrusts. He weaved his fingers into her hair and tilted her head back even farther than it already was, and she responded by arching her back so that her body strained against his. He pushed her dress up over her hips and positioned his knee between her thighs.

Over and over, he kissed her, until her head reeled and her lips felt bruised and her body pulsed with a passion she didn't even know she possessed. All the sensations he had previously aroused in her returned tenfold. The friction of his thigh against her womanhood quickly brought her to the brink of losing control. She felt as if something inside her was about to explode.

Adam pulled away from her, and a cry of protest escaped Regina's lips. She couldn't bear to have him leave her now. She needed him to finish what he had started, to assuage the throbbing heat that threatened to consume her. She struggled to pull herself up from the spinning abyss that nearly swallowed her, and became dimly aware that Adam was removing his clothes. Dazed and shaken, and feeling like a madwoman for what she was about to do, she untied the drawstring at her waist. Her hands trembled as she removed her underdrawers.

He returned to the bed and claimed her lips in a kiss that was even more fiery, even more demanding, than before. She clung to him, burying her fingers in his hair, pulling him to her, pressing her breasts against his chest. He settled his weight between her thighs, and she instinctively opened to him and wrapped her legs around his waist. She felt his hand between them, his fingers parting the hidden folds, followed by the pressure of his manhood against her heated flesh, stretching her, filling her. He withdrew slightly, then drove full length into her.

A strangled cry tore from her lips.

Too late, Adam felt the delicate membrane barring his entrance give way as he buried himself inside her. He pulled back to look at Regina's face, and the disbelief in his eyes reflected in the pain that darkened hers. He never dreamed she still was a virgin. How could he have been so wrong about her? "I'm sorry," he whispered hoarsely.

Fresh tears welled in her eyes. She tried to smile, and her mouth trembled. "It's all right. It doesn't hurt . . . much." A sob broke in her throat.

Adam lowered his head to hers and caressed her lips with tender kisses as he began to move inside her with a caution that tested the limits of his control.

When the pain finally subsided, Regina felt herself responding to yet another kind of longing. This time, the passion he aroused in her was not heated and frantic, but deep and slow moving like the river, carrying her along on a gentle current. His thrusts deepened and became faster, and soon she forgot the pain altogether as the current swept her away. Then he withdrew one last time and buried himself deep inside her, filling her with a shuddering warmth.

Adam wrapped his arms around her, carrying her with him as he rolled onto his side. He held her tightly, never wanting to let her go, wishing he could hold on to her forever. He didn't know what had happened to him, but making love to Regina had been therapeutic, cleansing his soul of the poisoning anger that had haunted him ever since Elise's betrayal. He just wished he had taken his time and been more gentle with her. If only he had known this was her first time.

He brushed her hair away from her face with his hand and kissed her forehead, and Regina stretched languorously against him, reveling in the hazy warmth that surrounded her like a cocoon. "I'm sorry I hurt you," he said softly. "I didn't know you were a virgin."

Regina stiffened as the full meaning of his words struck her like a slap. The contentment that had, only moments ago, left her feeling warm and safe, drained away like water through a sieve. She lay very still, hardly even breathing. When she finally managed to speak, her voice was little more than a strained whisper. "What did you think I was? A whore?"

Too late, Adam realized what he had done. He silently berated himself. Again, without meaning to, he had hurt her. What, in the name of God, was the matter with him?

Not wanting to make the situation worse than it already was, he chose his next words carefully. "I think you're a beautiful, desirable woman. I never thought you were a whore."

Yes, you did, his conscience accused.

Although Regina wanted desperately to believe him, Izzy's words echoed in her head. *You're just what everyone says you are. A whore!* Her chin quivered. "Everyone else does."

In that instant, Adam began to realize how badly he had misinterpreted the signals she had been sending him. What he had perceived as the intentional seduction by a worldly young woman was in reality the naive flirtation of an inexperienced schoolgirl. An adolescent testing the limitations placed on her by her elders. Except for that brief slip with Elise, he had always thought himself to be a good judge of character. How could he have been so mistaken this time?

He stroked Regina's hair, but this time she lay stiffly in his arms, not responding to his touch. An occasional muffled sound, so slight he could barely hear it, told him that she had started crying again. But instead of the gut-wrenching sobs that had consumed her earlier, the tears she now shed were eerily silent, a quiet cry of desperation that tore at his heart.

After what seemed an eternity, Regina stopped crying and drifted into a deep, exhausted sleep.

Moving carefully so he wouldn't awaken her, Adam extricated his arm from beneath her. He got up from the bed and got dressed, then straightened Regina's rumpled clothes. A light coverlet lay across the foot of the bed. He unfolded it and spread it over her.

He stood beside the bed for a long time, staring down at her tear-stained face framed by damp curls, wishing he could undo the hurt he had caused her. He even wished, for a moment, that he could turn back the clock and allow her to have her tryst with Fitzhugh, if that would repair the damage he had done.

But he knew that James Fitzhugh didn't really love Regina. If he had, he wouldn't have so readily taken the money. Regina's broken heart would mend in time. But if she learned the truth about how he had paid Fitzhugh to stay away from her, she may never learn to trust him again, and that was a chance he didn't want to take.

He knew what he had to do.

Chapter 11

The setting sun that streamed in through the tall windows cast long shadows across the study, illuminating the two men who faced each other across the top of the massive oak desk. A low growl sounded in Richard's throat, and there was the thirst for blood in his eyes. He swiped an arm across the top of the desk, sending papers and writing implements flying. "You bloody bastard," he bit out. "You already have everything that's ever belonged to me. My house. My land. My shipping business. I'll be damned if I'll let you have my sister, too!"

A muscle knotted in Adam's jaw. He regarded the man opposite him with contempt. Richard was unwashed and unshaven, and his clothes reeked of soured ale. At least in London, when Richard was recklessly gambling away his inheritance, he had taken care to groom himself and dress meticulously. Now, the only difference between Richard Langley and the filthy curs that populated the most sinister alleys was in the cost of their shirts.

Adam calmly straightened the items on top of the desk. "I'm prepared to make you a settlement of a thousand pounds in gold, five hundred acres fronting the river, and a limited partnership in the new shipyard." He removed a heavy leather pouch from the bottom desk drawer and placed it before him on top of the desk with a dull *thud*.

Richard stared at the pouch, speechless. A thousand pounds! In comparison, Charles Toliver's offer had been a mere pittance.

Suddenly his eyes narrowed and he regarded Adam with suspicion. "Why?" he demanded. "Until today, you were prepared to strip me of everything I owned, right down to the clothes on my back. Why are you being so generous now?"

Adam wondered that himself. What he really wanted to do was throw Richard Langley out of the house and never lay eyes on him again. Why he hadn't done just that he considered more a question of his sanity than his generosity. "You are going to be my brother-in-law. For Regina's sake, I don't want there to be any ill will between us. Besides, you are not completely lacking in redeeming qualities, Langley. When you're not drinking yourself into oblivion or wagering your shirt at the faro table, you have been known to make an occasional intelligent decision. I'm willing to work with you. With a little effort from both of us, I think we could realize a healthy profit from the arrangement."

"Ah, yes, so the man wants me to stay so he can take advantage of my shrewd business accumen," Richard said sarcastically. His eyes darkened. "Don't treat me as if I were stupid, Burke. What is the real reason you want me to stay at Summerhill?"

"In all honesty," Adam said slowly, deliberately, "I don't want you to stay at Summerhill. I don't want you anywhere near me. But you have something I don't, something I can't even buy." He placed his palms flat on the top of the desk and fixed Richard with a hard look. "The Langleys are one of the oldest families in Virginia. Descendants of one of the founding fathers, so to speak. No matter how destitute you become, no matter how badly you destroy your honor and your life, you will always be one of the colony's elite. You will always be acceptable to the local aristocracy in a way that I never will."

Richard snickered. "You're right about that."

"Between the two of us, we can create an empire the likes of which this colony has never seen. However, I can't do it without your social acceptance, and you can't do it without my money."

Richard stared at him for one long, disbelieving moment. Then he threw back his head and laughed. "You are amazing, Burke. Have you given any thought to Regina's reaction when she learns you purchased her for the purpose of furthering your own interests? She's a proud one, my sister. She'll never forgive you."

"The flip side of the coin, Langley, is that *you* will have sold Regina in order to further yours. Not a significant difference from the typical marriage contract negotiated in this county. Give yourself some credit, Langley; you didn't sell your sister to some strutting peacock like Charles Toliver."

"At least Toliver fancies himself in love with her. Whereas you, Burke, are one cold-blooded bastard. A man would be insane to entrust his sister to you."

Adam shrugged nonchalantly and reached for the bag of gold. "If that's the way you want it. But I think it is only fair to warn you: I intend to marry

Regina, with or without your blessing."

Richard seized Adam's wrist, pinning it to the desk. He stared at the money. He took a deep, quivering breath and nervously ran his tongue over his lips. Sweat beaded across his brow. "All right," he said shakily, his bloodshot eyes never leaving the leather pouch. "I give you... permission... to marry Regina."

In that instant, Adam felt a contempt for Richard Langley unlike anything he had ever felt toward any man. Nor did he want to look too closely at himself because he knew he was not likely to admire what he saw there either. Still, he told himself that this was best for all concerned. For Richard. For himself. For Summerhill.

But mostly for Regina.

He opened another desk drawer and withdrew a stack of documents, which he placed in front of Richard. "These are for you to read and sign. They spell out the terms of the marriage, including your rights as Regina's legal guardian. You'll receive the gold as soon as your sister and I are wed. And, lest you fear that I might try to renege on the agreement, a clause is included to prevent that from happening."

A deflated expression passed over Richard's face, making him look like an old man. He had hoped to get his hands on the gold right away. He wouldn't put it past Regina to spoil everything by doing something utterly foolish. "You've thought of everything."

"I try to be thorough."

Richard picked up the documents and carried them across the room to the side table, where he poured himself a drink. "If you think Regina will consent to this without a fight, you are mistaken," he tossed over his shoulder. He took the papers and his glass to a chair by the window and sat down. "She hates you, you know. She has hated you ever since she learned you stole Summerhill from our family."

Adam sighed as if the conversation bored him. "I can deal with Regina's moods," he said wearily. "She'll learn in time to accept that I know what is best for her."

Richard rolled his eyes in disgust. "You're so cocksure of yourself, aren't you, Burke?"

"I always get what I want." Adam turned his back on Richard, signaling the end of the discussion. He went to one of the tall windows and stared across the yard. Dusk was quickly falling, shrouding everything in a gray gloom not unlike what he was feeling. If Richard Langley ever caught the slightest scent of his fear that his plans might destroy Regina's tenuous trust in him, Langley would not hesitate to use that information against him.

Regina poked absently at the food on her plate with her fork. She had no appetite, only a dull ache in her temples that made her wish she had stayed in bed. The cold water she had splashed on her face and the cucumber compresses Bertie had given her for her eyes had done little to reduce the swelling. There was no pretending that she hadn't been crying. The evidence was glaring.

She couldn't stop thinking of James, of the way he had turned his back on her. She couldn't stop thinking of the things Izzy had said. *Why?* And why now, just when they were going to be married? James knew she loved him. And he loved her.

Yet something had happened to change all that. But what? She couldn't just sit back meekly and accept that James had suddenly decided to hate her. She needed answers. She needed to talk to James, to find out what had happened.

"Regina?"

Although Adam had spoken softly, his voice sliced through her like a blade, laying open her already broken heart. She jerked her gaze up to his face. "Yes?"

Adam winced at the sight of her tear-ravaged face. Her cheeks were pale and lifeless, and there were dark circles beneath her swollen eyes. The memory of her lying in his arms, crying inconsolably, hardened his resolve. If it was the last thing he did, he wanted to protect her from ever hurting like that again. He didn't love Regina, but he could not deny that she had touched something that had been buried deep inside him since that fateful day he had caught Elise in bed with another man. He lifted the decanter toward her. "More wine?"

She blanched. Just the thought of putting anything else in her mouth, whether it was food or wine, made her feel as if she would be ill. She shook her head.

Adam put down the decanter, and Richard reached for it. He bumped his glass with his elbow, knocking it over. The dark ruby liquid splashed across the white linen tablecloth and on his clothes. He swore aloud.

Adam moved the decanter out of his reach. "You've had more than enough to drink today. I suggest you give some thought to sleeping it off."

Richard glared at him. "Go to hell."

"This is a dining room, not a tavern," Adam said

curtly. "I won't permit that kind of language at my table."

"I forgot. It's your table now, isn't it, Burke?"

Regina shoved away from the table and leaped to her feet. "Stop it, you two! You've been sniping at each other all evening, and I'm tired of listening to you." She turned to leave.

Adam put down his napkin and stood. "Regina, wait! I'd like to talk to you."

"Well, I don't wish to speak with you. I just want some peace and quiet."

"You'd better learn to listen to him, Reggie. The man's going to be your husband."

Regina froze in the doorway. Slowly, she turned around. "What did you say?"

Adam ran his hand through his hair in frustration. "Damn you, Langley. I asked you to let me tell her."

"Go ahead and tell her." Richard got unsteadily to his feet and picked up the decanter of wine. He lifted the decanter in a mock toast. "She's all yours, Burke. Bought and paid for, like a side of beef." He left the room.

Regina gripped the doorframe as the floor swayed beneath her. She looked at Adam. "What did he mean by that, bought and paid for?"

"It was nothing, Regina. Forget it."

"What did he mean?"

Adam was dangerously close to going after Richard and beating the hell out of him. The calmness of his voice belied the rage that roiled just beneath the surface. "I asked Richard for your hand in marriage. He said yes. We signed the contracts this afternoon."

Regina stared at him, horrified. "Just like that.

Without consulting me? Did it never occur to either of you to ask me what *I* wanted? After all, it's my life we're talking about here. Don't I have any say in what happens to me?"

"I know this is sudden, but if you will give me a chance to explain, I'm sure you'll agree that we will both benefit from the arrangement."

"The arrangement?" Regina's voice broke. "My God, you make it sound like a business proposition."

"In a way it is. I can't pretend to be in love with you. You'd see through the falsehood in an instant. But I do admire your intelligence. Your spirit. Your courage. And I'd be lying if I said your beauty didn't figure into my decision."

Regina regarded him with disgust. "I wish you could hear yourself talk. You could just as well be describing a horse you intend to buy. Perhaps you would like to inspect my teeth to be certain you're getting what you paid for!"

Adam's frustration was quickly reaching dangerous levels. While he had not expected Regina to readily endorse his decision, neither had he expected it to go so badly. The fact that he had bestowed a financial settlement upon Richard in return for releasing Regina to him did nothing to improve his disposition. There was an uncomfortable truth in her implied accusation that he was indeed purchasing her. "You might already be carrying my child," he pointed out. "If so, then you have no choice."

Understanding dawned in Regina's eyes. She shook her head in denial. "Mr. Burke, if you think I lay with you for the purpose of trapping you into marriage—"

"Don't be ridiculous."

"It has been known to happen, sir. Father Tidewell will be the first to tell you that women as a lot are naught but scheming shrews who like to lure innocent men into their beds with the intention of forcing them into wedlock."

Adam's eyes narrowed until they were angry slits in his rigid face. "Regina, you are testing my patience."

"And you are testing mine!" Her voice rose to a shout. "You negotiate a marriage contract without troubling yourself to take *my* wishes into consideration, and you can't even give me a credible reason why!"

"Stop it."

"I need an answer! Why do you want so badly to marry me?"

Adam exploded. "Because you'd make the perfect wife! Haven't you ever heard that what every man wants is a lady in his drawing room and a whore in his bed? With you, I get both. All men should be so lucky. Is that a good enough reason for you?"

Regina's lips went white.

No sooner had the words left Adam's mouth than he regretted them. Until now, he didn't even know he was capable of being so cruel. He started toward her. "I'm sorry."

She felt as if someone had yanked the ground out from under her feet. She felt numb, as if all the life had been sucked out of her.

Adam reached for her, and she retreated a step. There was a hollow, vacant look in her eyes. "Get away from me," she choked.

"Regina, I'm sorry. I never meant to hurt you. Please forgive me."

She turned and fled.

"Regina!" Adam started after her, but came up short as he nearly collided with Bertie in the back hall.

The old woman folded her arms across her chest and stood her ground, blocking his way. There was murder in her dark soulful eyes. "Haven't you done that child enough damage for one day, Mr. Burke?"

"Please get out of my way, Bertie. This is between Regina and me."

"No, sir, it ain't. This old nigger don't have no qualms about slitting your throat while you sleep. You hurt Miss Regina again, and that's just what'll happen, and I won't even bat an eye doing it."

Adam fought for composure. Venting his frustration on Bertie would do more harm than good. "Bertie, I never meant to hurt her. I just need to talk to her."

"You can talk to her in the morning, when you've both calmed down. Right now, she needs to be with folks who love her, and that don't include you."

But I do love her, Adam thought, surprising himself. He opened his mouth to speak, but nothing would come out.

Bertie thrust out her chin in acknowledgment of her victory. Carrying herself like a queen, she turned and marched away.

Adam swore under his breath. How could he have been such a callous bastard? How could he have hurt Regina that way? How could he have hurt the woman with whom he was falling in love?

Impossible! The entire situation was impossible. How could he even *think* he loved Regina when he hardly knew her?

Returning to the dining room, he started toward the table with the intention of finishing off the decanter of wine, but it was gone. He'd forgotten that Richard had taken it.

"Damn it all!" he swore, furious with Richard. Furious with himself. He turned and smashed his fist into the wall.

Morning dawned hot and sticky. It promised to be one of those humid, sultry summer days that would inevitably end in a thunderstorm severe enough to beat down the maturing tobacco plants and snap off tree limbs the diameter of a man's forearm. There would be a mess to clean up afterward; there always was.

From the dining room window, James Fitzhugh watched the gray clouds gathering on the horizon and wondered sourly why it was so necessary that he follow in his father's footsteps and become a planter. He would rather go to London and become a businessman. He took a sip of coffee and grimaced. The coffee was strong and bitter. He went to the sideboard and shoveled several teaspoons of sugar into his cup.

"Excuse me, sir."

James turned around. One of the field hands stood in the doorway, clutching his hat in front of him. He was drenched with sweat, causing his homespun shirt to cling to his ebony skin. "What is it, Calvin?"

"You better come quick, sir. Some of the men found Miss Regina sleepin' out in the tobacco barn.

She looks like she been there all night."

James put down his coffee cup with a loud clatter and started toward the door. "Is she all right? Is she hurt?"

"She be just fine, sir. Just a little stiff and hungry, is all."

"Why didn't you bring her into the house?"

"I tried, sir, but she wouldn't come."

James followed the field hand across the lawn at a fast trot, leaping over hedgerows and perennial beds. As he ran, he prayed that the slave was right, that Regina wasn't injured.

Dear God, what was she doing here?

He hadn't meant to hurt her. He knew that she would be angry when he didn't show up at the mill as planned, but Adam Burke had been very explicit with his threats. And if he couldn't have Regina, then he didn't want to risk losing everything else that he would gain by marrying Lucy.

When he reached the barn, he found Regina standing beneath the bunches of tobacco leaves hanging from the rafters. Her gown was wrinkled and bits of grass clung to her tangled hair. She was pale, and had dark circles beneath her eyes. But there was something else about her today, something that made him uneasy, although he was at a loss to define it.

He quickly closed the distance between them. Worry clouded his eyes. "Reggie, what are you doing here? Are you all right?"

At the sight of him, Regina was suddenly overcome by the urge to throw herself into his arms, but somehow she managed to keep her head. She needed to be strong, at least long enough to find out the truth. If she didn't, she would crumble. "I'm fine, but I had to see you."

"You should have come up to the house."

"And risk encountering your father? You can't be serious!"

"Father's not home. He left early this morning. There was trouble at the Lees last night. One of the kitchen girls was raped by an indentured Scot."

Feeling her resolve weaken, Regina nervously moistened her lips. "Why did you tell Izzy I lay with Adam Burke?"

James gaped at her. "I never told Izzy that!"

"Don't lie to me! You told her that I was throwing myself at Adam, and that I—"

"For chrissake, Reggie, I told her that Adam Burke had paid me to keep away from you. Izzy drew her own conclusions."

It was Regina's turn to look surprised. "Adam *paid* you?"

"Yes, he paid me, damn it. God only knows why. It's not as if the bastard wants you for himself. He called it a wedding present to Lucy and me. He warned me to stay away from you." James angrily rubbed at his brow with his fingertips. "I felt like such an ass. After taking the money from him, there was no way I could face you."

Regina didn't know whether to laugh or cry. "You idiot! Since when have you ever let your conscience dictate your actions? You should have come for me anyway. That money would have given us a fresh start in Philadelphia."

"Reggie, it's not that simple."

"Of course it is."

"No, it's not. I don't expect you to understand. It's far too complicated."

Regina couldn't help feeling that he was being condescending toward her. "Then explain it to me."

"I can't. You'll just have to take my word for it."

"No, James, I won't just take your word for it. You're hiding something from me, and I want to know what it is."

"All right, damn it! He threatened me. He said if I came anywhere near you again, he would tell you about Lucy."

A discomfitting uneasiness gripped her. She had the feeling she wasn't going to like this one bit. "What about Lucy?"

James wiped his hands over his breeches, as if unconsciously trying to cleanse them. "I'd rather not talk about it."

"What about Lucy?" Regina repeated, more firmly this time.

"Reggie, I told you I don't want to talk about it. Can't you just let it go?"

"No! I'm not going to just let it go. You've always been able to talk to me before. Why not now?"

James's breathing was labored. "Because it's something I'm not very proud of! I made a mistake, all right?"

Regina realized with a vague sense of misgiving that she had never before heard James admit to any kind of wrongdoing. She also realized that whatever he had done, she had no choice but to forgive him. He was her only hope, her last chance to get away from Summerhill. Away from Adam Burke. Away from Richard. Away from Charles Toliver. She nervously moistened her lips. "James, whatever you've done, it won't change the way I feel about you. But I can't bear the thought of you keeping secrets from me. Please, just tell me. What is it about Lucy that Adam—Mr. Burke—is threatening you with?''

James hesitated for several tense seconds before finally blurting out, ''She's carrying my child.''

Regina felt as if he'd punched her in the stomach. She took a ragged breath. ''I see.''

''That's why Father and Mr. Carlisle changed the date of the wedding. They didn't want a scandal.'' James angrily ground his heel into the ground. ''Damn it, Reggie, I only lay with her once. I wanted you, but you kept insisting that we wait until we were married. You let me touch you, but then you wouldn't allow me to . . .'' His voice trailed off.

Regina cast him a sharp glance. ''Are you saying it's my fault that you bedded Lucy?''

''No! Yes . . . I don't know. All I know is that I wanted you so badly. I couldn't wait. I couldn't bear the thought of spending yet another night without you. You weren't there, and Lucy was. I tried to pretend she was you, but—''

''Don't say another word.'' Regina pressed her hands over her ears, shutting out the sound of his voice. That he could not restrain himself until after they were married was bad enough, but to place the blame on her hurt more than anything he could have done.

James gripped her wrists and pulled her hands away from her ears. ''Reggie, please, don't do this. I never wanted Lucy. I swear. I only want to be with you.''

His face blurred before her eyes. He had bedded Lucy Carlisle! Yet, who was she to judge? She had let Adam Burke—whom she hated more than any-one, except possibly Charles—bed her. She tried to tell herself that her situation was different, but in her heart, she knew it wasn't. "I'm sorry," she fi-nally managed to get out. "It's just that, of all the things you could have done, I never expected *that*."

"Neither did I! But I can't change the fact that it happened. My God, Reggie! Are you going to lord it over me forever that I made one small mistake?"

"Getting Lucy with child is not a small mistake! Damn you, James! I came here hoping to mend the rift between us. I just couldn't accept the way it ended. I was even stupid enough to hope that you might still care enough about me to want to marry me." Her voice waivered.

"I *do* want to marry you."

"But you're going to have a child! You can't just abandon your responsibilities!"

"I'll send Lucy money, for chrissake! She won't lack for anything. Neither will the baby." His hands tightened on her arms. "Reggie, let's do it. Let's run away and get married, just as we planned."

Regina didn't know whether to feel ecstatic that James still wanted her or revulsion at the thought of him deserting his unborn child. Never before had her feelings toward James been so conflicting. "I-I don't know—"

His hands tightened on her arms. "Do you still want to?"

Not trusting herself to speak, she nodded.

His forehead wrinkled as he tried to collect his thoughts. "We'll need to leave now, before anyone realizes you're missing. Did you bring a change of clothing?"

She shook her head. "I was so upset, I forgot."

"It's all right. You can wear something of mine. We'll need food. And water." He started to pull her toward the door. "We'll have to hurry. I don't know when Father will be home."

Regina balked. "James?"

"What is it?"

Fighting the overwhelming feeling of doom that threatened to engulf her, she swallowed hard. "I love you."

Chapter 12

Wind whipped along the river, kicking up whitecaps on the normally sluggish surface of the water, and causing the trees on the bank to bow and sway treacherously. Lightning slashed across a sky that had turned dark long before sunset, followed by a crack of thunder so loud Adam felt it reverberate in his teeth. In the warehouse office, an oil lamp illuminated the disarray of the changes he had ordered made to the building.

Adam faced the group of men who had gathered at his request, an unlikely mix of planters and indentures. "Randolph, I want you to take your group and head south. I know your daughter said Fitzhugh has relatives in Philadelphia, but there is still a chance they may have decided to go to Williamsburg instead, since it's closer.

"Sandhurst, you and your men are to search every house, every barn, every outbuilding on the Northern Neck. The rest of you will come with me. With any luck, we'll find them tonight. They can't have gone far in this weather."

The men went outside to get their horses. Richard pulled Adam aside. "I don't like the idea of giving *him* a horse."

Adam glanced at Duncan McLean. "Don't worry. He can be trusted."

"How do you know that? The man's a convicted murderer, for God's sake. He's also a Scot. After what MacDonnell did to that girl at Lee's place—"

"That has nothing to do with Duncan McLean. In truth, Langley, I have more faith in McLean's loyalty than in your ability to stay sober."

In the darkness, Richard's eyes glittered like live coals. "Have it your way. But if the son of a bitch escapes, I'm holding you personally accountable."

"I'll keep that in mind. Now go get your horse. We're wasting valuable time."

Adam, Richard, Duncan McLean, and Sam Eustis, a freeman who had entered Virginia nearly twenty years before as an indentured servant, set out on the road leading north by northwest, along the south bank of the Potomac. As they rode, Adam recalled his visit to Isabel Fitzhugh earlier in the day, a visit that had left him with a bitter taste in his mouth.

He had arrived at the young woman's house in the early afternoon. Izzy herself, her thin brown hair pulled back severely from her face and tied with a narrow ribbon, had answered the door.

"Why, Mr. Burke! This is such a lovely surprise! Please, do come in." Hastily touching her hair, she stepped aside to let him into the house. "My mother and I were just sitting down to dinner. Won't you join us?"

"Thank you, but I must decline. I can only stay a few minutes. Another time, perhaps."

Izzy's expression fell.

A tall black girl hurried into the hall, hastily wiping her hands on her apron. "I sorry, Miss Izzy," the girl mumbled. "I didn't hear the door."

Izzy squared her narrow shoulders and forced her mouth into a stiff smile. "It's all right. I'll take care of it. Please go back to what you were doing."

The surprised glance the girl cast Izzy told Adam that she probably wasn't accustomed to hearing kind words from her mistress.

Izzy led Adam to the drawing room. "It's a pity you can't join us for dinner, Mr. Burke. Perhaps you would have time for a cup of tea instead."

"I'm afraid this isn't a social call, Miss Fitzhugh. I'm here to ask for your help."

"By all means. Please, sit down."

Adam waited until she was seated, then took the chair opposite her. He saw her touch her hair again, and he couldn't help noticing how unappealing the thin, wispy strands were. She had styled it differently the night of the dinner party. The way she was wearing it now did nothing to soften the sharpness of her face.

Izzy folded her hands primly on her lap and looked at him with adoring eyes. "What can I do for you?"

"Regina has been missing since last night. She was seen early this morning with your cousin, James. Now neither of them can be found. I have reason to believe they've run away together. Can you tell me where they might have gone?"

The light in Izzy's eyes turned cold. She smiled thinly. "I haven't the slightest idea. I certainly wouldn't worry about them though. It wouldn't be the first time my cousin has disappeared without letting anyone know where he was going. And, of course, Reggie will do just about anything to get attention. I'm sure they're fine."

His jaw tightened. "I'm sure they are too, but until Regina is home where she belongs, I won't rest. Is there anyone to whom they would likely turn for help? Friends? Relatives?"

"I swear, I don't know where they are, or if they are even together. I wish I could help you, but I can't. The truth is, Reggie does outrageous things like this all the time. She thinks nothing of worrying the people who care about her."

As he sat there, looking at Izzy's pinched face and her hard eyes, he had wondered why he had ever thought her pretty. Features that had appeared delicate at first now seemed bony and angular. Her cheekbones. Her nose. Her narrow chin. Everything about her made him think of sharp little teeth.

He thought of the hateful things she had told Regina, and he longed to fasten his hands around Izzy Fitzhugh's scrawny little neck. That was one woman, he decided, who would never be welcome in his house.

Beatrice Randolph, on the other hand, had seemed genuinely concerned about Regina's disappearance. It was she who had revealed—albeit with some reluctance—James's and Regina's plans to run away to Philadelphia and get married. Even Arthur Randolph had set aside his annoyance with Regina and volunteered to start a search party.

He prayed silently that they were on the eloping couple's trail. If anything happened to Regina, he would never forgive himself.

Every time he thought of the vicious things he had said to her last night, he felt as if he would be

ill. He didn't know what had come over him. He
was not by nature a cruel man. Controlling, perhaps. Exacting. Even demanding. But not cruel. He
wasn't even certain from where the vulgar words
he had uttered stemmed. They had boiled up so
suddenly it was as if they had been buried deep
inside him for years, festering, until they finally exploded from his lips in a moment of weakness.

But why had he hurled them at Regina, who had
done nothing to hurt him? He certainly had never
said such things to Elise.

Elise. Elise. Elise. The name played over and over
in his mind, like a musical score that had no end.

As they rode, he drew his brows together and
squinted into the darkness. Regina reminded him
of Elise. Indeed, he had thought more about Elise
since arriving at Summerhill than he had in the
past ten years. Was that why he had exploded at
Regina? Because she reminded him of Elise?

Or because she reminded him of something he
didn't like to think about: how vulnerable loving
someone made him.

They had ridden more than four hours, stopping
only to search the three small cabins they had
passed on the way, when the road forked. The men
stopped. It was now fully dark, and the night was
damp and hostile. The wind howled through the
trees, and small branches littered the road.

Sam Eustis pointed into the darkness. "We
should go that way. There's nothing down the
other fork."

Adam did not have a good feeling about the situation. "Have you been there?"

"Many times."

"What about Fitzhugh? Does he know this place

well enough to have made the same choice?"

Sam shrugged. "I doubt it. But I can tell you one thing. If they went down that way, they wouldn't have gotten very far. That road leads straight into a tidal marsh."

"I say we split up," Richard said. "Two of us take the east fork, and the other two take the west."

"Not so fast," Adam cautioned. "With everything that has happened in recent weeks, we'd be wise to stay together. The larger our group, the safer we'll be. We'll all go west."

"Damn you, Burke! Regina is my sister. I have a right to decide what we do."

"Burke is right," McLean said suddenly, speaking for the first time since the search began. "With the Lee brothers flogging MacDonnell near to death last night for raping that girl, there's no telling what could come about. Had I an ounce of English blood in my veins, I wouldn't want to go anywhere in these woods without half the King's army for protection."

"What the hell do you know?" Richard shot back. "I've spent most of my life here in the Northern Neck. The indentures know that if they injure a planter, they'll find themselves hanging from the end of a rope."

"Silence!" Adam ordered. "Quarreling amongst ourselves isn't accomplishing anything except wasting valuable time. You may not think you are in danger, Langley, but your sister certainly is. The simple fact that she is female makes her vulnerable." Adam paused to let his words sink in, then said tersely, "We'll have a show of hands. Those who favor staying together?"

Adam, Duncan McLean, and Sam Eustis raised

their right hands. Lightning filled the clearing, making the surrounding woods seem even darker and more sinister than ever. "We'll stay together," Adam announced. "If we can't find them, we'll backtrack and try the other fork."

"He can't vote!" Richard protested, jerking his head toward McLean. "He's not a freeman."

"He's risking his life to find Regina," Adam reminded him. "His vote counts as much as yours."

"The hell it does!"

"We're staying together," Adam said curtly. Before Richard could voice another complaint, Adam snapped his reins, urging his mount forward. It began to rain. He pulled his cloak tighter about him and bowed his head into the wind.

They had gone no more than a mile when they came upon an inn. The building was small. Chances were, it contained no more than a common room on the ground floor and one or two private chambers upstairs beneath the steeply sloped roof. A newly built extension to the original building was being used as a stable, providing them with a place to rest their horses and get out of the rain.

The inside of the stable was warm and dry. A horse in one of the stalls neighed softly. Adam lit a sulphur-tipped splint.

"They're here," Richard said. "That's Fitzhugh's horse."

The light from the splint did not reach into the farthest corners of the stable. Adam approached the stall and raised the splint over his head. "Are you sure?"

"I should know; I've raced against Fitzhugh often enough." He paused, then muttered under his breath, "When the bastard wasn't trying to run me through with a blade."

Adam gripped the top of the stall with his free hand. Until now, he had not realized just how possessive he felt toward Regina. Although he had known her little more than a month, he had begun to think of her as belonging to him. Now that he had decided to marry her, the thought of her with James Fitzhugh—with any man—filled him with rage.

First Elise, and now Regina. The only two women he had ever loved. He could not bear to think that both of them had betrayed him with another man. Yet he had no one but himself to blame for Regina's betrayal. If he hadn't hurt her, if he hadn't said those unforgivable things to her, she wouldn't have run away.

Swearing aloud, he turned and headed straight toward the stable door.

The pounding on the downstairs door jolted Regina awake. She sat up in the middle of the uncomfortable bed with its sagging ropes and lumpy mattress, and rubbed the heel of her hand across her eyes. She was still fully dressed, wearing the shirt and breeches James had lent her. In the darkness, she could barely make out James's figure, slouched in the chair where he had fallen asleep shortly after they reached the inn. He hadn't even removed his boots.

Slipping out of bed, she went to the small, low window nestled beneath the eaves and pulled back the curtain. The rain still had not let up. The pounding at the door continued, with more urgency than ever. She leaned down and peered through the diamond-paned casements.

She gasped.

"James, wake up!" She went to the chair and shook him. "We have to get out of here. They've found us."

He groaned. "What the hell is going on? Where's all that noise coming from?"

Regina dropped to her knees and groped beneath the bed for her shoes. "It's Richard. He's downstairs with Adam and some other men."

"Hell," James mumbled. He dragged himself out of the chair. "How are we going to get out of here?"

"The window is our only hope. It's not very big, but I think we can squeeze through."

"We'll break our necks!"

Regina pulled on her shoes. "And so will Richard." The pounding on the door stopped. Going to the window, she turned the catch and opened the casements. Below her, lamplight spilled through the open door. She couldn't see her brother or the other men. They must be in the common room downstairs. Her heart pounded. She didn't want even to think about what Richard was going to do when he got his hands on her.

She sat on the window ledge and put one leg through the window. The opening was narrower than she had originally thought, and she banged her shoulder on the wood frame. "Ouch!"

Footsteps sounded on the stairs.

"Hurry, damn it! They're coming up the stairs." Panic surged through her. "I'm trying!"

Suddenly the chamber door slammed open.

Regina looked around just in time to see Richard grab James and swing him around. "James!"

Richard smashed his fist into James's face, and James staggered backward. Richard lunged at him, and both men stumbled across the room, crashing into the chair and knocking the tin basin off the washstand.

Regina screamed.

Adam's tall form darkened the doorway. Behind him, the innkeeper barked, "Destroy the place, y' rotten scoundrels, and I swear you'll pay for everything you break!"

Adam seized James by the collar and hauled him off Richard.

Richard drove his fist into James's stomach.

"Richard, stop it!" Regina jumped down from the window. She grabbed Richard's arm, but he flung her away from him, knocking her down.

Regina scrambled to her feet and plowed headfirst into the fray. An elbow collided with the left side of her face, and for several seconds, everything went black. She clutched a fistful of someone's shirt and held on as the floor seemed to drop out from beneath her feet.

Suddenly someone seized her and she felt herself being dragged backward. She tried to twist free, but a pair of strong arms closed around her and pulled her hard against a rain-soaked cloak. "Settle down!" Adam ordered.

"Take your fight outside," the innkeeper growled. "I'll not have you busting up the place."

Regina saw two men seize Richard and James, and pull them away from each other. She kicked wildly and clawed at the imprisoning arms. "Damn you, let go of me!"

Adam tightened his hold on Regina with a force

that drove the air from her lungs. "I said, settle down!"

Duncan McLean and Sam Eustis were battling to keep Richard and James apart. Richard wrested out of Sam's grip and started toward her. He shook his fist in her face. "You goddamned little slattern. I warned you to keep away from Fitzhugh. If Burke calls off the betrothal and withdraws the money because of this, I swear I'll beat you until you can't walk."

Regina stopped struggling. "What money?"

"Eustis, get him out of here."

"What money?" Regina demanded.

"Ask *him*," Richard spat, jerking his head toward Adam. "He's the one who bought you."

Sam Eustis reached for Richard, but Richard shrugged off his grasp. Pivoting, he strode from the room. His angry footfalls could be heard all the way down the stairs.

Adam spoke tersely to the other men. "Leave us."

James strained against McLean's hold on him. "Reggie, I'm sorry. I'll find a way to get us—"

"Now!"

Regina jumped when Adam's voice exploded in her ear. She twisted around. She couldn't see his expression clearly in the semidarkness, but it wasn't necessary. She could feel the rage that emanated from him in molten waves. "That's the second time in two days that Richard has said that I've been bought. What does he mean by that?"

Adam waited until the others were gone before he answered her. "I offered your brother a settlement in return for your hand in marriage."

"A settlement! You paid him money? For me?"

"I didn't want there to be any friction between our families. I thought the settlement would appease your brother and ensure his cooperation. It was never intended to hurt you."

She wrenched her arm from his grasp, hurting herself in the process. Tears stung her eyes. "How dare you! First you pay James to stay away from me, and now this. Yesterday, when Richard said I was bought and paid for, I didn't realize he meant *literally*." Her voice cracked. "Tell me, Mr. Burke, did you also pay Charles to keep his distance?"

"I didn't have to," Adam bit out. "The man's conscience kept his price low."

Ordinarily, she would have rejoiced at the knowledge that she would never again have to endure Charles's attentions. But the thought that Adam Burke—who had no legitimate claim on her whatsoever—could exercise such unlimited control over her simply because he had money made her livid. Drawing back her arm, she cracked her open hand across Adam's cheek. "Bastard!"

He seized her wrist and wrenched her hand down with a force that tore a surprised cry from her lips. When he spoke, his voice was low and frighteningly controlled. "That's not the first time you've struck me, Regina, but it *will* be the last. Do you understand me?"

"You deserved it!"

"And *you* deserve to have your backside blistered, but that's not the precedent I want to establish with the woman who is going to be my wife."

"I wouldn't marry you if you were the only man in the colony."

"You don't have a choice, Regina. Now that you've disgraced your family by running away and taking up lodgings with a young man, you can be assured that your parish priest will not rest until he has extracted a severe penalty from you."

Regina pried at his fingers, trying to break his hold on her, but his hand tightened around her wrist until it felt as if the slender bones would snap. "Don't be ridiculous," she bit out. "I'm a Langley. Father Tidewell won't dare do anything to me."

"He can have you flogged. Have you thought of that?"

"Not if Richard pays the fine."

Adam shook her so hard her head snapped back. "With what, damn it? Your good name and your privileged position? They won't buy your exoneration, Regina. Only money can do that, and right now your brother doesn't have a shilling to call his own."

Regina opened her mouth to object, but the words died in her throat. The horrible part was that Adam was right. The law was clear. For the crime of fornication—of which she and James would probably be found guilty since no one was likely to believe that nothing had happened between them tonight—James would merely be made to stand up in front of the church and confess his sins, something that would greatly distress his family, not to mention Lucy Carlisle's, but that would leave him virtually unscathed. She, on the other hand, would be ordered to pay a fine of five hundred pounds of tobacco or, if unable to pay, sentenced to receive thirty lashes on her bare back.

Tears flooded her eyes and her throat constricted as a desolation unlike anything she had ever known swept over her. Richard was broke. Neither he nor Uncle William had access to five hundred pounds of tobacco, and this year's harvest now belonged to Adam. She felt as if she would be ill. The thought of being stripped naked and publicly flogged was more than she could bear. "I hate you," she choked.

Adam released her wrist. "You're not the only one," he said wearily. "Meet me downstairs. I'm taking you home."

Furious that she had come so close to breaking down in front of him, Regina squared her shoulders and took a ragged breath. "Mr. Burke!"

Adam stopped with his hand on the door.

Scalding tears streamed down Regina's face. "I'll marry you," she blurted out, "but only because I have no choice. You might own me, but you can't make me fall in love with you."

In that moment, Adam came closer than he ever had to telling Regina to go to hell and booking himself return passage to England. He was sorry he had ever laid eyes on her. He was sorry he had ever come to her brother's rescue. He should have left the arrogant young fool to rot in a debtors's prison. It would have served him and the rest of the Langleys right. Without a word, he left the room.

Five minutes later, Adam was waiting in the common room with his black felt tricorne hat tucked beneath his arm when Regina descended the stairs. Although he had known when he saw her upstairs that she was wearing men's breeches, it wasn't until she stepped into the full light of the lamp that he realized how snugly they hugged her hips and her long legs, or the way the softly draping fabric of her white shirt hinted provocatively at the fullness of her breasts. She had not bothered to comb her hair, and now it fell about her shoulders with a wildness that made him ache to bury his fingers in the unruly tresses and tame them.

Made him ache to tame her.

Resentment glittered in her dark eyes as she approached him. He could tell she had been crying. Her eyes were puffy and reddened, and her lashes clumped together in long black spikes. The faint purplish beginnings of a bruise had spread across the curve of her left cheek.

His initial response was to reach for her and draw her into his arms, but the thought of her upstairs in that bedchamber with James Fitzhugh rekindled his rage and destroyed any sympathy he might have felt for her. He folded his arms across his chest, deliberately placing a wall between them. "Did you bring any clothes with you?" he asked curtly.

She thrust out her chin and glowered at him. "Only what I'm wearing." In spite of her open display of defiance, her voice quavered.

"We'll be traveling all night," Adam continued, his tone brisk and businesslike. "I want to have you safely back in your own bed before dawn. In the morning, I'll speak with Father Tidewell and make arrangements to have the wedding ceremony performed immediately, before rumor of a scandal has time to circulate." He went to the door.

Behind him, Regina clenched and unclenched her fists as the anger she had thought she was too exhausted to feel erupted inside her. Scandal or not, she seriously doubted this latest transgression of hers would go unpunished. And if she was going to be made to suffer, she wanted him to suffer too. She took a deep breath. "Your haste alone, Mr. Burke, would be enough to cause a scandal," she taunted softly. "Wouldn't you prefer to postpone the marriage until you're certain I'm not carrying James's child?"

Something inside him exploded. Adam abruptly turned around. His eyes blazing, he started toward her.

The look of triumph on Regina's face fled and she took a retreating step.

"Don't you ever," Adam bit out, closing the distance between them, "mention that man in my presence again. I don't want to hear his name spoken. He's not welcome in my house. If he's caught trespassing on my land, I'll give orders to have him shot. Do you understand me?"

Regina backed into a table.

"Answer me!"

"Y-yes."

He loomed over her. "Nor do I ever wish to hear you speak of this night. As far as I'm concerned, it never happened. Is that clear?"

She nodded jerkily.

Adam noticed the innkeeper standing in the shadows, eavesdropping, and he had to bite back the angry words that sprang to his lips. Fishing a guinea from the small leather pouch he carried in a pocket sewn inside his cloak, he tossed it onto the table. "That's for the damages."

The innkeeper's eyes widened when he saw the gold coin. He jerked his gaze up to Adam's face.

Adam's hard gaze penetrated the innkeeper's. "And for your trouble," he added with a deliberation that gave an unspoken meaning to his words.

Understanding dawned in the man's eyes. He nodded vigorously. "Aye, sir. Thank you, sir."

With a tenuous grip on his fury, Adam rammed his hat onto his head. He grasped Regina's elbow and steered her toward the door.

She had to run to keep up with his long-legged strides. "I can't believe you just gave that man a gold guinea!" she blurted out. "He doesn't have a guinea's worth of furnishings in this entire place!"

Adam jerked open the door. "For your information, Regina, what I bought was his silence. If anyone comes here asking questions, he'll say he's never seen you."

If Regina had ever before doubted the power of money, she was quickly getting an education. For as long as she could remember, she had believed that social standing was determined at birth. Except for the royalty, who were ordained by God, one was either a member of the small but privileged aristocracy, or was a commoner doomed to a life of hardship and poverty. Now she was beginning to see that man was not judged by his birthright, but by the depth of his purse.

The thought made her sick.

Outside, the rain had slowed to a steady drizzle. The other men had already mounted their horses and were waiting for them. Their curious gazes followed them as they made their way across the muddy yard.

Regina saw Duncan McLean watching her with his cold blue eyes, and hot color flooded her face. This was the second time that he had witnessed her humiliation.

Spotting James seated on his horse, she started toward him, but Adam hauled her back, nearly causing her to lose her footing on the soggy ground. He steered her toward his own mount. "You're riding with me. I don't want to take the chance that you'll attempt anything stupid."

He lifted her up onto his own horse, then swung up into the saddle behind her. Regina sat stiffly in an attempt to put as much distance between them as possible, but the effort was for naught. Adam opened his cloak and folded it protectively around her, pulling her back against him. She gritted her teeth when his hand brushed against the underside of her breast. If he touched her like that again, she swore silently, she was going to slap him silly.

As they rode, Adam's mind repeatedly assaulted him with torturous visions of Regina and James together, in bed, making love, until he was riddled with an overwhelming urge to kill them both.

He told himself he must be demented to still want to go through with the wedding after all that had happened. He was practical enough to know that the daughters of any number of fine Virginia families would be willing to marry him, for his money alone, thereby assuring him a place in the community.

So why did he still want Regina?

He looked down at the rain-darkened head pressed against his chest. Although she had not made a peep since leaving the inn, he knew she was not asleep; he could feel the anger in her tense body. He wondered what she was thinking, then decided he was better off not knowing. Most likely, she was probably plotting his demise.

He pulled the cloak tighter around her and wondered again at both his own sanity and the wisdom of the contract he had negotiated with Richard for Regina's hand in marriage.

He was beginning to think that what he had purchased was a place for himself in hell.

Chapter 13

William Langley, still in his traveling clothes, impatiently paced the length of his study. Within an hour of receiving Richard's note informing them that Regina had disappeared, he and his wife and sons were on their way back to Summerhill. The jarring carriage ride, made at breakneck speed, had put him in a foul temper, a dangerous mood that deteriorated even further when he arrived at Summerhill to find his niece safe and sound, and sulking over her thwarted elopement with James Fitzhugh. "Damn it, Regina, I ordered you to stay away from him!" he ground out between clenched teeth.

"I said I was sorry!"

"William, please calm down," Caroline begged. "I'm sure Regina didn't intend to worry us."

"I wasn't worried; I was humiliated." William stopped in front of Regina and pointed his riding crop at her. "Everyone in the county knows that you and Fitzhugh ran away together. How in God's name do you expect Toliver to continue with his suit after what you've done?"

"But, I don't *want* to marry Charles!"

"I doubt you need concern yourself with the pos-

203

sibility of that ever happening. After the scandal you've created this time, I would be surprised if Toliver even acknowledges you, much less courts you. Why, Regina? What is it about the scoundrel that makes you so eager to destroy any chance you might have of marrying a decent man?"

"I *love* James!"

"Damn you, if I hear you say one more time that you love that son of a bitch, I swear I'll knock you senseless!" William raised the riding crop, and Regina threw her hands protectively over her face.

Caroline seized her husband's arm. "William, don't. It's not important that Regina marry Charles. She can come to Williamsburg with us. She can start over, without the stigma of the elopement hanging over her head. We'll talk to Richard again. I'm sure that under the circumstances, he'll not be so against the idea this time."

"Regina's not going anywhere," Adam said from the doorway. He handed his hat to a houseboy.

William's face darkened. "What the hell do you mean by that?"

"William, please!" Caroline shot her husband a pained look. "Adam, thank you for finding Regina. We came home as soon as we heard she was missing."

"Burke, I realize this house belongs to you now," William said tersely, "but I would appreciate the opportunity to discuss family matters in private. This conversation does not concern you, so, if you would, please leave us."

"Actually, sir, this conversation does concern me. Regina isn't going to wed Charles Toliver, and she isn't going to Williamsburg with you. She and

I are to be married in three weeks. I've already made the necessary arrangements with your parish priest."

"What!" William's eyes bulged. "I didn't give you permission to marry my niece."

"No, but your nephew did." Going to the desk, Adam unlocked a drawer and removed a sheaf of papers. He tossed them on top of the desk. "You may peruse the contract if you wish. I assure you everything is in order."

Regina glanced up from beneath her lashes to find Adam watching her, his expression unreadable. A telltale fluttering in the pit of her stomach reminded her that, no matter how angry she was with him, he still had the power to make her tremble with longing. "I can't believe Father Tidewell agreed to this," she said sarcastically. "How much did you have to pay *him?*"

William rounded on her. "I don't want to hear another word out of you."

"But, Uncle William—"

"I said, silence!" William bellowed. Turning to Adam, he shook the riding crop in his face. "And you, sir, have overstepped your bounds. This contract of yours may be legal, but it was negotiated in bad faith. Yes, Richard is Regina's legal guardian, but I'm the one who has taken care of her since my brother's death. I know what is best for her. And I know *who* is best for her."

"Will you people stop talking about me as if I'm not even in the room!"

Adam held up his hand, silencing Regina, all the while keeping his gaze fixed on William Langley. "Five minutes, sir," he said. "That's all I ask of you.

If, during that time, I cannot convince you that Charles Toliver is not the man you want your niece to marry, then I'll tear up the contract."

William's jaw worked ominously. He clasped the riding crop behind his back and regarded Adam through narrowed eyes. "Five minutes," he agreed.

"Uncle William, surely you're not going to listen to him!"

William pointed the riding crop toward the door. "Out!"

Caroline took Regina's elbow. "Come help me unpack," she said firmly. "We'll leave the men to discuss this."

Knowing there was no way she could protest without creating a scene, Regina followed her aunt. She glowered at Adam as she and Caroline left the room.

Caroline did not speak again until they were safely behind the closed door of the upstairs bedroom. She turned to face Regina. "Why is Adam so insistent upon marrying you?"

"I-I don't know."

"What happened at the inn?"

"Nothing! I've told you a dozen times I didn't lie with James. I slept on the bed and he fell asleep in the chair."

"I'm not talking about James."

Unable to meet her aunt's gaze, Regina fidgeted. "Answer me."

"Nothing happened at the inn!"

"If not at the inn, then where? Here? In this house?"

The color fled Regina's face. She started to shake her head.

Caroline's expression gentled. "It was Adam, wasn't it?" she asked quietly.

Tears welled in Regina's eyes. Her chin quivered. "I didn't mean for it to happen. It just did."

"Did he force you?"

Regina wiped her eyes with her fingertips. "No."

"Then it seems to me as if he wants to do right by you."

"Doesn't it matter that I don't want to marry him?"

Caroline threw up her hands in frustration. "I don't know what to say to you anymore, Regina. You don't want to marry Charles. You don't want to marry Adam. For God's sake, who do you want? That spoiled, pampered *boy* you ran off with?"

Regina started to say yes, but she couldn't make herself say the word aloud. She shook her head. "I-I don't know. I just . . . I want to marry someone who is willing to accept me as I am, without trying to change me or make me into someone I'm not or ask me to put on airs for his fashionable friends. I want to marry someone who cares about *me*."

"And James does?"

"He says he does." Her voice shook.

"Don't you think it's possible that Adam could care about you as well?"

"Adam Burke doesn't care about me; he simply wants to own me. Just like he owns Summerhill."

"You're not being fair to him."

"Why should I? No one is being fair to me!"

Caroline sighed wearily. "Regina, for all your uncle's blustering, if that contract Adam and Richard signed is legal, and I have no reason to believe otherwise, then there's nothing any of us can do about it. You and Adam Burke are going to be married."

The next three weeks were the longest in Regina's life. If news of her attempted elopement had created a stir, the announcement that she and Adam were to be married set the entire county on its ear. For three successive Sundays, after the reading of the banns, Father Tidewell would launch into a lengthy discourse on the sins of the flesh, never once failing to look meaningfully at her as he spoke.

But if listening to Father Tidewell slander her virtue before the entire parish cut her to the core, seeing James and his new wife sitting together in the Fitzhugh pew made her feel confused.

James and Lucy had gotten married almost immediately after James's return from his illfated elopement, dashing for good Regina's hopes that the two of them could ever have a future together. Yet, to her surprise, she was more relieved than upset by James's marriage. When she first learned that James had fathered the baby Lucy was carrying, she had told herself it didn't matter. James didn't love Lucy. Then, the more she thought about it, she found herself unable to ignore the fact that not only had James been unfaithful to Lucy; he had been unfaithful to *her*.

Although it irked her to admit it, she was almost glad Adam had come after them and put a stop to the elopement. She didn't want to be married to a man she couldn't trust.

"It's so bizarre," she told Beatrice one Sunday

afternoon after church. The two girls had sneaked away from their families and met at their usual spot at the top of the cliff overlooking the docks. "I loved James so much, but when I ran away with him, I started remembering all the things he did that annoyed me. Whenever we were supposed to meet, he was always late and when he did arrive, he was usually drunk. And he never stopped pressuring me to lie with him. I'm glad now that I didn't."

"Especially since he was already bedding Lucy. I swear, Reggie, the more I learn about James, the more I'm glad you didn't marry him." Beatrice held out one of the biscuits she had brought with her.

Regina shook her head. Her stomach was so tied in knots, the thought of eating anything made her feel as if she would be ill. She couldn't believe any of this was happening. Ever since she was a child, she had imagined her wedding as the celebration to end all celebrations, with everyone in the county present to bestow good wishes upon her and her cherished husband. Instead she was about to marry a man she didn't love, in a private ceremony limited to immediate family members. Even Beatrice, who was her best friend in the whole world, wasn't allowed to attend. "This wasn't the way I wanted it," she said thickly. She glanced up at Beatrice through the tears that stung her eyes. "I wish you could be there."

Beatrice plucked at a blade of grass. "Me too," she said uneasily. "But at least you're not moving away. I'll get to visit you whenever I want."

"If your father will let you."

"He can't stay angry forever," Beatrice pointed out.

"You're right." Regina took a shaky breath and looked out across the field. "Where's Izzy? Isn't she coming today?"

"I doubt it. She's not ready to forgive you for stealing the man she wanted."

Regina groaned. "Oh, Bea, I wish you'd stop saying that. I didn't steal Adam. I don't even *like* Adam."

"You'd better learn to like him, Reggie. Day after tomorrow he's going to be your husband."

"Excuse me, may I come in?"

Adam turned around to find Caroline Langley standing in the doorway of the study. "Of course. I'm about to pour myself a glass of port. Would you care for some?"

Caroline smiled weakly. "Perhaps a drop. I need something to calm my nerves."

"You and me both. How is Regina? Is she all right?"

"She'll be fine. Bertie is helping her get dressed." Caroline sat down on the edge of a chair and carefully smoothed her skirt. "I just wanted a chance to speak with you alone before we left for the church."

Adam carried the glass of port to her. "Shall I close the door?"

Caroline took the glass. "That won't be necessary."

Adam noticed that Caroline's hand shook slightly as she raised the glass to her lips. "I've been wanting to thank you and your husband for postponing your trip to Williamsburg until after the wedding. I wish you'd reconsider staying permanently."

"Your offer is very generous, Adam, but in all honesty, losing Summerhill was hard on William. Even though it never really belonged to him, he had come to think of it as his own. I'm not sure he could ever really be happy here again after all that has happened."

"I can understand that. Were I in his shoes, I too would probably want to start over elsewhere. But I hope that both you and your husband will continue to think of Summerhill as home. My door is always open to both of you."

"Thank you." Caroline nervously ran the tip of her forefinger around the rim of her glass.

Adam put down his glass and sat down opposite Caroline. "Something is troubling you. What is it?"

Caroline stared at the glass in her hand. Several minutes passed before she spoke. "I just want to be certain you are marrying Regina for the right reasons. That child means the world to me, and I don't want to see her hurt."

"Nor do I."

"Adam, I know that you and Regina have been together . . . intimately."

Adam wondered if it was Regina or one of the servants who had told Caroline. Either way, there was nothing to be gained by denying the truth. "Yes," he said simply.

Caroline took a deep breath. "If that's the only reason you're marrying her—"

"It's not."

"She's *not* pregnant."

"I know." God, did he know! In spite of his promise to marry Regina, he had not been able to forget that he was not the only man she had been with. The three-week wait imposed by Father Tidewell before they could marry had been a mixed blessing. Had Regina been with child, he knew he would have had to accept the very real possibility that he might go to his grave never knowing whether the baby she carried had been fathered by him, or by Fitzhugh. And not knowing was preferable to knowing the latter.

However, less than a week after the thwarted elopement, the gossip circulating among the household staff had included the tidbit that Regina need not start sewing baby clothes just yet.

He had breathed a sigh of relief as the agonizing uncertainty that had loomed over him from the moment he learned Regina had run away with Fitzhugh suddenly lifted, and had spent the better part of that night at the Boar's Head, thanking God over a bottomless tankard of ale, and trying to figure out how he had once again allowed himself to fall prey to a woman's charms. Regina had made him forget Elise. He hoped that, in time, he could forget—and forgive—the rest.

"I know Regina can be trying at times," Caroline continued. "But she's not a bad seed, as Father Tidewell would have everyone believe. She would never intentionally do anything to hurt anyone. It's just that she seldom stops to think before she acts."

Adam chuckled. "That's an understatement."

"Adam, please be patient with her."

Adam's expression turned serious. Leaning forward, he took the glass away from Caroline and set it on the table. Then he took both of Caroline's hands between his, and held them firmly. "Mrs. Langley, if you're worried that I might take undue advantage of my position as Regina's husband, let me assure you that I am not an abuser of women or children. I never have been, and never will be."

Caroline smiled wanly. "Thank you."

"I'm marrying your niece for a number of reasons, some practical, some not so practical, and all of them unquestionably selfish. However, I promise you that I will do everything within my power to see that she wants for nothing. I want Regina to be happy. Please believe that."

"I do. Thank you for putting my mind at ease." Caroline stood up. "I've already sent Jethro over to the Sandhursts with our trunks. We'll spend the night there."

"You don't need to leave so soon. You're welcome to stay here as long as you wish."

"It's best this way. You and Regina need your privacy."

Adam and Caroline turned to find Regina standing in the doorway of the study. Adam caught his breath. Never in his life had he seen anyone more beautiful. She was wearing a satin gown the color of rich cream. The high-necked, close fitting bodice and long sleeves that hugged her slender wrists had been embroidered with thousands of tiny seed pearls that caught the light and shimmered like fine jewels. The toes of her matching satin slippers peeked demurely from beneath a full overskirt that separated in the middle to reveal an elegant petticoat of silk cream and white brocade. Except for two fat shiny curls that rested on her right shoulder, the rest of her black hair had been swept up off her neck and elegantly arranged in soft curls that framed her mutinous face.

Adam slowly released his breath. "You're beautiful."

Caroline hurried toward her. "Regina, what are you doing in here? You know it's bad luck for the groom to see you in your gown before the wedding!"

Regina lifted her chin and fixed her glittering gaze on Adam. One black brow arched imperiously. "I just came to see if you two were ready to go. I would like to get this ordeal over with."

Caroline gasped. "Regina, that's no way to speak to—" Before she could finish, her niece had pivoted and marched from the room. She whirled around. "Adam, I'm so sorry."

"You have nothing to apologize for, Mrs. Langley. Don't worry. Regina will come around."

He hoped to God he was right.

If Regina had thought the trip to St. John's Church was long, the ride back to Summerhill seemed as if it would never end. Uncle William and Aunt Caroline had taken the small light carriage, leaving her to ride with Adam in the enclosed coach. She sat stiffly beside him on the velvet upholstered seat, not looking at him, not touching him, staring out the window. Her throat was so tight it hurt, and it was all she could do not to burst into tears.

Never in her life had she thought her wedding day would be a day she would dread. She had no happy memories from this day, nothing she could look back on with fondness. The ceremony itself had been a quiet, somber affair, more befitting a funeral than a wedding. All she wanted to do right now was go home, shut herself in her bedchamber, and cry herself to sleep.

"You haven't said a word since we left the church," Adam said quietly as they neared the house. He reached for her hand.

She pulled her hand away and sat anxiously twisting the slender gold band around the third finger of her left hand. "I'm sorry if you find my conversational skills lacking, Mr. Burke, but I truly have nothing to say."

"I'm your husband, Regina. I prefer that you start addressing me by my given name."

"And if I don't?"

"I won't force you to do anything you don't want to do."

She turned her head to glower at him. "Except marry you."

The coach rolled to a stop in front of the house. Regina started to rise, and reached past Adam for the door, but he extended his arm across the door, blocking her exit. "Sit down."

"I don't want to."

"I merely want to talk to you."

"I already told you, I have nothing to say."

"Regina, sit down."

So angry she felt as if she might explode, she obeyed, not out of deference to his wishes, but because she wasn't quite certain he wouldn't break his promise and *make* her sit down.

Adam placed two fingers beneath her chin and tilted her head up toward his. "I want to ask a favor of you."

Regina pulled her head away. "You have a lot of gall asking anything of me, Mr. Burke. You have Summerhill. You have the house, the business, the land. You've destroyed my brother, and broken up my family. And now you have me. What more could you possibly want?"

"Regina, I know you didn't want to marry me, and I'm sorry you're unhappy. But this is our wedding day, and I don't wish to spend it bickering with you. For this one day, I ask that we call a truce."

"Go to hell." Regina scrambled over Adam and thrust open the door, startling the groom standing outside awaiting directions. She jumped down from the coach and started toward the house at a furious pace, her angry footfalls striking the ground with a force that reverberated through her clenched teeth.

Adam caught up with her just as she reached the portico. He seized her elbow. "Damn it, Regina, slow down!"

She jerked her arm away and rounded on him. She glared at him through a haze of angry tears. "I'll grant you one day, Mr. Burke. I'll be civil to you this one day. But don't expect me to pretend to be overjoyed to be your wife, because I'm not. And if I'm going to be miserable, then you are too. Starting tomorrow, I intend to make every day of the rest of your life a living hell."

The muscle in Adam's jaw twitched ominously. "Thanks for the warning," he bit out.

Gathering up her skirts, Regina bolted up the stairs and yanked open the front door.

"*Surprise!*"

She skidded to a stop.

Yard upon yard of satin ribbon in every color imaginable had been draped and looped from the foyer ceiling, forming a colorful canopy the length of the broad hall. At the far end of the hall, the double doors leading out to the terrace had been thrown wide open, and the opening trimmed with garlands of nasturtiums and daylilies from the cutting garden. Virtually every slave and indentured servant from Summerhill stood along the walls of the foyer, clad in their best attire, their faces breaking into grins at her startled expression.

"Congratulations, Miss Regina!" they called out. "God bless you!"

A small black girl of about seven whom Regina recognized as one of the kitchen helpers thrust a bouquet of wilted black-eyed Susans into her hand. "These are for you, Miss Regina," she whispered shyly.

Regina knelt and gave the child a hug. "These are beautiful. Thank you."

Bertie was the next to engulf her in a hug. "God bless you, child."

Regina held onto the old woman as if her life depended on it. She didn't want to be married to Adam, yet she was. She was going to be married to him for the rest of her life.

She suddenly felt as if she would be sick.

Bertie finally pried her arms away. "Off with you," she scolded. "The others are waiting for you outside."

Moving slowly as if in a trance, Regina walked the length of the hall, shaking extended hands and returning the hugs of the well-wishers. She felt dazed, and helpless. Everything seemed like a dream, a very bad dream, from which she couldn't awaken. Finally she stepped through the double doors and into a shower of wheat grains and millet and polished rice. Shouts of "Congratulations!" and "Good luck!" filled the air.

From the back of the crowd, someone yelled, "Good riddance!" and everyone laughed.

She stood on the broad stone terrace, not believing what she was seeing. More than a dozen long tables, draped with white linen cloths and laden with colorful bouquets of flowers and greenery and platters piled high with food, had been arranged in a giant "U" in the middle of the expansive lawn. More tables, not as elegantly decorated, but still groaning beneath enormous amounts of food were set up close to the kitchen. The air was filled with the spicy aroma of woodsmoke from the cooking fires, and the mouthwatering smells of pit barbecue and roast pig.

Virtually everyone Regina knew, with a couple of notable exceptions, was present. The Lees were there, as were the Sandhursts, the Randolphs, the Carters, most of the Fitzhughs, and countless others that Regina seldom saw except on special occasions because they lived so far away. Beatrice, her coppery hair flaming in the sunlight, grinned from ear to ear and waved. Aunt Caroline and Uncle William stood arm in arm, and Aunt Caroline had tears in her eyes. Robert and Timmy and the other children were searching through the grass for seeds and rice to throw at each other. Even Richard was dressed for the occasion, and seemed to have put aside his hostility.

For now.

Adam placed his hands on Regina's shoulders.

"Welcome home, Mrs. Burke," he whispered in her ear.

Regina turned and looked up at him. Bits of wheat chaff clung to his dark hair and dusted the broad shoulders of his black silk jacket. He was smiling down at her, and there was a tenderness in his gold-flecked eyes that sliced through her defenses. Suddenly she felt like the most despicable person in the world. She folded her arms defensively across her chest. "I never expected any of this." Her voice trembled.

"I know you didn't," Adam said gently.

"I-I don't understand. Why did you do it?"

"Because this is your wedding day. And because I wanted to."

"But I said such terrible things to you."

"I probably deserved them."

She shook her head. "Not all of them. Some of them, maybe, but not—"

Sliding an arm around her waist, Adam pulled her to him and covered her mouth with his, silencing her with a long, passionate kiss.

Hoots and whistles erupted in the crowd.

By the time Adam released her, Regina was flushed and breathless and more than a little embarrassed that he had kissed her so boldly and so intimately in front of everyone.

Amusement glittered in Adam's eyes. He crooked an arm toward her. "Shall we?"

Feeling a little unsteady on her feet, Regina placed her hand on his arm.

As they stepped off the terrace, the crowd surrounded them. Caroline Langley kissed her niece on the cheek and smiled through her tears. "I know you're going to be happy, darling. I can feel it in my heart."

"Oh, Reggie, isn't this wonderful!" Beatrice burst out. She was clutching Captain Bebe's arm, and her face glowed through her abundant crop of freckles. "You were so despondent on Sunday that I wanted desperately to tell you what we had planned just so you would cheer up. I almost spoiled the surprise."

"I still don't know how we kept it from her," Caroline said, laughing. "If she hadn't spent most of the past three weeks in her bedchamber, *sulking*, she might have noticed that everyone else in the household was running around frantically trying to get all the preparations completed in time for the wedding."

"I guess I have been pretty awful lately," Regina said sheepishly.

"Awful!" William sputtered. "Young lady, if your aunt hadn't begged me not to, I would have hauled your rebellious hide out behind the garden shed and—"

"William!" Caroline interrupted, aghast.

William cleared his throat and composed himself. He extended his riding crop, handle first, toward Adam. "Son, consider this a wedding present. You're going to need it."

The crowd burst into laughter. Regina blushed furiously.

Adam drew Regina closer against his side. "Thank you, sir, but I believe I've found a much more effective way to entice your niece into doing my bidding."

Regina glanced up at him to find him watching her, restrained passion burning like a fever in his hazel eyes, and she felt her knees grow weak. Maybe being married to Adam Burke wasn't going to be such an ordeal after all.

Richard pushed his way through the gathering. He held up a tankard of ale in a toast. "To the loving couple," he said. His eyes were bloodshot and he slurred his words. "May you have a long and happy life together."

Regina felt uneasy. "Thank you, Richard."

Edward Lee slapped Richard on the back. "C'mon, Langley. Let's go get some of that barbecue. The smell is making my stomach growl." He nodded at Adam and Regina. "Congratulations, you two."

A dark look passed over Richard's face. "I think I'll stay here and chat with the newlyweds."

"That's a good idea you had there, Lee," Adam said suddenly. "I'm famished. Regina, are you hungry?"

Even though her stomach was too knotted to enable her to eat, it didn't take Regina more than a second to realize what Adam was doing. "A little. I'm more thirsty than anything."

"I'll bring you something to drink. Show me where that keg is, Langley. I could use a tankard myself."

After Adam and Edward led Richard away, Regina slowly released her breath. Inasmuch as she had started out dreading this day, she certainly didn't want Richard spoiling it for her now.

"Ignore him," Caroline said, as if reading her thoughts. "The rest of us are here to help you celebrate. We're all under orders from your husband to make this the happiest day of your life."

Her husband. The realization that she was *mar-*

ried struck Regina full force. She felt as if someone had yanked the ground out from beneath her feet.

Beatrice grabbed her hand. "Miles Jordan is starting up a game of cricket. Let's go watch."

Regina looked around for Adam.

"Go enjoy yourselves," William urged. "We'll point Adam your way when he returns."

"Besides," Beatrice whispered, "I have something to tell you."

"You ladies go on ahead," Captain Bebe said. "I'll get all of us some refreshment."

Beatrice waited until they were well away from the crowd before telling Regina her secret. "Silas asked me to marry him!

"What?"

"I'm going to be Mrs. Silas Bebe!"

"Bea, that's wonderful! But what about Richard? I thought you were in love with him."

"Richard who?"

Regina stared at her. "You're serious, aren't you?"

Beatrice's face pinkened beneath her freckles. "He asked me this morning, and I said yes. We haven't told Father yet, but I'm sure he will approve. He really likes Silas."

Regina shook her head. "I can't believe this. Everything is happening so fast." Then another thought occurred to her, casting a shadow over her happiness. "Does that mean you'll be leaving and going back to England with him?"

"Heavens, no! Adam has offered him a position here at the shipyard he's building. With the new ports opening upriver, Silas will have all the business he can handle, ferrying goods back and forth along the Potomac."

Regina stared at her friend in disbelief. "Adam did all this?"

"Of course. Oh, Regina, Adam is such a good-hearted man. When Silas told him he wanted to stay in Virginia with me, Adam gave him the job, and a share in the shipping company."

Regina turned her head. Across the yard, she spotted Adam with her cousin, Robert, and her breath caught in her throat as she was struck by the sheer masculinity that Adam exuded. He had removed his black jacket. His white shirt fell in elegant folds from his broad shoulders down to narrow hips encased in white breeches that fit his long muscular legs like a second skin. He had rolled up his shirtsleeves. His dark hair was tied back from his tanned face. His knee-high black boots shone like a mirror.

Adam motioned out across the yard, and Robert Langley started running in that direction. Adam threw the ball, and Robert landed a running catch.

Adam cheered, and in that instant, Regina thought her cousin seemed a little taller, a little more confident. He took several running steps backward and threw the ball back to Adam.

For several seconds, it was not her flaxen-haired, twelve-year-old cousin she saw running after the ball, but a slender, earnest youth with long legs and hair the color of midnight, and her heart swelled with emotion.

She knew instinctively that she could not have chosen a better man to father her children.

Never in her life had she been as confused as she was now. Adam affected her in a way that neither

James—nor any other man for that matter—ever had.

Lust. That's what Father Tidewell would say it was. Lust, plain and simple.

Although she could not deny that she felt a little weak in the knees whenever she saw Adam, it was more than physical attraction. There was something else, something she could not quite identify. Being married to Adam simply felt *right*. It felt comfortable. It felt . . .

She frowned. She didn't want to feel comfortable. She wanted excitement. She wanted to be courted. She wanted to be swept off her feet.

Beatrice followed her gaze. "Do you still hate him?"

Regina was pensive a moment before turning a bewildered gaze on her friend. "Bea, is it possible to hate someone one minute, and the next minute find yourself falling in love with him?"

Beatrice eyed her suspiciously. "You're joking."

Regina shook her head. "I don't think so."

Beatrice shook her head in disbelief at the same time that a smile of delight broke across her features. "With you, Reggie, I think anything is possible."

By the time the last guest left, night had fallen. Those who had come from farther away had invitations to stay the night at homes nearest Summerhill, most ending up at either the Randolphs or the Sandhursts. Regina bid a tearful farewell to her aunt and uncle and cousins, standing on the front portico and waving at the departing carriage long after it disappeared down the road. Finally, she went inside. She pushed the door shut, leaned back against it, and sighed wearily. "I'm exhausted."

Adam leaned down and kissed her gently, tenderly. "Did you have a good time?"

Regina smiled up at him. "I have a feeling that I'm going to regret admitting this, but I had a fabulous time. This was the best day of my life. I'll treasure the memories for as long as I live."

He blew out the candle in the wall sconce, and darkness surrounded them like a velvet shroud. Then he slid one arm around her waist and the other behind her knees, and picked her up. "It's not over yet."

Chapter 14

⟨‿⟩⟨⟩⟨‿⟩

Adam pushed the bedroom door shut and lowered Regina to the floor. She barely had time to get her bearings before he caught her and pulled her hard against him. His mouth came down hungrily over hers.

She instinctively leaned into his kiss, rising up on tiptoe and wrapping her arms around his neck, as something that was at once primitive and uncontrollable roared awake inside her. His strong hands roamed over her back and hips with restrained urgency, kneading the soft flesh and pulling her even closer to him.

Through her clothes, Regina could feel the granite hardness of his arousal pressing against her stomach, and that part of her that was soon to receive him began to ache with a longing so great it seemed to fill her up to the point of bursting. She tugged the narrow black silk ribbon from his hair, letting it fall free, then slid her hands down his chest to unbutton his shirt. Adam groaned, and she felt his heart leap reflexively beneath her fingertips. "God, I want you," he murmured in her ear.

Stepping away from him, Regina reached up and began pulling the pins from her hair.

His bride's silhouette against the moonlight streaming in through the open window, her slender arms upraised as if in offering, was more than Adam could bear. Holding her hips, he kissed her neck, her breasts, his lips forging a smoldering trail down her satin-encased midriff, then lower still, until he was kneeling before her.

He pressed his opened mouth against the layers of silk and satin at the juncture of her thighs, and a liquid warmth surged through her entire body.

Adam slid his hands beneath her gown, and Regina shuddered when he touched her bare skin above her garters. He unfastened a garter, then slowly, tantalizingly, rolled the silk stocking down her leg. She stepped out of her shoes, and he eased the stocking the remainder of the way off. By the time he had removed both stockings, she was trembling.

He caressed her buttocks, her abdomen, and the insides of her thighs, sliding his fingers up into the soft curls to part the sensitive flesh and tease the taut little bud with his thumb. Regina moaned softly as her world reeled around her. It was as if a dam had burst inside her, setting free a torrent of raw emotions over which she had no control.

The hairpins she had been holding clattered to the floor as her world shifted beneath her feet. She clutched Adam's shoulders, fighting to keep her balance. He breathed another molten kiss into the folds of her skirt, and her knees buckled. She gasped.

He rose and wrapped his arms around her, holding her close against his pounding heart. Shaken, she clung to him. Fragments of memories flickered through her thoughts. The time he caught her sneaking back into the house after her rendevous with James. The first time he made love to her. That godawful night at the inn, when she had taunted him about carrying James's child.

Adam standing on the terrace and murmuring tenderly in her ear, *Welcome home, Mrs. Burke.*

Remorse shot through her with a heart-rending pang. "Adam, there's something I have to tell you . . ."

"Not now," Adam growled. He buried his hands in her hair and covered her lips with his, and she groaned into his mouth. He kissed her tenderly, teasing her lips with his tongue, then gently parting them to taste the honeyed sweetness within. He kissed her fiercely, driving his tongue into her mouth again and again until she was delirious with longing.

One by one, he unfastened the tiny pearl buttons that extended down the back of her gown. He eased the gown off her shoulders and down over her hips, letting it slide to the floor in a symphony of rustling satin.

Still kissing her, he took her by the shoulders and slowly guided her toward the bed. One of the house slaves had already turned back the covers. Adam picked up Regina and laid her on the crisp, sun-scented sheets.

Dazed, she clutched the front of his shirt, pulling him down with her as he bore her down onto the bed. "Adam . . ."

"Shhh." Kneeling beside her, he pressed his lips against the fluttering pulse in the hollow at the base of her throat, then down to the sweetly scented valley between her breasts. Cupping her breasts, he lifted and stroked them, teasing the taut nipples through her chemise and lulling her into a hypnotic languor that made her feel as if she were floating. He pulled her chemise down over her shoulders, freeing her breasts from the soft silk, then lowered his head and drew a nipple into his mouth.

She sucked in her breath and her back involuntarily arched. "Adam!" she cried out. She threaded her fingers through his hair, holding his head against her breast as he alternately laved the sensitive crest with his tongue and sucked gently, until sharp, almost painful, stabs of desire shot through her body.

As he caressed her breasts, Adam marveled at her responsiveness. Even after all that had passed between them, including his careless breaching of her maidenhead, she accepted his touch with a trusting innocence that filled him with awe, and reminded him that tonight he was laying the cornerstone for their future together. No matter how badly he wanted to bury himself in her and assuage his own needs, he was determined to make this night perfect for her. He intended to kiss and caress and make love to every inch of her body until she was delirious with pleasure.

He intended to make her forget James Fitzhugh.

He worked her chemise up to her hips. Sliding one hand beneath her buttocks, he lifted her slightly and pushed the undergarment up to her waist, then settled his weight between her thighs, parting her legs with his knee. As he bent over her, his long hair fell forward and tickled her stomach. Regina choked back a giggle and jerked. Adam caught her hips, holding them motionless. "Ticklish?" he asked, kissing her abdomen.

"Yes!" she gasped.

He pushed her legs farther apart and brushed his lips over the petal-soft skin of her inner thighs. "Here?"

A small sob broke in her throat. She clutched the sheet. "Ye-es . . ."

He slid his fingers into the mound of soft curls, gently parting the feminine folds. He lowered his head. "And here?"

Something inside Regina exploded. A low scream tore from her throat and her hips surged upward. Adam cupped her bottom and lifted her even higher, and renewed his intimate exploring.

Wave after wave of undiluted pleasure washed over her and through her, carrying her from one incredible peak to another until she thought she could endure no more. No longer able to think coherently, she clenched her teeth in a fruitless attempt to keep from crying out, but the soft mewling sound that had started deep in her throat gave way to choked sobs that she could no longer hold back. "Adam . . . please . . ."

Suddenly the dam burst, filling her with a molten heat. She threw back her head and gripped the sheets as a tremor so violent it felt as if it would rip her apart shuddered through her. She didn't know what was happening to her. Never in her life had she felt anything that was so frightening, yet so wonderful. She felt consciousness slip away, then return in an altered form, bringing with it a sharpened awareness: of the velvet softness of the night air against her bare skin; of the sound of her breathing; of the blood pulsing through her veins; of her woman's fragrance filling the bedchamber.

Of wrongs yet to be righted.

Fighting her way back to reality, she became aware that Adam had left the bed and was removing his clothes. She raised up on one elbow and struggled to sit up. "Adam," she whispered, overcome by a gnawing sense of urgency. "I have to tell you something . . . about that night at the inn."

He flung his breeches aside and approached the bed.

Regina's breath caught in her throat. Even though it would not be the first time Adam had bedded her, it was the first time she had seen him completely naked. There was no denying that not only was her husband a handsome man, he was a strong one as well, tall and lean and powerful, with well-defined muscles beneath skin that shone like silvered bronze in the moonlight. The sheer size of him, not to mention his enormous arousal, made Regina feel small and vulnerable. She was no naive virgin, but she suddenly felt like one. He leaned over her and took hold of her chemise, and she started like a frightened rabbit. "Adam—"

He pulled the chemise off over her head. "I don't wish to discuss that night at the inn. Not now. Not ever."

The controlled anger in his voice made her heart pound. "Please, Adam, you have to know the truth."

Sliding one arm beneath her knees, he gave her a hearty jerk that put her flat on her back. The bed dipped beneath his weight. He parted her legs with his knee and settled between her thighs. Regina tensed briefly in expectation of the same pain she had felt the first time he had made love to her, and was surprised when there was none, only a pleasant fullness as he slid into her. Supporting most of his weight with his arms, Adam lowered his head and touched his lips to one corner of her mouth. "I don't want to hear another word about it. Whatever happened between you and Fitzhugh is in the past. It's forgotten. Don't ever mention it again."

The feel of the crisp hair on his chest brushing against her nipples and the proud heat of him deep inside her were almost more than Regina could bear. He began to move inside her, and she sucked in her breath. "Nothing happened between James and me," she blurted out.

He froze.

She nervously moistened her lips. For reasons she could not explain, not even to herself, she had to set right the lie she had told him, and she had to do it now. She took a shaky breath. "I only let you think I'd lain with James because I was angry with you. But the truth is, he never touched me. He wanted to, but I wouldn't let him. I was afraid if he found out I wasn't a virgin, he wouldn't go through ... with the marriage ..." Her voice faltered. "You're the only man I've ever been with."

Above her, Adam's face was hidden in shadow. She could feel the tension that emanated from him, but whether it was from anger or from the effort of supporting his weight, she didn't know. She was already beginning to regret having brought up the subject of that night at the inn. He had told her he didn't want to discuss it. Why couldn't she have let it be? "I'm sorry," she whispered. "I didn't mean to make you angry. I just couldn't let you go on believing something that wasn't true."

Angry? Good God, he was delirious! Although Regina was not the only woman he had ever bedded, he could not deny a certain pleasure—and relief—at hearing that she had never been with anyone else. Yet he also was quick to realize that her admission had the effect of diminishing the rage that was his only defense against her, his only protection against falling too deeply in love with her. "I'm not angry."

If he wasn't angry, why was his voice so taut? Then he started to withdraw and panic surged through her. "There's something else you should know." The words barely squeaked from her throat. "That same night . . . I also said you'd never be able to make me fall in love with you." She hesitated, then added shakily, "That, too, was a lie."

Adam's resistance shattered. He drove into her full force, again and again, possessing her with a hunger that came from the depths of his soul. He couldn't get enough of her. He wanted her. He wanted to possess her, to make her so inseparably a part of him that he need never fear losing her.

The almost brutal intensity of Adam's passion caught Regina by surprise, sending her senses reeling before she even realized what had happened. She wrapped her arms around him and held him tightly, instinctively lifting her hips to take him deeper inside her, and the exquisite feelings he had aroused in her earlier returned with a fury that struck her like a gale blowing in from the river, heady and exhilarating and dangerous.

She couldn't think clearly. Everything she was feeling, everything he was doing to her, was so utterly wonderful that she wished in her heart that it would never end. She felt as if she were standing on the edge of the cliff overlooking the river, her arms outstretched against the wind, letting it buffet her with its incredible power. Then what little control that remained in her was gone and she ceased to think at all. Her nails dug into the bunched muscles of his shoulders and she cried out as the wind lifted her and carried her over the edge.

Adam suspended his movements, absorbing the force of her climax, then drove into her one last time and poured his shuddering warmth at the mouth of her womb.

Totally spent, Adam gathered her in his arms and sagged against her. Burying his face into her softly scented hair, he fought to catch his breath. He had never before lost control like that, or surrendered so completely.

Or felt so goddamned vulnerable.

It wasn't a feeling with which he was comfortable.

Still holding Regina, he rolled onto his side, carrying her with him. He brushed the hair from her face and lightly touched his lips to her brow. He tilted her face up toward his with the intent to kiss her, and was surprised to see the glimmer of tears in her eyes. He raised himself up on one elbow. "Did I hurt you?"

She shook her head.

"Then why the tears?"

"I-I don't know. I'm just trying to understand everything that's happened."

"Such as?"

She uttered a small sigh of frustration. "It just doesn't make any sense. This morning I hated you. And now . . . I don't anymore."

"And that's why you're crying?"

"Adam, I really loved James," she blurted out. "And I thought I wanted to marry him. But when

I'm with you, I can hardly remember what he looks like."

"I'm glad."

She searched his face in the darkness, desperate for some sign of understanding. "But don't you see? If it could happen to me, then could it not happen to you also? Suppose you meet someone else, and suddenly you don't want *me* anymore?"

Her insecurity touched a resonant chord deep inside him. He too had felt that same self-doubt, for years, after Elise's betrayal. He stroked her cheek with his knuckle. "I won't let that happen."

"But it's possible."

"Regina, this morning, when I swore 'to forsake all others,' I did not take that vow lightly. I don't intend to let *anyone* come between us. Ever."

She trailed her hand over his chest. The crisp, dark hair curled around her fingers. "I just wish I understood why you married me, especially when I was so mean to you. There were so many other women you could have chosen. Izzy was besotted with you."

He captured her hand and held it still against his heart. "I don't love Izzy," he said quietly.

Regina stared at him, not quite certain she had heard him correctly. Or if she *had* heard him right, then perhaps she had misinterpreted his words. She opened her mouth to ask him directly if he loved her, then closed it again. If she was wrong, she didn't want to know. She took an unsteady breath. "I didn't want to marry you."

"I know."

"But I don't think I'm going to be sorry I did."

Adam chuckled. "Neither do I."

She nervously moistened her lips. "Make love to me again."

Adam started to tell her that he needed more time to recover, but the idea had already taken hold and he could feel himself growing hard again. He leaned down to kiss her. "You're going to be sore in the morning," he cautioned.

She wrapped her arms around his neck and pulled him down to her. "I don't care."

Regina didn't know what had startled her, but suddenly she was wide awake. For several moments, she lay motionless, listening to the night sounds: the hum of the cicadas, the rustle of leaves outside the bedchamber window, the comforting sound of Adam's breathing. She glanced over at him, sleeping soundly beside her, one arm draped possessively around her waist, and felt herself blush all the way to her toes.

Never in her wildest dreams had she imagined that she would be married to such a handsome man, or to one who was such a wonderful lover. Just remembering the way he had touched her and the delightfully decadent things he had whispered in her ear were enough to send shivers of desire down her spine. If she lived to be a hundred, she would never tire of having Adam in her bed. Of that she was certain.

Careful not to wake him, she scooted out from under his arm and sat up.

She choked back a gasp.

Adam had not exaggerated when he said she would be sore. Every muscle in her body felt as if it had been stretched to its limit, and beyond. She clutched the edge of the bed and waited for the wave of pain to pass. Perspiration beaded across her upper lip, and for several seconds, she felt as if she might faint. So much for the glory of love-making, she thought wryly. She felt as if she had been trampled by wild horses.

Determined to find out what had awakened her, she eased her way out of bed, then picked her chemise up off the floor and put it on. She swore inwardly. "Damn you, Adam Burke," she whispered into the darkness. "If I survive 'til morning, I swear I'll make you pay for this."

She limped across the room to one of the windows that faced the front of the house and pulled back the curtain.

At first she saw nothing, then as her eyes adjusted to the darkness, she was able to make out the lone figure of a man standing beneath the grand old oak tree on the front lawn. A tall man, broad of shoulder, and with hair as black as Satan. It was Duncan McLean! She was certain of it.

He wasn't doing anything; he was just standing there, staring out across the lawn toward the woods in the distance, almost as if he was watching—or waiting—for someone.

"Couldn't sleep?"

Startled, she dropped the curtain and spun around. "Adam! I-I'm sorry. I didn't mean to wake you."

"You didn't. Is something wrong?"

She turned back to the window, but when she looked outside, Duncan McLean was gone. She released the curtain and rested her forehead on the window frame. He couldn't be gone! He had been there only seconds ago. She shook her head. "I-I thought I heard something . . . outside . . ."

Surely I didn't imagine it?

Adam pulled back the covers and patted the mattress beside him. "Come back to bed."

The husky note in Adam's voice told Regina that going back to bed did not necessarily mean going back to sleep, and she felt a pleasant heat surge through her loins, taking the edge off the pain and dulling her memory. Had it only been moments ago that she had cursed him and sworn retribution for the ache that gripped her body? She started toward him.

As she neared the bed, one glance at her husband's fully aroused body told her that her intuition had been on the mark. Adam had no intention of going back to sleep right away.

Reaching out, he grasped a fold of her chemise between a thumb and forefinger and tugged gently. "Take it off."

Regina could not suppress a smile. "Is that an order?" she asked coyly, already reaching for the hem.

His grin flashed in the darkness. "It could be interpreted as such."

A quick study, Regina was already gaining an understanding of what pleased her new husband. Taking her sweet time, she inched up her chemise, exposing first her legs, then her hips, then her breasts, finally pulling it up over her head and casting it aside. She shook her head and her long hair tumbled around her shoulders.

She could have sworn she heard Adam groan.

She climbed back into bed and leaned down to plant a kiss on his lips. Her breasts brushed against his chest. "There's something I should tell you," she murmured into his mouth.

In a move so swift it caught Regina by surprise, Adam lifted her by her hips and set her down on top of him. Regina gasped as she felt him penetrate her. After several seconds, the pain subsided, and there was only the proud heat of him sliding into her, filling her completely. Straddling his hips, she leaned forward and her hair fell around them, surrounding them like a silky black curtain.

Holding her hips, Adam began to guide her movements until she grasped the rhythm and began moving on her own. "What did you want to tell me?" he prompted.

Above him, her eyes shone mischievously in the darkness. "Remember this morning, at the church, when I promised to obey you . . ."

"Yes."

"I had my fingers crossed."

Chapter 15

~~~~~~~~~~

Regina kept her eyes closed, determined to steal a few more minutes of sleep, but Bertie had already seen through her ruse. " 'Bout time you decided to join us," the old woman chided. "I was beginning to think you planned on sleeping all day." She pushed open the curtains.

Regina covered her eyes with her hand, shielding them from the bright sunlight that spilled into the bedchamber. "What time is it?" she mumbled sleepily.

"It's time for decent folk to be up and about; that's what time it is. If Mister Adam hadn't insisted that you not be disturbed, I'd have rousted your lazy bones out of bed hours ago. If you ask me, too much sleep is as bad for the body as too little."

Clutching the covers over her breasts, Regina sat up, wincing at the stiffness in her muscles. "Did Adam say where he was going?"

Bertie stooped to pick Regina's wedding gown up off the floor. "Down to the waterfront. Said to tell you he'll be back in time for dinner. Then he wants to take you riding and show you some of the changes he's making to Summerhill."

240

Regina shoved her hair away from her face and frowned. "What kind of changes?"

"Don't know. He didn't tell me, and I didn't ask." Bertie draped Regina's gown over her arm, then her chemise, and finally her stockings. "I can see that taking a husband hasn't cured you of any bad habits," she said dryly. "Maybe Mister Adam will be able to teach you how to pick up after yourself. I certainly haven't been able to."

The reminder that she was now a married woman brought a flush of embarrassment to Regina's face. "Bertie, thank you for yesterday. That was the most wonderful wedding party anyone could wish for."

Bertie harrumped. "It wasn't nothing. I was just happy that Mister Adam finally decided to do right by you. If he'd got you with child and didn't do nothing about it, I was going to kill him. And I told him as much."

Regina's eyes widened. "You *knew* about that?"

"And about you sneaking out to see Mister James, and a whole host of other things you think you've been getting away with all this time." The old woman stopped at the door and glanced back. She grinned conspiratorily. "Your dressing gown is on the chair over there. Get out of that bed and get your bones downstairs. There's a hot bath waiting for you in the kitchen."

After Bertie had gone, Regina sat back against the pillows, not certain whether to laugh or worry. The thought of Bertie threatening to kill Adam amazed her. Obviously, Bertie had figured out long ago something that she was only beginning to realize: Adam Burke was an extremely forgiving man.

Memories of last night's lovemaking danced through her thoughts, making her entire body tingle with a delicious warmth. Smiling to herself, she lifted her hands high above her head and pointed her toes and stretched so hard she got a cramp in her foot.

"Ouch!" she muttered. As she reached beneath the covers to massage her foot, her gaze fell on the handsome brick fireplace across from the bed, and a completely unrelated thought flashed through her mind: There was one advantage to being married—she wouldn't have to sleep in a cold bedchamber this winter.

Suddenly the day seemed too bright and too wonderful to spend sleeping.

The hot bath Bertie had prepared for her was the perfect remedy for her sore muscles. A folding screen blocked the copper tub from view of the rest of the kitchen, giving her a measure of privacy. Ordina.ily she would have been tempted to sit in the tub and soak until her fingers and toes puckered and the water turned cold. But she had slept far later than she had intended, and the midafternoon meal, which was the main meal of the day whenever there were no guests to entertain, would be served soon.

In her haste to hurry and finish her bath before Adam returned to the house, she got soap in her eyes.

She splashed water on her face, over and over, but the stinging would not go away. Squeezing her eyes shut, she groped for the towel, but couldn't find it. "Bertie, please hand me the towel."

No answer.

"Bertie!"

Still no answer.

"Blast it all! I can't see!"

Suddenly a towel was shoved into her hand.

"It's about time," she muttered ungraciously, pressing the towel against her burning eyes. "Bertie, where did you—"

She broke off as her blurred gaze came to rest on a pair of men's work boots, the hide still new and unbroken.

She jerked her gaze up to find Duncan McLean towering over her. His black hair was pulled back and tied away from his face. Long hours spent in the hot Virginia sun had turned his skin dark and leathery. Were it not for his clear blue eyes, he could easily have been mistaken for a savage.

A scream rose and lodged in her throat. She clutched the towel in front of her. "What are you doing here?" she choked.

"You wanted a towel, and I handed you one," he said, the musical lilt in his voice at odds with the sheer size of him. He seemed in no hurry to leave.

Regina's voice shook. "Get out."

He didn't move.

"I said, *get out!*"

Amusement flickered in his eyes. He inclined his head toward her. "Good day to you too, Mrs. Burke," he said dryly. He disappeared around the screen.

Regina didn't realize she was holding her breath until it exploded from her lungs in a strangled gasp. "Bertie?" she called out. Her heart pounded so hard it hurt. She pushed herself to her feet, sending water surging over the sides of the tub. "*Bertie!*" In her hurry to get out of the tub, she bumped into the screen, sending it toppling over. It hit the floor with a crash.

"Good Lord, child! I can hear you all the way out in the garden!" Bertie dumped an apronful of green beans onto the table.

Regina clutched the towel in front of her. "That man was in here," she said, struggling to catch her breath.

"What man?"

"Duncan McLean! Bertie, didn't you see him? He was just here!"

Her forehead creased in bewilderment, Bertie crossed the room toward her. She took the towel from her, and Regina turned around. Bertie began briskly rubbing her back with the towel. "I didn't see nobody. I didn't go no farther than the garden. No one could've come in this kitchen without me seein' him."

"I'm not crazy, Bertie. I know I saw him. I *spoke* to him."

"No one ever said you was crazy. I just said I didn't see nobody come in here."

Regina shuddered. "He didn't even have the decency to turn his back; he just stood there, looking at me. The man is insufferable. I don't know why Adam bought his term of indenture."

Bertie didn't say anything, and Regina suspected that the old woman thought she was making way too much of the situation.

She dressed hastily. Several times she glanced over her shoulder, certain she was being watched. It was all she could do to sit still while Bertie brushed out her hair. By the time Adam returned to the house for dinner, her nerves were so taut the slightest noise made her jump.

"Adam, I have to talk to you!"

His brow furrowed, he pulled back from kissing her. "That's a fine welcome for your new husband," he said dryly.

"I'm sorry. But this is important."

"Come upstairs. We can talk while I change for dinner."

Shocked by the suggestion, Regina started to shake her head, then remembered that she was Adam's wife. It was perfectly acceptable for her to be with him when he changed clothes.

She followed him up the stairs.

No sooner had the bedchamber door closed behind them than Adam turned and scooped her up in his arms.

"Adam, put me down!"

He chuckled. "Good idea." Carrying her across the room, he deposited her on the bed.

She started to sit up, but he pressed her back into the pillows. His mouth captured hers, silencing her protest.

He parted her lips and delved his tongue into the honeyed sweetness of her mouth, and Regina forgot what she had been about to say.

The feel of his weight pressing comfortably against her, his erotic kisses, and the velvet roughness of his hand beneath her skirt, was like touching a flame to dry kindling. She opened her legs, and he responded without hesitation to the invitation, sliding his fingers into her wet warmth and touching the pad of his thumb to her most sensitive spot, and the flame burst into a million sparks. She wrapped her arms around his neck and returned his kisses full measure, demanding as much as she gave, and more, as Adam stoked the blaze, quickly bringing her passion to a fevered pitch. Then, just when she thought she couldn't bear another second without having him inside her, he withdrew.

He kissed the tip of her nose and rose from the bed. Amusement danced in his hazel eyes and a knowing smile touched his mouth as he gazed down on her flushed face. He began to unbutton his shirt. "We're going to be late for dinner," he remarked offhandedly.

Rising up on her elbows, Regina glowered at him from beneath her lashes. "Do you mean to tell me you got me all worked up just to walk away and leave me all . . . all . . ."

"Hot?" Adam finished for her. His hazel eyes smoldered. "Feeling as if your entire body is on fire? As if you might die if the blaze isn't extinguished soon?"

She blushed furiously. "Yes."

"Good. Now you know how I feel when I can't have you."

Regina seized a pillow and hurled it at him. "Damn you, Adam Burke! I'm going to make you pay for this!"

Adam's hearty laughter filled the room. "Later, love," he drawled suggestively.

Dinner passed most pleasantly. To Regina's relief, Richard failed to appear. At least they would be able to enjoy their meal without worrying if Richard was going to get drunk and create a scene. Because the day was comfortably warm, without the oppressive humidity that was more common this time of year, and because it was just the two of them, Adam suggested that they eat on the terrace.

As they ate, they talked about the future, about

Adam's plans for Summerhill, and the improvements he wanted to make to the plantation.

The ease with which they were able to talk surprised Regina. It was almost as if Adam was more than just her husband; he was quickly becoming her best friend. She felt as if she had known him for years. Every time she looked at him, she was struck by how handsome he was. And every time he looked at her, she remembered how it felt to have him inside her, and her face would turn a brilliant red.

When she was with him, she felt beautiful and vulnerable and safe, all at the same time.

She felt loved.

"Miles Jordan took the surveying crew upriver this morning," Adam said as he refilled Regina's glass of wine. "There is a strip of land with a natural deepwater harbor a few miles from here that would be an excellent spot to build a shipyard."

Regina stared at him in surprise. "But what of the docks here? And the warehouses?"

"I'll continue to use them. They're convenient for the families living on the Northern Neck. But upriver, we're seeing fewer plantations and more settlements. The colony's population is growing much more quickly than anyone would have thought possible. Germans are settling in the valleys to the west and iron ore is now being mined where there were once only Indian trails. Soon there is going to be a pressing need for ships and shipping companies, and for business and services to support them."

"It sounds as if you're building a city!"

"In a sense, we are. At the very least, we are laying the foundation for one. Would you care to see the plans for the shipyard? You might be able to think of something I've overlooked."

Regina stared at him in amazement. She could not believe he was soliciting her advice. She had spent her entire life at Summerhill, and not once had anyone ever asked her opinion on anything even remotely connected to the family businesses. In fact, most people treated her as if she didn't have a brain in her head. "I'd love to!" she said when she finally found her voice.

"We'll go after dinner." Feeling extraordinarily pleased with himself in his choice of a wife, Adam watched Regina over the rim of his glass as he took a drink of wine. She was a beautiful woman. An extremely beautiful woman. If they were lucky enough to have daughters—and if those daughters resembled their mother in the least—he knew he was going to have his hands full keeping overly eager young suitors at bay.

There was nothing prissy or artificial about Regina. She was intelligent and articulate. And, for a novice, she was an amazingly passionate lover. He almost regretted even suggesting the ride; he would have preferred to carry her upstairs and spend the rest of the day making love to her.

Just then, she glanced at him from beneath her lashes and caught him studying her. Her face turned a delightful shade of pink. "What are you thinking?" she asked, suddenly sounding uncharacteristically shy.

A smile tugged at the corners of his mouth. His gold-flecked gaze smoldered as he allowed it to roam boldly over the length of her. "Probably the same thing you are."

Her cheeks went from pink to crimson.

Adam chuckled. "Later, love," he teased. "I promised you a different kind of ride this afternoon."

It was a glorious day for a ride. As she sat next to him in the open carriage, Regina saw Summerhill as if for the first time: the lush bronzed green of the tobacco fields, the dainty blue blossoms of wild chickory peeking through the masses of orange black-eyed Susans that grew alongside the road, the playful zigzag of the split-rail fence. Somehow, today, the colors seemed brighter, the sky clearer, the air sweeter than she remembered. Feeling at peace with herself and with the world, she tilted back her head and closed her eyes and savored the soothing warmth of the sunlight on her face. She sighed blissfully.

Watching her, Adam chuckled softly. He never tired of watching Regina. And he never knew what side of her she was going to show him next. In the short time that he had known her, he had seen her angry. He had seen her happy. He had seen her petulant, jealous, conniving.

God, was she ever conniving!

Yet there was another side to Regina, a side she kept hidden so well that it was only by chance that he had even glimpsed it.

The first time he saw her—down at the docks when Father Tidewell had dragged her unceremoniously into his office and berated her in front of both him and her brother—he had thought she was a spoiled brat who needed to be taken down a notch.

He didn't know when he first started to see through the rebellion that Regina sported like a suit

of armor, or realized that her blatant acts of dis-
obedience, far from being spawned by malicious-
ness, were instead pleas for attention. Perhaps it
had been a gradual process. But it wasn't until yesterday, standing on the terrace after the wedding,
surrounded by well-wishers, that the truth finally
struck him: Even in the midst of friends and family,
Regina was lonely.

Painfully lonely.

Her aunt and uncle, while they certainly cared
for their niece, were not the most demonstrative
people. Adam couldn't remember ever seeing William kiss his wife, or hug her, or give either her or
his children a word of encouragement. While his
own childhood had been cut short by the untimely
loss of his parents in a carriage accident, he clearly
remembered the warmth and affection that had
marked their marriage. He believed that children
learned to love by watching their parents, and had
noticed that children who were denied such a pos-
itive example often grew up showing signs of star-
vation. Not for food, but for affection. Elise had
been such a person. He was beginning to think Regina was, too.

It wasn't that he thought Regina was incapable
of loving; had that been the case, he could never
have married her. But he did suspect that she
found giving love far easier than receiving it. He
was going to have a hard time convincing her that
his love for her was unconditional.

As they rode, Adam pointed out the fields that
he planned to return to pasture after this year's tobacco harvest, and he talked of bringing cattle from
Scotland to start a herd that would provide additional income. They drove past the timber-framed

houses that had recently been built for the newly arrived indentures, handsome square structures, each a story-and-a-half high, with a common room downstairs and a sleeping loft upstairs and a massive fireplace on one gabled end. Even though they were entitled to take their meals with the rest of the servants and slaves, some of the indentures had already cleared away plots for their own gardens.

Regina wondered which of the houses belonged to Duncan McLean, and she felt the heat rise in her face. The man had seen her naked, for God's sake!

She took a deep breath. "Adam, there's something I need to tell you."

"Is something wrong?"

Regina opened her mouth to tell him about the incident in the kitchen, but she couldn't make the words come. A nagging voice in the back of her mind told her that it wasn't worth creating a stir over something so inconsequential. After all, Duncan McLean had done her no harm; he had merely handed her a towel. That he had seen her without her clothes had been an accident. An unfortunate accident, but an accident nonetheless. Swallowing her pride, she gave him an embarrassed half-smile and shook her head. "It's not important."

Adam cast her a puzzled glance, but said nothing. Ahead of them, the river came into view.

The waterfront swarmed with seamen and laborers. The *Lady Anne*, which had only returned from Belhaven a few days ago, was being outfitted for the long voyage to England.

Regina noticed immediately the new roof on Uncle William's old office, as well as the new chimney. Adam had certainly lost no time putting his mark on the building.

But when he lifted her down from the carriage and escorted her inside, the changes he had made to the office took Regina's breath away. She stared in amazement at the clean white plastered walls and crown moldings, the brick fireplace, and the polished oak floor. A new desk anchored one end of the room, and several upholstered chairs were arranged around it. A huge tapestry depicting a medieval battle hung on the wall behind the desk. The new door that had been installed in the wall behind the desk was propped open. Through it, in the part of the building that had once been used to store tobacco, Regina could see tall storage cabinets, shelves laden with books, and a portable cot.

She shook her head. "I can hardly believe this is the same place," she said. "Uncle William never intended this to be more than a warehouse. He planned to build himself a real office one day, but he never got around to it."

Adam went into the back room and returned with a large sheet of paper like the kind upon which maps were drawn. He unrolled the paper and spread it across the top of the desk. "With the warehouses I plan to build at the new location upriver, I won't need as much room for storage here, so I turned the entire building into an office. The fireplace will keep the place warm in the winter, so I can conduct most of my business here instead of bringing strangers into the house."

"Oh." Regina could not keep the note of disappointment from her voice. Until now, she had not realized how much she was looking forward to having Adam work out of Uncle William's old study where she would be able to see him during the day. She looked up at the tapestry hanging on the wall. "That must be very old."

"It is. It's been passed down in my family for generations. I couldn't tell you its exact age. But as a boy, I used to lie on the floor in front of the fireplace and stare at it, and pretend that I was the king leading the battle charge."

Adam came up behind Regina and wrapped his arms around her. He rested his chin on top of her head. "I also thought this would be a pleasant place to come to be alone together," he said quietly. "Can you imagine being here during a storm, with the wind whipping at the trees and the rain lashing at the windows? We could make love in front of the fire."

Regina leaned back into his embrace and smothered a giggle. "On the floor?"

"On the carpet."

"What carpet?"

He leaned his head down and nibbled on her ear. "The one I'm ordering from England."

A little abashed by the suggestive turn the conversation had taken, Regina changed the subject. "What does Richard think of all these changes? He used to hate coming to this office."

Adam abruptly released her. "Your brother hasn't been in here since I started rebuilding." The note of stiffness in his voice brought Regina up short.

She turned and fixed him with a bewildered gaze. "I don't understand. I thought he was working with you."

"I thought so too." Adam went to his desk. "This is a working drawing of the new shipyard. Silas is going to oversee the day-to-day operations of the place, which will allow me to spend more time here." Glancing up at her, he grinned and added meaningfully, "With you."

Regina approached the desk. "I forgot to tell you! Did you know that Beatrice and Captain Bebe are getting married?"

"That I did. They're going to build a house about a quarter of a mile from the shipyard, where they'll have a fine view of the river."

Regina eyes him warily. "How far is that from here?"

Adam chuckled. "Don't worry. They'll still be close enough for you and Beatrice to visit regularly."

Regina looked at the drawing. Buildings were laid out in an orderly fashion, separated by thoroughfares, like city blocks, with the buildings on the innermost rows noticeably smaller than the others. "What are all these?"

"The larger buildings will house warehouses and factories. Some of these smaller ones I hope to lease to merchants, solicitors, tavernkeepers, and other small business owners. These smallest buildings here on the periphery will house the dock workers and their families."

"That's quite an ambitious undertaking."

"Ambitious, yes. Impossible, no. We have all the resources we need right here. It's just a matter of seeing the plans through to fruition."

Regina could not shake the sinking feeling that had settled in the pit of her stomach. Adam always seemed to know exactly what he wanted and how to go about getting it. He didn't need her to make his plans succeed. And he certainly didn't need her brother. No matter how much she tried to ignore it, both of them were at Adam's mercy. Without them, Adam could still build his shipyard and run the plantation. But without Adam, she and Richard were paupers.

"What's wrong?" Adam asked quietly.

Regina shrugged. "I don't know. I guess it's just that you have all these dreams and plans, and I feel rather ... useless ... like I'm not really needed."

Adam took her by the shoulders and turned her to face him. "Look at me."

"Adam, please ..."

"Look at me."

Reluctantly, almost wary of what she was going to see, she obeyed.

Adam's gaze, honest, forthright, unwavering, bored into hers with an intensity that raised prickles of anticipation on her skin and made her knees suddenly feel weak. But there was something else in his eyes, something she couldn't quite identify. Something she had never associated with him. *Vulnerability? Desperation?* His hands tightened on her shoulders. "*I* need you."

Bewildered, she shook her head. "Why?"

"Regina, this shipyard isn't mine. The plantation isn't mine. They're *ours*. They're the legacy we're going to leave to our children someday."

It was the first time Adam had mentioned having children, and the thought made Regina feel a little self-conscious. She looked away, but Adam caught her chin and tilted her face up toward his.

"When I first purchased Summerhill from your brother, it was strictly a business decision. I saw an opportunity and I took advantage of it. My original plan was to stay in the colony for a few years, make the plantation profitable, then sell out and return to England. I had no intention of staying here permanently."

"What made you change your mind?"

"You."

Regina's eyes widened. "Me? You hated me!"

"I thought you were a spoiled brat. I didn't hate you."

"I hated *you*."

Adam pulled her toward him and slid his arms around her waist. "Do you still?"

Her brows knitted together as if she were giving the question serious consideration. "Not as much. You do have a few redeeming qualities."

"Oh really?" Adam lowered his head to hers. "And what might those be, Mrs. Burke?"

Regina glided her hand down over the taut, flat muscles of his abdomen, then lower still. Mischief danced in her dark eyes. "Well, that's one . . ."

Adam caught her hand and brought it back to a respectable—and safe—place. He kissed her. "You're treading on dangerous ground," he murmured against her lips. He kissed her again.

Regina tugged her hand, but Adam kept it firmly imprisoned against his chest. "I always tread on dangerous ground," she murmured back. "In case you haven't noticed, Mr. Burke, *I* don't have any redeeming qualities at all." Rising up on tiptoe, she wrapped her free arm around his neck and returned his kiss fully, boldly thrusting her tongue into his mouth.

"I wouldn't say that," Adam replied when he was finally able to take a breath. His body's response to Regina's antics was straining the limits of his control. He wasn't certain how much longer he was going to be able to restrain himself from taking her right there on the floor of his office.

Regina kissed his chin, then his jaw, then the corner of his mouth. "It's true. I'm not a very good housekeeper. I can't sew more than three consecutive stitches without tangling my thread. I'm neither meek nor obedient. And I hold grudges."

Adam grinned down at her. "It would appear, madam, that I may have been rather hasty in choosing a wife."

In spite of his playful tone, Regina felt a twinge of insecurity. "Too late," she teased, struggling to keep the uncertainty out of her voice. "You're stuck with me." Her arm still wrapped around his neck, she pulled him down toward her. "Oh—I almost forgot: I can also be very demanding."

She had just touched her lips to his when they were interrupted by a loud knocking at the door.

Chuckling at the look of disappointment that flashed across Regina's face, Adam gently extricated himself from her arms, then went to the door and opened it.

A bearded man wearing dirty breeches and a leather jerkin stood on the steps. Regina didn't recognize him. "Sir, you better come quick. There's trouble!"

His demeanor changing abruptly from pleasure to business, Adam rounded on Regina. "Bolt the door, and don't open it for anyone. I'll be back as soon as I can."

She started after him. "Adam, what is it?"

"Bolt the door!" The door slammed after him.

Regina hesitated a split second, then hurried to bolt the door behind him. The iron bolt was new—

there had never been one on that door until now—
and slid easily into place.

She ran to the window.

She barely caught a glimpse of Adam before he
disappeared into the crowd. Whatever was happening on the dock, she couldn't see it from here.
She cursed silently. The last place she wanted to be
right now was behind a bolted door.

It was then that she noticed the iron bars on the
outside of the window. All the windows had bars.
And in addition to the bolt, the door also had a
new lock that required a key.

Regina couldn't make sense of what she saw. Uncle William never had bars on the windows or
locks on the doors of his office; now the place was
a veritable fortress. She wondered uneasily if
Adam intended to do the same to the house.

She didn't know Adam very well, she realized.
Unlike the men she had grown up with on the
Northern Neck, she didn't know where Adam
came from, or who his family was, or anything
about him. For all she knew, he could be a murderer, or worse. *He could already be married to
someone else!* He was practically a stranger to her.
And yet he was her husband.

For better or for worse.

Of course, they had an entire lifetime to get to
know each other, Regina rationalized. But what if
she learned something about him that she couldn't
possibly live with?

Feeling distinctly unsettled, she looked around
the office, her gaze finally settling on the drawing
of the new shipyard he had left lying on his desk.
Adam's words echoed in her mind: *They're the legacy we're going to leave to our children.*

She wrapped her arms defensively around herself. She had to trust him. If she didn't, she would make herself crazy with unfounded doubts and suspicions. Yet how could she trust him when she had never, for as long as she could remember, trusted anyone?

It was going to be the hardest thing she had ever done.

After what seemed an eternity, the crowd parted, and Adam emerged from the throng. Captain Bebe was with him. Between them, they were supporting a man who appeared to be barely conscious. The man's head hung down and his dark hair covered his face. His white shirt was bloodstained and dirty.

As they neared the building, Regina gasped.

The injured man was Richard.

Chapter 16

Regina threw back the bolt and opened the door. Adam and Captain Bebe half led, half carried, Richard up the stairs. Regina's stomach lurched when she saw the extent of her brother's injuries.

His face was battered almost beyond recognition. One eye was swollen shut, and his nose appeared to be broken. Blood dripped from his mouth and nose.

"Richard, are you all right?" Regina blurted out. "My God, what happened to you?"

"Get out of the way!" Adam ordered.

Regina stepped back to let them pass. The men took Richard into the other room and lowered him to the cot.

Regina gripped the door frame. She felt as if she was going to be ill. "Adam, what happened? Is he going to be all right?"

Adam and Captain Bebe eased Richard down onto the cot. Adam straightened and began pulling his own shirt free of his breeches. "He'll be fine," he said tersely. He stripped off his shirt, sending buttons scattering across the wood floor. He tossed the shirt to Regina. "Go wet this."

Regina caught the shirt.

Adam turned back to Richard. "Let me see that eye."

For several seconds, Regina stood in the doorway, clutching Adam's shirt to her breast, unable to move. Dropping to one knee beside the bed, Adam took Richard's chin and turned his face toward him.

"Damn you!" Richard bellowed, his whole body coming up off the cot. He swung wildly.

Adam threw up his arm, deflecting the blow.

Captain Bebe caught Richard's wrists and pinned them over his head. "You've got to lie still, lad."

Richard bucked, but Silas held fast to his wrists. Blood ran in rivulets down Richard's temples and onto the pillow, staining the crisp white cotton pillowcase red.

"This is going to hurt," Adam said, his voice surprisingly calm. "But you have to be still. I don't want to risk injuring that eye any more than it already is."

"Go to hell," Richard muttered. .

Regina's stomach rebelled, and for a frantic second, she thought she was going to lose her dinner. Unable to stand still any longer, she turned and bolted from the building.

She ran to the rain barrel that had been placed at the end of the building to catch the runoff from the roof, yanked off the mesh covering designed to keep out insects and debris, and plunged Adam's shirt into the cool water. She twisted the excess water from the shirt with shaking hands, splashing water all over the toes of her slippers and soaking the front of her gown. She hurried back to the office, taking the stairs two at a time.

Adam took the shirt from her.

Regina stood in the doorway, her fist pressed against her mouth to keep from crying out as Adam used the wet shirt to clean Richard's face. Yet she was too fascinated to turn away. Richard gritted his teeth and clutched Captain Bebe's hands so tightly his knuckles whitened. From where Regina stood, she could see his face. The bleeding from his nose seemed to have diminished, but his right eye was a bloody swollen mass, so bruised that she wondered if he would lose it.

Richard's body involuntarily lurched. "Son of a bitch! When I get my hands on the bastard, I'll kill him."

"You'll keep away from him," Adam said firmly. "If you had minded your own business, none of this would ever have happened."

"He started it!"

"That's no excuse, Langley. There are better ways to deal with a man's foul mouth than by putting your fist in it. I'll speak with McGrath. I want you to stay away from him."

"The man deserves to be horsewhipped!"

"Stay away from him," Adam repeated firmly. "And be still!"

Regina's brow wrinkled in bewilderment. The only McGrath she knew was Gordy McGrath, a Scot indentured to Arthur Randolph. From what Beatrice had told her about him, she had gathered that he was a rather unsavory character, given to surliness and fighting.

If it was the same McGrath, what was he doing on Summerhill?

Regina nervously moistened her lips. "Adam . . . may I speak with you a moment?"

Adam turned his head to look at her, and from the expression on his face, Regina knew he had forgotten she was standing there. He got to his feet.

Richard glowered at her through his one good eye. "What in the hell are you doing here, Reggie?"

Adam folded his bloodied shirt until the most soiled areas were concealed inside. He handed the shirt to Captain Bebe. "Hold this over his eye."

Richard, who had managed to pull his hands free, snatched the shirt from Adam. "I'll do it myself."

His expression grim, Adam took Regina's elbow and led her to the outer office, out of her brother's sight. "What is it?"

"Is Richard going to lose his eye?" In spite of herself, her voice shook.

"It's too early to tell, but I think not. The swelling makes it look worse than it is."

"That man, McGrath, was he the one who beat up Richard?"

"Why?"

"Because if he's the same man I think he is, he has no business even being here. He works for Bea's father."

"I'm well aware who he is."

"Adam, it's a criminal offense for an indentured servant to attack a planter!"

"I promise you, I'll get to the bottom of the matter. In the meantime, I don't want you to concern yourself with it. It's not your problem to deal with."

"But it is my problem! It's everyone's problem. If there is trouble brewing between the planters and the Scots, it affects all of us."

"Enough! I told you I'll deal with it. Right now,

I want you to take the carriage and go home. You'll be safer there."

"I want to stay here!"

"Go home."

"But, Adam—"

"Bebe, get in here!"

Regina groaned.

Captain Bebe appeared in the doorway. "Yes, sir?"

"I want you to take Regina back to the house."

"Adam, I'll be fine here. I'll stay out of your way. I promise."

"No."

Regina opened her mouth to protest, then clamped it shut again. If there was one thing she was quickly learning about her new husband, it was that there was no arguing with him once he'd made up his mind about something.

Of course, there were a few things he had yet to learn about her.

He couldn't say she hadn't warned him.

Regina used the ride home to try to wheedle information from Silas Bebe, but the sea captain was nearly as closed mouthed as Adam. "I'd tell you if I could, Regina," he said wearily, "but the truth is, I don't know any more about what happened down on the dock than your husband does. I reached the fight only moments before Adam did, and all it got me was a busted lip for attempting to break it up."

Regina glanced sharply at Captain Bebe, realizing for the first time that he had been injured in the brawl. His bottom lip was swollen, and blood had crusted across the fullest part where the skin had split. She winced. "Does it hurt?"

Captain Bebe chuckled. "I won't be kissing Bea so heartily for a day or two, if that's what you mean."

He deposited her in front of the house and turned the carriage around. "If I find out anything, I'll let you know," he reassured her. "Although, you'd probably do best to ask your husband. That man has a talent for gleaning information the rest of us aren't privy to."

Captain Bebe drove away.

Regina waited impatiently on the front steps until the carriage disappeared from sight, then gathered up her skirts and broke into a run across the lawn.

Bertie appeared around the corner of the house nearest the kitchen, drying her hands on her apron. "Miss Regina, wait! What happened? Where's Mister Adam?"

Although Regina heard her, she kept running. There would be time enough later to tell Bertie what was going on.

By the time she reached the cliff overlooking the docks, she was out of breath and had a stitch in her side. Pressing her elbow into her side in a futile attempt to alleviate the pain, she dropped to her hands and knees. Hidden from below by the dense brush that grew wild along the edge of the cliff, she separated the branches and peered down at the riverbank below.

She saw Adam's carriage roll to a stop in front of the office. Captain Bebe jumped down from the carriage and bolted up the office steps. She swore silently. She was too far away to be able to see through the windows. Until the men left the building, she wouldn't be able to see much of anything from her perch.

She could, however, clearly see the bars on the windows, and the sight of them brought a crease of worry to her forehead. Had Adam anticipated trouble? Was that why he had ordered bars to be put on the windows and locks on the door?

Or did he simply know something he wasn't telling her?

She glanced upriver where a crowd of servants and slaves had gathered near the auction block. Although she couldn't hear what they were saying, the men appeared to be arguing among themselves. She recalled the discussion among the men at the dinner party when Richard first returned from England, and wished she had paid more attention to what they had said. While she knew that a slave uprising like the one in Hampton was always a possibility, she had thought the probability of it ever happening in Westmoreland County was minimal. It was as if she lived in a cocoon of her own making, sheltered from reality by walls she had built in her mind.

Finally the door to the office opened, and the three men emerged from the building. Richard, walking on his own now, managed to climb into the carriage unassisted. Adam and Captain Bebe talked between themselves for several minutes, then Adam joined Richard on the seat. Adam took the reins and turned the carriage around. As the carriage moved out of the long shadows, the late afternoon sunlight glinted off his broad shoulders, making them gleam like polished bronze. Next to him, Richard sat stiffly, clasping his right arm with his left, his face ashen.

Captain Bebe lifted his hand in farewell.

Adam snapped the reins, and the carriage surged forward.

Determined to be back at the house before Adam discovered that she was gone, Regina scrambled to her feet.

She froze.

She stood motionless, not even daring to breathe, the pounding of her heart the only sound to break a silence that suddenly seemed threatening rather than peaceful. She didn't know why, but she had an eerie feeling that she was not alone, that someone was watching her.

Suddenly the secluded glade above the river where she and Beatrice and Izzy had met in secret nearly every Sunday for the past two years no longer seemed so inviting. The trees were too close together, the surrounding underbrush too dense, and the clearing where she liked to lie on the soft grass and let the sun warm her face too small and confined.

Furthermore, no one knew where she was. If anything happened to her, it might be days before anyone found her body.

You're being morbid! she chided herself. *Nothing is going to happen to you.*

Still, she could not dispell her uneasiness. She started back toward the house, walking swiftly, but surely, every nerve in her body alert, her ears trained to the sounds coming from the woods around her. By the time she reached the open pasture, she was so tightly wound, she felt ready to snap. Glancing back to make certain no one was behind her, she took off running.

Duncan McLean waited in the semidarkness of the forest, his sense of duty turning into anger as he watched Regina leave the woods and head back toward the house.

Stupid woman, he thought, furious that someone like her, who showed a blatant disregard for common sense and who carelessly placed herself in danger time after time, should dance through life unscathed while his kind, gentle sister, who never dared wander out of sight of their home, had been made to suffer so cruelly at the hands of brutal men.

His throat tightened. "Jenny, why?" he whispered, his tortured mind searching for answers that never came. The image of his sister, huddled in the corner of the kitchen of the crofter's cottage where they had lived, her body battered and bloodied, returned to haunt him. The silent rage that had become so much a part of him that he couldn't remember what it had been like to live without it welled up in him. For as long as he lived, he would never understand the minds of men who violate women.

Nor would he ever forgive himself for not being there to save her from the attack.

He took a deep breath to calm himself, and once again focused his attention on Regina. He had failed Jenny. He would not let it happen again.

He waited until Regina was halfway across the pasture before emerging from his hiding place. Keeping a cautious distance behind her, he followed her home.

Chapter 17

ⵯⵯⵯ

"Child, where did you run off to? Look at
your gown! You got all dirty! I swear,
between you and that brother of yours, the two of
you are diggin' me an early grave."

Regina struggled to catch her breath. "Bertie,
where's Adam?"

"Mister Adam done changed his clothes and
took off for the Randolphs. Didn't say what for or
when he'd be home." Bertie wrapped a towel
around the handle of a kettle of hot water and
hoisted the kettle off its hook over the fire. "Get
those bandages there and that pot of salve, and
come with me. Mister Richard needs tending to."

"Do you have your bag of herbs?"

"In the pocket of my apron."

Regina grabbed the stack of clean linen strips
that Bertie had laid out on the table and the small
stoneware crock covered with cheesecloth, and followed her to the main house.

"You mind tellin' me where you ran off to in
such a hurry?" Bertie asked over her shoulder as
she lugged the heavy kettle up the stairs.

"I wanted to see what was going on down at the

docks, but Adam sent me home. Bertie, is Richard going to be all right?"

Bertie snorted. "Mister Richard got his pretty face busted up good this time. Might've even broken his nose." She stopped outside Richard's bedchamber. "Mister Richard, you open this door. This kettle weighs as much as you do."

Footsteps sounded on the floorboards. Richard opened the door.

Regina gasped when she saw him. His face looked worse now than it had in Adam's office, when the flow of blood had hidden much of the damage. His eye was swollen completely shut and his once aristocratic nose was smashed to one side and crusted with blood.

Richard glowered at her. "If you're going to throw up, Reggie, go do it somewhere else. It was your bloody honor I was defending."

Regina gaped at him. "What?"

Bertie pushed past Richard and carried the heavy kettle into the room. She set it down on the hooked wool rug beside the bed.

"You heard me," Richard muttered. "Word's all over the county about how you and Burke got married in a hurry because you're carrying Fitzhugh's bastard."

"That's not true!"

"Tell it to Burke. He's the laughing stock of the entire parish."

Regina bristled.

"That'll be enough of that," Bertie said sternly. She took the bandages and the pot of salve from Regina. "I can take care of this. You go get yourself cleaned up, child."

Before Regina could respond, Bertie closed the door.

For several minutes, Regina stood outside the closed door, too numb to move. *Adam was the laughing stock of the parish? Because of her?*

It wasn't possible!

Adam was the only man she had ever been with, and until then she had been a virgin. Adam knew that. And he believed her. *Didn't he?*

Yet what did it matter that he believed her if no one else did? What if Adam's shipyard and his standing in the parish suffered because of malicious gossip? What if he grew to hate her because of it?

It just wasn't fair! For the first time in her life she was beginning to feel as if someone truly cared about her, and now everything was going to be ruined. And if Gordy McGrath was spreading such filth about her, who else was?

Oh, to hell with all of them, she thought, suddenly angry. She had never cared before what people thought about her. She even enjoyed antagonizing them with her outrageous behavior. So why should she concern herself with them now?

Because it's no longer just your own reputation you're damaging, a chastising voice whispered in her mind. She was a married woman now, and everything she did reflected, not only upon herself, but upon Adam as well.

She suddenly felt sick at heart.

Disdain darted across Charles Toliver's features as he brushed an imaginary piece of lint from the sleeve of his pale blue silk brocade coat. "Why don't you invite Burke to join us?" he said coolly.

"He might be interested in our proposition. After all, he does have a number of Scots working for him."

Arthur Randolph glanced toward Adam, who had just unexpectedly arrived, with a look that was part apology, part unease. "Please, Burke, do come in. Would you care for a glass of port?"

"No. Thank you." Feeling as if he had just walked into an ambush, Adam glanced around Randolph's office at the half dozen faces that stared back at him. In addition to Randolph and Toliver, he recognized Edward Lee, Thomas Parke, and John Sandhurst. The sixth man was unknown to him, a situation that was soon corrected.

The dark haired young man grinned. "So you're the lucky fellow who managed to snare our Reggie," he said. He extended his hand. "I don't believe we've met. I'm Harry Lee."

Adam glanced from brother to brother, taking a mental note of the family resemblance as he shook the younger Lee's hand. "Adam Burke."

"I'm sorry I wasn't able to attend your wedding party, but I wish you both the best."

"Thank you. And you are right: I am a lucky man. A very lucky man." Adam could feel the enmity that emanated from Charles Toliver. "Now tell me, what is this proposition you gentlemen were discussing?"

"Most of the Germans working at the mines and the foundry left when their terms of indenture ended," Arthur Randolph said. "Governor Spotswood is eager to find replacements as soon as possible. He has offered to purchase the terms of anyone willing to serve the remainder of his time at the ironworks."

Edward Lee snorted. "God help them if they don't want to go to the ironworks; the decision isn't theirs to make."

"Aw, c'mon, Edward," Harry said. "Do you always have to be so hard on poor fools? They haven't done anything to you."

Edward's jaw tightened. "In case you've forgotten, little brother, one of those 'poor fools' raped Sarah. And I consider an assault against my property to be an assault against me."

It was obvious to Adam what direction this discussion was taking, and he felt himself growing impatient. "Let me guess: Your intention is to round up the Scottish indentures and sell the balance of their terms to the governor."

A cold smile touched Toliver's mouth. "Do I detect a note of disapproval in your voice, Burke?"

"Not at all," Adam said evenly. "Getting rid of the troublemakers will make life easier for all of us."

"I'm surprised to hear you say that," Edward Lee said. "I was under the impression you harbored a certain fondness for foreigners."

"I said I favored getting rid of the troublemakers. I did not say I approved of a mass expulsion of large segments of the population for reasons of personal bias."

Charles's face reddened beneath his white wig. "You are treading on dangerous ground when you start accusing us of being incapable of sound moral judgment. Were it not for the landowners, this colony would still be in the hands of wild savages."

"I am accusing you of nothing, merely cautioning you against setting a precedent you may later regret. You might also remember that most of you became landowners, not by your own efforts, but by accident of birth."

An ominous hush descended over the room and everyone present stared at Adam in openmouthed shock. To question the social order of the English gentry was tantamount to heresy, and Adam knew it. A fundamental tenet of the aristocracy was that one born into the peerage was destined to be there. But losing his parents at an early age had effectively destroyed that myth for him. He had quickly learned that being the son of a viscount did not guarantee a roof over his head or assuage the rumblings of an empty belly.

John Sandhurst was the first to break the silence. "An interesting philosophy. Let's hope it's not contagious."

An uncomfortable laughter erupted throughout the room.

As Adam looked around at the men who were going to be a part of his world for a long time to come, he was struck by the realization that at the moment he wanted nothing more than to return home to his wife.

He wanted to spend the evening with her. He wanted to talk with her, to plan their future together. He wanted to take her to bed and make love to her.

Because of Regina, Summerhill was beginning to feel like home.

Arthur Randolph coughed nervously. "Gentlemen, now that we've had our fun, we must get on with more serious matters. The governor's offer is a good one, but Burke is right: We must not act without having first considered the consequences."

"Randolph, you were the one who first proposed

we take advantage of Spotswood's offer," Charles said hotly. "Are you now suggesting that we reconsider?"

Not wanting to get embroiled in an argument, Adam took his leave. "Randolph, I came here to discuss a different matter with you, but it can wait until another time. If you gentlemen will excuse me, I'll leave you to your discussion."

"Burke, wait," Randolph said, following Adam to the door. "I don't want you to have made a wasted trip. We can step outside and talk in private."

The two men stopped on the circular portico that adorned the front of Randolph's square, hiproofed, red brick house. In as few words as possible, Adam told Randolph about the fight between McGrath and Richard. "I hold Richard equally responsible for the brawl," he added. "However, there is no getting around the fact that your man had no business being on my property. I don't wish to see him there again."

"You're right, of course. I'll take care of it. And I apologize for McGrath's actions. The man has been a thorn in my side since the day he arrived in Virginia."

"I don't want there to be any trouble between us, Randolph. Not only are you my nearest neighbor, your daughter is my wife's dear friend."

Randolph chuckled. "A situation I've rued more often than not, I can assure you. But I must say, I believe you will be a good influence on Regina."

Adam hoped he would be a better influence on Regina than Randolph apparently was with Marion. He couldn't help wondering if Randolph had even the slightest suspicion his wife was having an affair with Charles Toliver.

Uncannily discerning the object, if not the nature, of his thoughts, Randolph asked suddenly, "You don't like Toliver much, do you?"

"I don't trust him. There is a difference."

"It's no secret that he *hates you*. He's not likely to forgive you any time soon for marrying the woman he wanted."

At least in Regina he had set his sights on a woman who was free to marry, Adam thought dryly.

"What I haven't figured out," Arthur mused aloud, "is why Toliver didn't fight to keep her. He truly loves her."

"Regina didn't want to marry him."

"She didn't want to marry you either."

"But she did marry me. And Toliver is going to have to accept that."

Randolph was pensive a moment before continuing. "There is something else that doesn't sit well with Toliver. With any of us, for that matter."

"Which is?"

"Your man, Duncan McLean. For a nine-year-indenture, he enjoys an inordinate amount of freedom."

"Oh, really?"

"Burke, the man is a convicted murderer! He deserves to be in fetters, on a short chain. I wouldn't have let him off the ship, much less let him roam the countryside as if he were a free man!"

"Has he done anything to you or to any of your people?"

"Not yet. But he will, you mark my words."

"If anyone—anyone at all—comes to harm be-

cause of McLean, I will take full responsibility."
Adam turned to leave.

"It's rumored that he's armed."

Adam stopped. Anger snapped in his eyes.
"Yes, he's armed. When he's clearing away brush,
he's armed with a saw. When he's building a
cabin, he's armed with an ax. When he's turning a
field, he's armed with a plowshare—just as your
people are."

"My people aren't cold-blooded killers."

"Neither is McLean."

Randolph shook his head. "I must warn you,
Burke, you make people around here nervous. If
you intend to make your home here in the parish,
you need to make more of an effort to accommo-
date the other landowners' wishes. If you don't,
you'll never succeed here."

Adam eyed the other man coldly. "Is that a
threat?"

"Consider it a piece of neighborly advice."

Night had fallen by the time Adam returned to
the house. The visit to Arthur Randolph's had left
him with an unpleasant taste in his mouth, as if he
had bitten into something that was as disagreeable
as it was enticing. Randolph had known something
that he was not divulging; Adam was certain of it.
He didn't know what Randolph and his friends
were up to, but he suspected that when he arrived
they had been discussing something other than the
governor's proposal.

In the study, he picked up the flint decanter and
poured himself a glass of port. As he lifted the glass
to his lips, he made a mental note to have the rest
of William Langley's personal belongings crated

and sent to Williamsburg. Of the furnishings that had once belonged to Regina's parents, he intended to keep those that Regina had expressed a preference for; the rest he would turn over to the Langleys to divide as they saw fit.

"Adam?"

He turned around.

Regina stood in the doorway in her nightdress and wrapper. The light of the candle in the wall sconce near the door gently illuminated her face. The sight of her with her feet bare and her hair hanging down her back in tangled curls sent heat coursing through his loins. It was when she was like this, soft and vulnerable, that he wanted her the most.

"You were gone a long time," she said.

"Too long. I thought you'd be in bed by now."

"I couldn't sleep. What happened at the Randolphs? Did you speak with Bea's father about Gordy McGrath?"

Adam frowned. "What do you know about that?"

"Richard told me that he was spreading tales about me."

"And about a number of other women in the parish."

Regina fidgeted. "Adam, the things he was saying about me . . . they're not true."

"I know that."

"You're the only man I've ever . . . been with."

"I believe you. I believed you last night when you told me, and I believe you now. Nothing has changed between us because some weasel with too much idle time on his hands tries to slander my wife. McGrath had best keep his distance from me, because if I ever hear him utter anything like that about you, I'll likely kill him."

Regina said nothing. She plucked nervously at the folds of her nightdress.

Adam frowned. "Did you think I would be angry with *you*?"

She defensively crossed her arms in front of her. "I didn't really know what to think. I mean, I barely know you. How am I supposed to know how you might react to different things? The only thing I'm really certain of, and that's only because I've seen it, is that you don't like it when I mention . . ."

"Fitzhugh."

"You said his name. I didn't."

Adam chuckled. "I can see we have some getting-acquainted to do." Putting down his glass, he crossed the room toward her. "Do you want to talk down here, or would you prefer to go upstairs?"

She swallowed hard. "I just want you to hold me," she whispered.

The insecurity in her voice caused Adam's throat to tighten. He folded his arms around her and held her tightly. He buried his face in her soft, sweetly scented hair and thought that he was the luckiest man alive. He kissed the top of her head. "Is that better?" he murmured into her hair.

Regina nodded. All evening she had worried that Adam might be furious with her, that he might have believed the things Gordy McGrath had said. Over and over, she had told herself that it really didn't matter what Adam believed; she knew she was innocent.

Except that it did matter. More than anything

else in the world, she wanted him to believe her. She needed him to believe her.

"Let's go upstairs," Adam said.

They blew out the candles and went up the long staircase together. Adam undressed and joined Regina in the bed. The night was warm, so they left off all the covers except a single sheet. Lying down, Adam slid one arm beneath Regina's shoulders and rolled her against him. Although he ached to bury himself in her, he didn't try to caress her or make love to her. He simply held her. And talked.

He told her about his early life in Warwickshire. "We lived in an old stone manor house that was impossible to keep warm in the winter. My father earned a living as a country physician. We had no servants, only a girl from the village who came to the house twice a week to help my mother with the laundry. We had very little money, but we were happy.

"My parents were killed when I was six. They were going to a Christmas party, and their carriage slid off an icy road and rolled down an embankment. I was sent to live with an elderly uncle for several years before I was old enough to strike out on my own."

Nestled comfortably against his side, Regina tilted her head back to look at him. "How old were you when you left?"

Adam's forehead creased. "I don't know. Eleven. Twelve."

Her cousin Robert was twelve, an age that suddenly seemed incredibly young. "My God, you were just a child," she said, her voice filled with awe.

Adam couldn't resist a bemused laugh. "At the

time, I thought I was quite the grown man."

"How did you survive?"

"Miles Jordan's father was a vicar who had a small parish outside London. He hired me to tend the church cemetery. In all honesty, I think he felt sorry for me, so he created the job as an excuse to take me in. I was a proud one in those days, refusing to accept a handout. I stayed with the Jordans until I was seventeen. They treated me as if I were their own. Father Jordan tutored me in a wide variety of subjects, impressing upon me the importance of a good education, not only in the classics, but in what he called 'the university of life.' He taught me how to invest money and make it grow. He taught me how to recognize the difference between the cost of an item and its real value. He taught me how to spot at a glance someone who might try to cheat me in a business deal, and how to recognize opportunities to expand my own wealth. He was pretty adamant though, that I never cheat anyone out of what was rightfully theirs, and that if I did profit from someone else's misfortune, that I do it in such a way that I've gained a friend rather than made an enemy."

Regina thought it was a shame that Adam had not succeeded in his endeavor where Richard was concerned, but she said nothing. Nor did she think it was the appropriate time to reveal what she had learned from Miles Jordan about Adam's childhood. She sensed a vulnerability in Adam, that he was telling her things he had never told anyone else, and she didn't want to destroy the closeness that it brought them.

Adam continued. "Using Father Jordan's connections, I started my own shipping business in

London. It didn't take me long to learn that there was money to be made in tobacco. By the time I was twenty I had amassed what seemed to be a small fortune as well as a reputation on the waterfront for being honest. It was through a contact in Williamsburg that I started doing business with your father."

Regina raised up on one elbow. "Bea told me you had been doing business with my family for years, but I never knew. I mean, your name sounded familiar, but—"

"Actually, your father worked directly with Samuel Peterson who was an employee of mine for several years. When Peterson left and opened his own business, he took the Langley account with him, although I continued to advise him regarding the best way to handle different investments. The rest of the story you already know."

Regina frowned in concentration. "I've heard of Samuel Peterson. Richard mentioned him. So did Uncle William."

"He was handling the Langley shipping accounts when your brother inherited Summerhill. He's a good man, and a competent one. I intend to retain his services."

Regina mulled over the things Adam had told her. It still seemed incredible to her that he had once been homeless and penniless. Like she and Richard would have been had he turned them out. There were still so many things about him that she wanted to know. Not about his past so much as about him now. His likes and dislikes. His beliefs. How did he feel about having children?

How did he feel about *her*?

She trailed her fingers through the dark hair on

Adam's chest. "Were you ever in love?"

Adam was silent for a long moment before answering. "Once."

Regina folded her arms on Adam's chest and rested her chin on them so she could see into his face. "Tell me about her."

Again Adam was quiet. "It happened a long time ago," he said at last. "I was very young and very much in love, and she was very beautiful. Her name was Elise Haverly. She had black hair and dark brown eyes. She looked very much like you."

Did that mean Adam thought that she too was beautiful? Regina didn't know whether to be flattered or jealous.

Adam absently stroked her hair. "Elise was rather bold and daring. She liked to do things to shock people, such as wear men's breeches, or stay out all night without a chaperon. She used to say she would rather live a very short exciting life than a long dull one. She was terrified of being forced to fit into society's mold."

Regina could understand that. Having to spend one's entire life doing only what society dictated, with no regard for one's personal desires, was tantamount to a slow death. "Did you ask her to marry you?"

"Yes."

"And she turned you down?"

"No. She accepted. We were betrothed for three months."

"What happened to her?"

"I found her in bed with one of the grooms."

Regina froze. Now she understood why Adam had become so furious when she ran away with James. She would never forget that night at the inn, or the unforgiving look on his face, or his barely constrained rage.

What she didn't understand was why he had still wanted to marry her even after he thought she had betrayed him just as Elise had betrayed him. "I'm sorry," she said softly. "You must have been devastated."

Adam slid his hand beneath her nightdress to caress her hip. "I was. At the time. But if it hadn't happened, I wouldn't be here with you."

Regina sighed with contentment and lay her head on Adam's chest. The feel of his hand beneath her nightdress, stroking her bare skin, awakened all the delicious sensations he could so easily arouse in her. "What's going to happen to Gordy McGrath?" she asked after a long, leisurely silence.

"I don't know. This isn't the first time he's been in trouble. Randolph may decide to send him to work at the iron mines."

Regina's brows dipped with bewilderment. "What mines? The ones inland that the governor owns?"

"The same. Spotswood needs replacements for those indentures whose terms have ended. Tonight, Randolph and some of the other planters were talking about selling the Scots to the governor just to get them out of the county. I'm willing to bet Randolph sells McGrath."

"Are you going to sell your indentures?"

"Unless there are any who prefer working the mines over working a field, I have no reason to."

Without warning, Adam shifted his weight, rolling Regina onto her back and parting her legs with his knee. "I don't want to talk anymore," he said hoarsely before covering her mouth with his.

*   *   *

Regina lay on her side in the darkness, facing Adam, listening to the reassuring sound of his breathing and watching him sleep.

It had been an exhausting day, yet sleep eluded her. She kept thinking about the things Adam had told her—as well as the things he hadn't—the horrible details that she had learned from Miles Jordan.

Life had dealt Adam one cruel blow after another, she thought sadly. The tragic loss of his parents. The years he spent with an uncle who beat and starved him. Betrayal by the woman he loved and had planned to marry.

Scandal surrounding the one he finally did marry.

Tears stung Regina's eyes. If anyone deserved a chance at happiness, Adam did.

"I'll try harder to be a good wife to you," she whispered achingly. "I promise."

Chapter 18

❝❝I wish it were safe for Aunt Caroline to travel. I want to give a harvest party here at Summerhill just like the ones Uncle William used to have, with dancing and games and lots and lots of food. And I want to invite everyone in the parish.''

Bertie frowned over a particularly stubborn tangle in Regina's hair. "Seems to me someone already wore her red dress.''

Regina glanced up at Bertie's reflection in the dressing table mirror, and grinned. "Then I'll get another one. You know Adam; he'll buy me anything I want.''

Bertie harrumphed. "That man spoils you rotten,'' she said peevishly, but her expression gentled as their gazes met in the mirror. "It's good to see you so happy, Miss Regina. For a long time there, I didn't think I'd ever see you smile again.''

Uncertainty and wonder softened the light in Regina's dark eyes. She and Adam had been married a month now, and she still could not believe the unexpected turn her life had taken. Nor could she believe her good fortune. Adam doted on her. He granted her her every whim. And he treated her with respect, seeking her opinion on different matters, including her ideas in his plans to expand Summerhill, and—most of all—asking her what *she* wanted. She couldn't quite get used to it. Every morning she awoke half expecting it all to have been a dream.

"Oh, Bertie, I love him so much."

"I know you do, child. And he loves you too, even though he don't say it. You can see it in the way he looks at you."

Regina's expression became pensive. "I saw James and Lucy at church yesterday. James doesn't even seem like the same person anymore. Bertie, when I think of how close I came to throwing my life away for him, I feel sick inside."

"You ain't the only one. I thought Mister William was going to burst a blood vessel when he found out the two of you had run off." Bertie twisted the final lock of Regina's hair into place and secured it with a pin.

Regina turned her head slightly to one side and studied Bertie's handiwork in the mirror. She lifted a silver filigree ear bob and held it beside her face, and then a gold one. A dimple appeared at one corner of her mouth and mischief danced in her dark eyes. "Green," she said definitively. "Emerald green."

Bertie looked at her as if she had lost her mind. "I don't know what you're talking about." She started straightening the bed.

Regina put down the earbobs and got to her feet. "My dress for the harvest party," she said, twirling around in the middle of the room. "I want it to be emerald green."

Bertie's lips tightened in disapproval. "You'd

best get busy plannin' this harvest party of yours, or there ain't going to be one."

They were interrupted by the thunder of horses' hooves and the rumble of carriage wheels approaching the house. Regina went to the window and pulled back the curtain. The driver was standing up in the box, driving the team forward at breakneck speed. Regina frowned. "It's Bea!"

She bolted out the bedchamber door and down the stairs. She threw open the front door just as Beatrice Randolph climbed down from the carriage, her clothes askew, her red hair falling out of its pins, and her eyes puffy. She was crying.

"Bea, what happened? Are you all right?"

"Oh, Reggie, the most terrible thing has happened. Please say I can stay here with you. I just can't go back home."

"Of course you can stay here. Please don't cry. Come in the house. Bertie, find Jethro and have him take care of Bea's carriage."

Regina put her arm around her friend's shoulders and led her into the house. "Come sit down and tell me what happened. Bea, are you all right? Are you hurt?"

Beatrice sniffled loudly and shook her head. "I'm fine, truly I am. Oh, Reggie, you'll never believe what happened!" She burst into tears all over again.

Not knowing what else to do, Regina took Beatrice into Adam's study and led her to a chair. "Sit here."

Beatrice sat down on the edge of the chair and buried her face in her hands. Her sobs filled the room.

Regina went to the side table and poured a hefty

portion of port into a glass. Her hand shook, causing some of the ruby colored liquid to splash on the table. She carried the glass to Beatrice. "Here. Drink this."

Beatrice took the glass from her and lifted it to her mouth. She drained it in several huge gulps and handed it back to Regina. "Thanks," she said hiccuping.

"Do you want more?"

Beatrice shook her head. "I'm fine, really." She sniffled again and wiped her eyes with her fingers.

Regina returned the glass to the side table and snatched up a small hand towel that was used to clean up spills. She shoved the towel into the other woman's hand. "Use this."

Beatrice blew her nose and dabbed at her eyes. "I'm sorry. I don't mean to be such a baby. I just didn't know where else to go."

Regina dropped to her knees beside the chair. "You still haven't told me what happened."

Beatrice shuddered. "Reggie, it's so awful. Mother and Father have been fighting since yesterday. I couldn't stand the screaming anymore. I just had to get away from there. I can't go back. I can't live there anymore."

"Bea!"

Beatrice took a shaky breath. "Mother's been carrying on in secret . . ." Her voice quivered. "With Charles Toliver."

Regina's mouth fell open. "You mean, she and Charles—"

Beatrice nodded. "Oh, Reggie, it's been going on for years, and no one ever knew about it until yesterday. Father came back from Williamsburg a few

days early, and he caught them...together..."
Her voice trailed off.

Regina was speechless. *Mrs. Randolph and Charles Toliver?* It didn't seem possible! The Randolphs were the most upstanding citizens she knew. She couldn't believe Marion Randolph was even capable of cheating on her husband. And yet she had. With Charles Toliver, no less.

Regina's shock turned to rage. Why that sneaking, lying, no good weasel, she fumed. Pretending to be in love with her while at the same time he was bedding Mrs. Randolph. If Uncle William had known about that, he would never have given Charles permission to court her.

Or would he?

Uncle William was certainly no saint. Although no one had ever spoken about it to her directly, she had heard enough gossip to suspect that he had been far from faithful during the years he had been married to her aunt.

Regina took Beatrice's hand. "Bea, I'm sorry. I didn't know. Of course you can stay here as long as you want."

Beatrice gripped Regina's hand. "I wish Silas were here."

"I know. He'll be back in a few days."

"He wanted me to make this trip to Belhaven with him, but Mother and Father said no. They said it wasn't proper because we aren't yet married. But I wish I'd gone anyway. I wish I'd been brave like you and done what I wanted."

"I was never brave," Regina corrected her. "Just contrary. Besides, defying your parents would only have caused an uproar, and they might have forbidden you from ever seeing Silas again."

"God, I hate her!"

"Bea, don't say that!"

"Reggie, you just don't understand. Father loved her more than life itself. He worshiped her."

Regina had to bite her tongue to keep from blurting out that she thought Beatrice was overstating her father's fondness for her mother. While Mr. and Mrs. Randolph were openly polite to each other, no one would ever go so far as to suggest that either one of them harbored any great passion for the other.

Beatrice rubbed her temples. "I've been crying so much my head hurts."

"I'll have Bertie make you some chamomile tea, and then you should lie down and rest for awhile. You can use my old room."

New tears welled in Beatrice's eyes. "I wish everything could go back to the way it was before, when we were all happy."

Regina was tempted to remind her that during the times Bea was happy, *she* had been miserable. Instead, she said with mock innocence, "Back when you were in love with Richard and I was in love with James?"

Beatrice rolled her eyes. "Oh, God!"

Regina grinned. "You mean, *King George's codpiece*, don't you?"

Beatrice choked on a giggle. Tears rolled down her face. "I miss Izzy. I wish the three of us could be friends again."

"I do too."

"Oh, Reggie, what am I going to do?"

"Take a nap. After that, I don't know. The only thing I can promise is that I'll always be here for you."

Beatrice's shoulders began to shake with suppressed sobs. Regina got up and wrapped her arms around her friend. The two women clung to each other while Beatrice cried.

Regina nervously followed the tall, gangly black girl through the wide central hall to the double doors that led out to the terrace. Regina noticed with a sinking feeling that one of the glass panes in the door was broken and that the paint around the door frame was cracked and peeling. Of all the houses on the Northern Neck, it was rumored that the Fitzhugh mansion was one of the most costly to build. Now, after years of neglect, the once elegant home wore a cloak of shabbiness.

She had not been in Isabel Fitzhugh's house since last spring, several months before Adam first entered their lives. And she and Izzy had not spoken since that awful night when Izzy had shown up at the mill instead of James. She felt like a criminal breaking into a place where she was no longer welcome.

Izzy was on the terrace with James and Lucy. The three were sitting at a small table bathed in sunlight, enjoying a late breakfast and laughing over some private joke. Izzy, who was sitting facing the house while the other two had their backs to the door, was the first to see her. She had just been about to take a drink of her coffee when she froze, her hand poised in midair. Her smile fled and the color drained from her small, pointed face.

Following his cousin's gaze, James suddenly turned around. His pale blond brows shot upward. He jumped to his feet, nearly knocking over his chair. "Reggie, what are you doing here?"

Lucy turned to stare at her. Regina did not miss the hatred that glittered in her eyes. Nor did she fail to notice the pronounced swelling of Lucy's belly beneath her pale pink summer gown. "I came to see Izzy."

Izzy put down her coffee cup. "Have you considered that I may not want to see you? Or do you still think only of yourself, Reggie?"

Regina braced herself against the pain that Izzy's hatred caused her. She knew in her heart that she and Izzy could never resume their former friendship, no matter how much she wished it. "Please, Izzy. It's important. It's about Bea."

Izzy's antagonism faltered. After several indecisive seconds, she finally pushed back her chair and stood. "We can go into the receiving room," she said stiffly. "Lucy. James. Please excuse us."

Her head held unnaturally high, Izzy led the way back into the house. Regina followed her into the drawing room with its cornflower blue walls and ornamental white plaster moldings that had been imported from France when Izzy's father was still alive.

Izzy rounded on her, her eyes blazing. "You have a lot of nerve, Reggie, coming here after what you did to James. How could you? How could you break his heart that way, then dally with him after you knew he and Lucy were finally going to be married?"

"Izzy, I never meant to hurt James—"

"Oh, stop lying! You knew exactly what you were doing. Because of your stupid elopement, Mr. Carlisle was going to call off the wedding and have James charged with rape. The only reason he didn't was because Lucy wouldn't lie and say that James forced himself on her."

Regina felt her frustration rising. It didn't make sense that Izzy would be so protective of her cousin. She and James had never been especially close, and most of the time she had criticized him for his roving eye and his prowling tomcat ways. Now it seemed as if James could do no wrong in Izzy's eyes. Now Izzy blamed *her* for everything.

Then another thought occurred to Regina. She cast Izzy a questioning glance. "Is it James you're so angry about," she asked quietly, "or is this really about Adam and me?"

Sudden tears replaced the fury in Izzy's eyes. "You knew I wanted Adam," she sobbed, her voice shaking. "I confided in you. I told you how I felt about him. And he liked me, too. At least, he did until you poisoned him against me."

Regina shook her head. "Izzy, I never—"

"I don't want to hear any more of your lies, Reggie. I trusted you, and you used that trust against me."

Regina fidgeted. She knew that she could talk until she was blue in the face and Izzy would never believe that she had not stolen Adam from her. Izzy's anger was like a cancer, eating away at her from the inside. And there was nothing Regina could do about it. On the other hand, Izzy might listen to Adam. She nervously moistened her lips. "Perhaps if you talked to Adam—"

"No!" Izzy clenched her fists. "I don't want to see him!"

"Izzy, please—"

"I don't want to see you either. Just say what you came here to say and get out."

Regina's heart sank. She took a steadying breath. "Bea's parents had a terrible fight—it would be best if she told you about it herself. Anyway, Bea is staying at Summerhill, at least for the next few days. She's really upset. She hasn't stopped crying since she arrived."

Izzy said nothing.

"Izzy, it would help if you came to see her. She needs her friends right now. She needs to have people around her who love her."

"Then go fetch Captain Bebe," Izzy said caustically.

Regina's frustration exploded. "Blast you, Isabel Fitzhugh! I thought you cared about Bea, but you don't. You're so wrapped up in feeling sorry for yourself that you can't even take the time to comfort a friend who needs you."

Izzy's mouth fell open.

"And I'll tell you something else," Regina continued, just warming up, "I'll be damned if I'm going to spend the rest of my life feeling guilty because Adam wanted to marry me, and not you. I'm not the one who is being selfish, Izzy; you are. I didn't want to marry Adam. If you don't believe me, you can ask Bea. Or ask Richard. For that matter, you can ask Adam.

"It wasn't my fault that Adam chose to marry me. But I can tell you one thing: If someone were to try to take Adam from me now, I would fight to keep him with everything that I have in me. For the first time in my life, I'm happy. And I'm not going to let you destroy that."

Izzy glowered at her through her tears. She clenched and unclenched her fists. "Get out."

Regina's shoulders slumped. An ache of defeat

in her throat, she asked thickly, "Are you going to put aside your anger at me long enough to come visit Bea? I'll stay out of your way. I promise. You won't even have to see me."

"I said, get out!" A sob broke in Izzy's throat. She shoved past Regina and bolted from the room. Her footfalls echoed on the wooden treads as she ran up the stairs.

Regina stood in the middle of the drawing room for several long, painful moments, fighting back her own tears. It wasn't fair! She loved Adam. She had also treasured her friendship with Izzy. Why couldn't she have both? Why did having one mean she must give up the other? Why did her happiness mean that someone else must suffer?

Why did Adam choose her over Izzy?

Unable to find answers to the questions that tormented her, Regina found her way to the front door through a haze of blinding tears. She had to get out of there.

"Reggie, are you all right?" James asked from behind her.

She stopped and hastily wiped her eyes with her fingertips. "I'll be fine."

James nervously glanced over his shoulder toward the terrace door, then turned back to Regina. He took her elbow. "Let's go outside where we can talk in private."

Too shaken to protest, Regina let him walk with her out to the carriage.

"Are you sure you're all right?"

She nodded. "I'm fine. Really. I guess I never realized how much Izzy's friendship meant to me until . . . until I lost it." Her voice broke.

"Come here."

Regina unthinkingly went into his arms. She burst into tears.

James pressed his face against the top of her head and held her tightly while she sobbed out her misery against his chest, wetting the front of his shirt with her tears.

Gradually, she stopped crying.

Feeling a little self-conscious about standing there with James's arms around her, she pulled away. She hiccuped and wiped her eyes with her fingertips. "I-I'm sorry. I don't mean to bl-blubber so much."

James pressed a handkerchief into her hand.

Regina blew her nose. "I must be a sight. My eyes always swell up when I cry." She hiccuped again. "And between Bea and me, we must have cried gallons today."

"That was one hell of a shock, learning that Toliver was in the hay with Mrs. Randolph. That's one scandal that everyone will be talking about for a while. In comparison, our elopement seems almost trivial."

Regina dragged the back of her hand across her eyes. "You know about Charles and Bea's mother?"

"Everyone in the county does. If they don't by now, they will soon."

"I didn't tell Izzy; I thought it would be best if Bea told her herself."

"She already knew. We found out this morning." James chuckled, more to himself than to her. "Now I know what Burke had on him."

Bewilderment creased Regina's brow. "What do you mean?"

"Aw, c'mon, Reggie. Your husband paid *me* to stay away from you, didn't he?"

"Yes, but . . ." Regina broke off as a long forgotten memory tugged at the far corners of her mind.

Tell me, Mr. Burke, did you also pay Charles to keep his distance?

I didn't have to; the man's conscience kept his price low.

Suddenly Regina felt as if she would be sick to her stomach. *Adam knew!* He had to have known about Charles and Mrs. Randolph. And he must have used that information to get Charles to drop his suit for her hand. There was no other plausible explanation.

"Reggie, are you all right?"

James's voice jolted her back to the present. "I-I'm fine. James, I'd better go. I don't want to leave Bea by herself for very long."

"Give her my regards?"

Regina nodded. "Will you try to get Izzy to come see her?"

"I'll try. But I can't promise you she'll listen."

"Oh . . . here's your handkerchief."

"Thanks." Taking her by the shoulders, James pulled her toward him. Before Regina realized what he intended, he lowered his head to hers.

Regina's first instinct was to shove him away, but she gradually relaxed and let James kiss her. Oddly, the feel of his lips on hers failed to invoke any of the old sensations that his kisses had once aroused in her. She felt pleasure, but not passion.

Her love for James was dead.

Finally James pulled away and released her.

Regina climbed into the carriage and took the reins. Genuinely sorry that he was no longer going to be a part of her life, she smiled sadly at him. "Good-bye, James."

At an upstairs window, a curtain fluttered and then was still.

For the second time in as many nights, Regina was jolted awake, her heart pounding furiously and her nightdress clinging to her sweat-dampened skin. She glanced over at Adam sleeping soundly beside her, his back toward her.

She listened intently, but could hear nothing out of the ordinary. Something had awakened her. But what? She thought of her wedding night when she had seen Duncan McLean standing in the front yard, near the oak tree. Was he there again tonight? Was it possible that it was not a noise that had awakened her, but something less tangible? Was it possible that she could *feel* his presence?

Moving carefully so she wouldn't awaken Adam, she slid from the bed. She crossed the room and pulled back the edge of the curtain, just enough to see out the window.

Nothing.

She saw nothing. For a long time, she stared out the window, waiting, for some movement in the yard or in the distance, along the edge of the woods. There was none.

So what had awakened her?

Glancing back to make certain Adam was asleep, she left the bedchamber and tiptoed down the hall.

The door to Richard's bedchamber stood ajar. He had left the house shortly after dinner. No one needed to ask where he was going; he came home drunk more often than not. "Richard?" she whispered.

No answer.

She pushed the door farther open. "Richard?"

His bed was empty. He still had not returned from the Boar's Head.

Regina tiptoed to the stairs. The floorboards creaked beneath her feet. She stopped at the top of the staircase and stood, staring down into the darkness, her heart still beating unnaturally fast. She knew she should go back to bed, or at the very least, go get Adam. If someone was down there, it wouldn't be safe for her to venture downstairs alone.

On the other hand, Beatrice was down there, as was Bertie. Chances were, one of them was up and around, and that was what had awakened her.

Feeling a little foolish for worrying over something that was probably no more than a figment of her imagination, she returned to the bedchamber she shared with Adam.

Adam stirred when she crawled back into bed. He rolled toward her and wrapped his arms possessively around her. She snuggled against him, grateful for his closeness, even though it failed to bring her any reassurance that all was as it should be.

Her heart continued to pound, and it was a long time before she finally drifted into an uneasy sleep.

Richard flung his cards down on the table. "Damn!"

Harry Lee chuckled. "Five hundred acres of riverfront property. I never thought I'd see the day when I'd own a piece of Summerhill."

"You don't own it yet," Richard reminded him,

ale slurring his voice. A haze of tobacco smoke filled the air.

"But I will." Harry signaled the tavernkeeper.

Arthur Randolph, Jr., glanced up from the initials he was gouging into the top of the table. "You'll win it back, Langley. Lee's luck can't hold out forever."

"Sure it can," Thomas Parke said. "Although if I were Lee, I'd be after Langley's shares of Burke's shipping company."

The tavernkeeper brought three more tankards to the table. "You boys hungry?"

Randolph deftly slid his arm over the damage he was inflicting on the table top, hiding it from the tavernkeeper's view. "You got any more of that chicken?"

"Coming right up."

The door opened, and a half dozen indentured servants and landless freemen entered the tavern. Richard bristled when he saw McGrath. He still hadn't forgiven the Scot for breaking his nose. He jerked his head toward the group. "What's *he* doing here? I thought your father was going to keep him locked up until he packed him off to the mines."

Randolph looked flustered. "I don't know."

Hatred burned red in Richard's eyes. He reached for the knife in Randolph's hand.

The other men at the table glanced uneasily at each other. "Let it go, Langley," Lee cautioned.

"The hell I will." Richard started to rise. "I got some unfinished business to take care of."

Lee seized Richard's wrist, pinning his arm to the table. "I said, let it go."

The muscle in Richard's jaw twitched. He slowly sat back down. He'd had about all he was going to take from Harry Lee. From any of them. This wasn't over yet.

Chapter 19

Adam handed Miles Jordan the bank note. "This should cover passage for both you and Mary, and the cost of shipping your household furnishings."

Miles folded the bank note and put it in his waistcoat pocket. "I think Mary will like it here. She hasn't been the same since we lost Roy to pneumonia. This will give her a new start away from the painful memories."

"You have the name and address of my solicitor in London," Adam said. "Before you leave, I'll provide you with a letter of reference. If you need anything at all, contact him. He'll take care of it. And one more thing: Give your parents my regard."

Miles tucked his hat beneath his arm. "I'll do that. And I'll follow up on your inquiry about Duncan McLean. If we're lucky, by the time I return, we'll have an answer from the courts."

Adam walked him to the front door. "I want you back here by next spring. There'll be plenty of work for you to do. I wish I had more men with your talents."

Miles chuckled. "Surveying or investigating?"

"Both."

Miles shook his head. "It was a pity about the Randolphs. They seem like good people. I hate to see a marriage go sour."

"So do I." Although Adam had little sympathy for either party involved, he could not help noticing that Mrs. Randolph was paying a high price for her indiscretion, while Toliver had emerged from the scandal virtually unscathed. Rumor was already circulating the parish that he had lost no time shifting his attentions to a well-to-do young widow from Henrico County.

"I'm going to do some more work here and then I'll meet you down at the waterfront," Adam said. "We'll inventory your surveying equipment, and I'll give you a receipt."

"Thanks for permitting me to store it here until I return from England. I appreciate the favor."

"It only makes sense. There's no point in paying shipping charges if you're only going to bring it back again. One more thing. If you see Langley, tell him I need to speak with him."

After Miles took his leave, Adam returned to his study.

It annoyed him that Richard was nowhere to be found. His brother-in-law had a bad habit of showing up for work whenever he felt like it, and even then it was not unusual to find him in the back room of the office, sprawled on the cot, sleeping off the previous night's excesses. Adam knew he was going to have to take a stand. If Richard Langley wasn't going to take his responsibilities seriously, then he was going to have to replace him. He needed someone he could depend on.

Adam was deep in the ledgers, trying to make sense of William Langley's accounting, when he heard a knock at the front door. Marking his place in the ledger with a ruler, he went to answer it.

Somehow Adam managed to conceal his surprise. And his distaste. "Father Tidewell, please come in." He stepped back and held open the door. "To what do I owe the pleasure of this visit?"

The priest stepped into the hall. "I'm afraid this isn't a social call, Mr. Burke."

"I don't know, Reggie. I really don't feel up to going anywhere or seeing anyone," Beatrice hedged. "Adam invited Silas to dinner. I'll see him then."

"Why wait when you can see him sooner? Adam said we could ride with him when he goes down to the waterfront." Regina took the stocking Beatrice was mending and placed it on the sewing table. "It'll be fun. Besides, you haven't been out of this house since you came here."

Beatrice groaned.

Regina took her hands and pulled her up out of the chair. "The *Triumph* dropped anchor this morning, and we're going down to the docks, just like we used to. Except that we no longer have to hide at the top of the cliff and spy on everyone . . . unless you want to."

Beatrice choked on a laugh. "I really don't want to go."

"No arguments! You go freshen up and I'll tell Adam to wait for us."

While Beatrice went to her bedchamber to get ready, Regina went to find Adam.

She worried about Bea. Ever since coming to Summerhill, Beatrice had spent most of her time bent over some piece of sewing that one of the servants could easily have handled, or curled up in bed with a book whose pages seldom got turned. Getting out of the house would be good for her. She was glad Silas Bebe was back from his trip to Belhaven. Maybe he could raise her spirits.

When Regina reached Adam's study, he was standing at one of the tall windows that looked out over the front lawn. His back was toward her, and he was staring out the window. "Adam, I'm glad you're still here. I talked Bea into going down to the waterfront with us. She put up a fuss, but once she's there, I'm sure she'll—"

She broke off, the words dying in her throat as he turned to look at her, fury blazing in his hazel eyes. "Adam, what's wrong?"

"Close the door." The ominous quiet in his voice sent a tremor of dread through her. Her heart pounding, she pushed the door shut.

Adam inclined his head toward a chair. "Sit down."

Regina's stomach knotted. She had a feeling she wasn't going to like this. She went to the chair and sat down on the edge of the hard seat. "Has something happened?"

Adam moved around to the front of Uncle William's big oak desk. He leaned against the desk and folded his arms across his chest. His gaze drilled into hers. "Father Tidewell came to see me."

Regina almost relaxed. Ever since the wedding, Father Tidewell had shown her a great deal more courtesy than he had been wont to do. It was as if being married gave her a respectability that maidenhood lacked. Or perhaps he was merely trying to ingratiate himself to Adam. She suspected it was the latter. "What did he have to say?"

Adam stared at her so long and hard that Regina began to squirm inwardly. "Adam, talk to me!"

He came at her so fast that Regina instinctively recoiled, thinking he meant to strike her. Instead, he leaned down and placed his hands on the arms of her chair, trapping her. His face was only inches from hers. It was all she could do not to shrink away from the churning rage in his eyes. "Did I, or did I not, tell you to keep your distance from James Fitzhugh?"

Regina gaped at him. "What?"

"Answer me!"

"Yes, but—"

"But, what? What possible excuse do you have for going to see that scoundrel after I gave you explicit orders to stay away from him?"

So that was it! Father Tidewell must have told Adam about her trip to Izzy's. Yet who had told Father Tidewell? Whoever the informant was, he certainly had his facts wrong. "I didn't go to see James. I went to see Izzy. Had I known that James was going to be there, I'd never have—"

"Don't lie to me!"

"Adam, I'm telling you the truth! James was there with his wife. They were having breakfast, for God's sake. It's nothing out of the ordinary. After all, he is Izzy's cousin."

The look in Adam's eyes turned so hard and so brittle that Regina thought she was going to be ill. It took every ounce of courage that she had to keep her gaze fixed on his. She didn't dare glance away for even a second. She didn't dare let him think she was afraid—or guilty.

Adam pushed away from the chair. He turned his back toward her and took several steps, and

Regina slowly released her breath. "Adam, I didn't go to Izzy's with the intention of seeing James. I swear. Until I saw him, I didn't even know he was there."

Without warning, Adam rounded on her. "And I suppose you didn't intentionally kiss him either!"

Regina's courage fled. She started to shake her head.

Rage exploded in Adam's eyes. He seized Regina by the shoulders and hauled her up out of the chair. "Did you kiss him?"

"Adam, please—"

"Answer me!"

"Yes!"

From the pained expression that shot across Adam's face, Regina knew that he had been hoping she would deny the charge. Anything, even a lie that he knew to be a lie, was more tolerable than the truth. His fingers tightened on her arms until tears sprang into her eyes and she gasped, then he released her so abruptly that she stumbled backward.

He stalked across the room, dragging his fingers through his hair in rage and frustration. Without warning, he took an angry swipe across the top of his desk, sending the ledgers and inkpots hurtling to the floor with a loud crash. An oath exploded from his lips.

Regina winced.

She rubbed her bruised arms and fought for composure. Her first impulse was to go to Adam and beg for forgiveness. It would never happen again; she would make certain of that. She didn't even love James anymore, if she had loved him at all. She needed to make Adam understand that.

Yet at the same time that her anguished mind was scrambling to find a way to make Adam forgive her, she felt herself growing angry. She hadn't intended to kiss James; it had just happened. And it wasn't as if she planned to do it again. If Adam couldn't forgive her for so trivial an incident, what would happen if she committed a truly serious blunder? Was she destined to spend the rest of her life fearing that she might do something to jeopardize her marriage simply because she wasn't perfect? Was she destined to spend the rest of her life trying to compensate for another woman's infidelity? If that was the kind of existence she had to look forward to, she would rather not live at all.

"It was only a good-bye kiss, Adam," she said shakily. "It didn't mean anything. The only reason I even let James do it was because I wanted to find out if I still felt anything for him. And I didn't. I didn't feel anything at all. And do you want to know why I didn't feel anything?" Her voice quivered. "Because I love *you*. And no matter what you choose to believe, I would never betray you. I'm not Elise!"

Adam rounded on her, his eyes blazing. "That is enough! I did not tell you about Elise just to have you hurl her name at me every time you lose your temper. I don't ever want to hear you mention her again."

"You need not worry about that, Mr. Burke. Until you apologize, I won't even *speak* to you again!"

"Apologize! *I* wasn't the one who was seen in my lover's arms!"

Regina clenched her fists. "James Fitzhugh is not my lover. And I'm not going to stand here and allow you to accuse me of something I haven't done, simply because you've forgotten how to trust anyone. I'm sorry Elise broke your heart. But that doesn't give you the right to break mine!"

She threw open the study door and ran blindly from the room, nearly colliding with Beatrice, who was standing in the middle of the foyer, her face pale with shock.

Regina bolted past her and ran up the stairs.

"Regina!" Adam bellowed. He stopped short and glowered at Beatrice. It was evident from the look on the girl's face that she had overheard a significant portion of their argument. "Don't you have anything better to do than to eavesdrop?"

Beatrice backed away from him. "I-I'm sorry. I didn't mean to . . ." She inched several steps backward, then turned and fled.

His mood dangerously strained, Adam went back to his study, but didn't go inside. Instead, he stood in the doorway, fighting to get his temper under control. The mere idea of Regina locked in James Fitzhugh's arms—letting him kiss her— pushed him to the point of blind rage. He didn't want to think about what he might do if he got his hands on Fitzhugh. If Regina thought he was angry now, she hadn't seen anything yet.

Anxious to get away from there and let his temper cool, lest he do something he might later regret, Adam turned on his heel and stalked from the house, slamming the door shut after him.

Regina dumped an armload of shoes on the bed in the downstairs bedroom. She turned to find Bertie standing in the doorway, her hands on her hips and her lips pressed into a thin line. "Just what do you think you're doing, child?"

"I'm doing exactly what it looks like I'm doing. I'm moving back into my old bedchamber."

Bertie clucked her tongue in disapproval. "Mister Adam isn't going to like that one bit."

Regina thrust out her chin. "Good." She squeezed around the old woman and headed for the staircase.

Marching over to the bed, Bertie scooped up an armload of shoes and followed Regina up the stairs. "You shouldn't be doing this, child. You don't want to upset Mister Adam any more than he already is. The man has a heap of worries on his mind these days."

"And I don't?"

"Not by half, you don't."

Regina cast her a petulant look over her shoulder. "I thought you were on my side, Bertie."

"I am. That's why I don't want to see you do anything foolish." Bertie followed Regina into the upstairs bedchamber that she shared with Adam. She bent and placed Regina's shoes in a single row against the wall. "Talk to your husband. Don't let this poison fester between you."

"I'll talk to him when he apologizes," Regina said. In spite of her efforts to control it, her voice wavered.

"And if he don't?"

"Then he can just sleep in this bed by himself. I'll be damned if I'm going to just sit back and let him accuse me of being unfaithful."

"He didn't do no such thing."

"It's what he was thinking."

Bertie rolled her eyes. "What am I going to do with you, child?"

"Well, to begin with, you can stop carrying my

things back upstairs." Regina sat down on the edge
of the bed as a wave of despair washed over her.
Her throat constricted. "Oh, Bertie, why did this
have to happen? Why couldn't we go on being
happy?"

"Because life ain't always happy, that's why.
Some days are good ones, and some not so good.
But in the end, it's what you make of them that
counts."

"That doesn't help me, Bertie. What am I supposed to *do*?"

"You could say you're sorry."

"But I didn't do anything wrong."

"It don't matter whether you did or not. The
whole purpose is to get you two talking, so you
can iron out this wrinkle."

Regina caught her bottom lip between her teeth
and battled the urge to burst into tears. She had
been doing a lot of crying lately, far more than was
ordinary for her. She didn't know what was wrong.
She was loath to forgive the least little slight. And
she was tired. More tired than she had ever been
in her entire life. She sighed wearily. "Maybe
you're right."

"You know I'm right. You love that man. And if
you're not careful, you're going to lose him to foolish pride just as surely as to another woman."

Regina continued to sit on the bed, mulling over
Bertie's words long after the old woman left the
room.

Bertie was right. She should apologize. Not because she had done anything that she need be
ashamed of, but because she loved him.

Her throat tightened. For the first time since they

were married, she was afraid—genuinely afraid—
of losing him.

A soft tap at the door dragged her thoughts back
to the present. She glanced up to find Beatrice
standing in the doorway. "Are you all right?" Beatrice asked.

She nodded. "You heard everything, didn't
you?"

Beatrice smiled sheepishly. "I heard enough."

Regina plucked at the bedcovers in nervous frustration. "It makes me so mad that someone would
run to Father Tidewell and tell him that James and
I were together. Yes, I let James kiss me, but it
didn't happen the way Adam thinks it happened.
Everything was twisted out of proportion."

Bertie appeared in the doorway. "Miss Beatrice,
your brother is here to see you. He says it's urgent."

Beatrice groaned. "How much do you want to
bet Father sent him to bring me home?"

"Don't go if you don't want to. You can stay here
until you and Silas get married."

"I wish it were that simple. You know Father.
Once he gets a notion into his head, he doesn't relent until he has his way."

Regina certainly did know how stubborn Mr.
Randolph could be, at least where *she* was concerned. "Maybe you should go see what your
brother wants. It might really be something important."

Beatrice let out her breath in an exaggerated sigh.
"I suppose you're right. But if all he wants is for
me to go home, I'm not going to give in." She
paused, and defeat flickered across her face. "At
least, I hope I don't give in. Oh, Reggie, why

couldn't I have been born brave like you? I would never have the courage to stand up to Father the way you did to Adam."

If Beatrice knew how miserable she was right now, she wouldn't say that, Regina thought, suddenly feeling sick to her stomach. She smiled wanly. "Good luck."

"Thanks. I'm going to need it."

After Beatrice left the room, Regina scrambled for the chamber pot and heaved up her breakfast.

Adam smelled the smoke even before he saw the flames. He dug his heels into his horse's sides, sending the animal leaping forward.

An inferno met him at the waterfront. His office was engulfed in flames, as was the tobacco warehouse.

When he had left the docks earlier that morning, the waterfront had been teeming with men busy unloading cargo from the hold of the *Triumph*. Now, except for Captain Bebe, Miles Jordan, and a handful of seamen trying to douse the flames with buckets of water, the waterfront was deserted.

Dismounting, he bolted up the steps and into his office. Smoke filled the building, burning his eyes and lungs. Hurrying into the back room, he yanked the covers off the cot and carried them outside. He ran to the river and plunged them into the water.

For what seemed like hours, although it may have been no more than a few minutes, the men battled the blaze. They threw buckets of water and shovelsful of dirt on the fire. Adam swung the wet blankets, beating out the flames, until his arms ached. Someone else attacked the flames with the wet sheets.

Finally, they managed to get the blaze under control.

Adam struggled to catch his breath. Sweat poured down his face, forming muddy rivulets in the dirt and soot there. He stared at the blackened ruins of what had been his office. The warehouse had also been destroyed, as was the disabled ship his people had been trying to salvage. Wagons of cargo had been overturned, and the crates smashed. Fortunately the *Triumph* was anchored far enough offshore to have escaped damage.

Fortunately, he had insurance.

Captain Bebe limped to where Adam was standing. His clothes were torn and blackened, and he seemed to have aged ten years.

Adam dragged his filthy sleeve across his face. "What happened?"

Captain Bebe shook his head. "I'm not sure," he said, exhaustion and defeat slurring his voice. "One minute we're bringing barrels of dried beef ashore, and the next minute the men are fleeing as if for their lives. Someone knocked me down from behind, then all hell broke loose."

"Any idea who started the fires?"

"I'm afraid not," Captain Bebe said. "It all happened so fast."

Adam was at a loss. He might have expected such trouble at one of the neighboring plantations, but not at Summerhill. He had gone out of his way to treat his people fairly, and he rewarded them generously for work well done.

While most of the other landowners had used Governor Spotswood's proposal as a way to get rid of indentures they didn't want, he had asked for volunteers. Anyone who wanted to leave Summerhill to go work for the governor could do so; no questions asked. Only one man requested to be transferred. The rest had chosen to stay. So why had they revolted now?

"There is something else you need to know," Captain Bebe continued. "Do you remember that Scot your brother-in-law got into the bout of fisti-cuffs with?"

Adam's forehead furrowed. "Gordy McGrath."

Captain Bebe nodded. "Some men pulled his body out of the river this morning. He'd been stabbed several times. As soon as McGrath's fol-lowers heard he was dead, they went after Ran-dolph and demanded retribution. It's rumored that your brother-in-law killed him."

"What!"

"The last time McGrath was seen alive was at the Boar's Head yesterday evening. Your brother-in-law was there too. He went for a knife, but one of the Lee brothers stopped him."

"Did anyone actually see Langley attack Mc-Grath?" Adam asked.

"If they did, no one's talking."

Adam swore under his breath. It was definitely Langley's nature to threaten people and to try to bully them into doing his bidding. But was he ca-pable of murder? "Did Langley ever show up this morning?"

"He was in your office early this morning. He looked like hell. I don't think he'd even been to bed yet."

Alarm surged through Adam. Had Richard gone into the back room to sleep and been trapped in the burning building? Had someone set fire to the building as an act of retaliation? If the indentures truly believed that Richard Langley had slain one of their own, it would not be unreasonable to expect that at least some of them might take the law into their own hands and seek revenge against the perpetrator. Or his family.

Adam froze.

Regina.

Chapter 20

❦❦

❝It had to be the bacon, Bertie. It didn't agree with me.❞

The old woman folded the wet cloth and placed it on Regina's forehead. "I don't think so, child. We all ate it too, and you don't see any of us clinging to a chamber-pot like our lives depended on it. Now you just lie there and rest, and I'll go get you something to settle your stomach."

"Don't worry. I'm not leaving this bed. At the moment, I feel too weak to sit up."

Bertie stopped in the doorway and looked back at her. She clucked her tongue in sympathy and shook her grayed head. "Just like your mama," she said. "She couldn't keep nothing down neither."

Regina closed her eyes and waited as another spasm gripped her stomach. She wished she knew what was wrong with her. She wasn't by nature a sickly person. She couldn't even *pretend* to be sick with any degree of credibility; she had certainly tried often enough as a child, whenever she didn't feel like practicing her stitches or polishing silver.

She wished Beatrice had not returned home with her brother; she could have used the company. But Arthur had been adamant, telling Bea that there had been trouble at home, without telling her what had happened. "A family matter," was all he would say. Bea had reluctantly caved in.

Suddenly, Regina's eyes flew open.

Just like your mama. She couldn't keep nothing down neither.

Exactly what did Bertie mean by that?

Unless . . .

Delight, awe, and concern surged through her at once. Surely it wasn't *that*. She and Adam had not been married that long. Was it possible that she was already carrying his child?

She still didn't know how he felt about having children, although most of the men she knew welcomed the idea. Of course, they didn't have to walk around for nine months with their bellies getting bigger and bigger and looking as if they had swallowed a watermelon. And they didn't have to endure labor or give birth, or, worst of all, risk death from childbirth.

On the other hand, those risks didn't stop most women from wanting to have children either. They certainly hadn't frightened *her* away. When she was younger, she had had misgivings about having children. But now, more than anything in the world, she wanted to have a baby. She wanted to hold in her arms a child who had been conceived out of the love she felt for Adam, and who, day after day, would serve as a constant reminder of that love. Even on days like today, when that love seemed precariously in danger of shattering.

Especially on days like today.

Willing her stomach to cooperate, Regina got up from the bed and went to the window. Bertie was right, she thought. She should swallow her pride and apologize, she thought, staring absently out across the yard. She really shouldn't have let James kiss her anyway. She certainly wouldn't have liked it if Adam had kissed Izzy—

"Here's your tea," Bertie said from the doorway. She stopped just inside the room. "What are you doing up, child? You were supposed to stay in that bed."

Regina only half heard her. Far across the yard, beyond the tree line, thick black smoke was billowing into the sky. She motioned to Bertie. "Come here and look at this. It's coming from the docks. Bertie, something is on fire!"

Bertie set down the tea tray and joined her at the window. "Lord have mercy! Whatever caught, there's not going to be much left of it."

Another sick feeling settled in the pit of Regina's stomach. What if something happened to Adam? Her last memory of him would be their unfortunate argument, a stupid quarrel over James Fitzhugh, of all people!

She turned and bolted for the door.

"Miss Regina, get back here! Just where do you think you're going?"

Regina didn't answer her. She was already halfway down the stairs.

Before she could reach the front door, the door flew open and Duncan McLean burst into the hall. He slammed the door shut.

Regina stopped short, caught by surprise.

He towered over her. His shirtsleeves were rolled up, exposing arms that bulged with muscle, and hands so massive they could probably snap her in two. His face was flushed, as if he had been running, and brilliant blue eyes burned with a light that seared through her defenses and sent a tremor of fear down her spine. He started toward her and she instinctively retreated. "You have no business being in here," she bit out, masking her fear with a show of anger. "Get out, or I'll—"

McLean seized her arm, and she screamed. "Bertie!"

"I'm not going to hurt you."

"*Bertie!*"

McLean backed her against the wall. "Be silent!"

Through sheer dint of will, Regina stopped struggling. Her heart pounded fiercely.

His gaze bore into hers. "I'm not going to hurt you, lass," he repeated.

Regina's knees threatened to buckle beneath her. "You had better have a good explanation for this, Mr. McLean, or I'll see to it that my husband flays you alive." Her voice trembled, making her threat seem pitifully weak.

An unfathomable sadness flickered through the Scot's eyes, and then was gone. "Randolph's men have revolted," he said quickly. "They've already set fire to the warehouse, and now they're on their way here."

Regina gaped at him. "Why?"

McLean hesitated a second before answering. "They believe your brother killed one of their own, and now they're out for blood." He glanced up to where Bertie stood on the landing, her eyes bulging with terror. "Get everyone out of the house," he ordered. " 'Tis not safe to be here."

Gripping Regina's arm, he hauled her through the dining room and down the back stairs. Regina had to run to keep from being dragged. She twisted around to see if Bertie was following, but McLean nearly jerked her off her feet. "Hurry up," he barked. "There's no time to lose."

By the time they reached the door leading out to the kitchen, Regina's stomach was halfway into her throat. She didn't know whether to trust the Scot or to try to get away from him. She wished Adam was here. Her stomach roiled. She needed to find a chamber pot.

Richard killed a man?

McLean yanked open the door and Regina caught a glimpse of men armed with shovels and axes just before he quickly pushed it shut again. He rammed the bolt into place. "Is there any other way out?"

"Just through the windows."

Outside, a man with a thick Highland accent shouted, "We know ye're in there with Langley and his sister, McLean. Turn them over to us, and no harm will come to ye."

A muscle in McLean's jaw knotted. "Langley's not here," he shouted back.

Regina glanced frantically back toward the staircase. Where was Bertie?

The man outside shouted again, "Then send out the girl!"

McLean's grip tightened on Regina's arm. "Come with me." Steering her back the way they had come, he pushed her down into the shadowy recess beneath the stairs. "Stay here," he ordered. "I'll tell ye when it's safe to come out."

Regina grabbed his sleeve. "Why are you risking your neck to help me?"

"Your husband asked me to watch over you whenever he couldn't be there to look after you himself."

"You've been following me?" Regina asked, taken aback.

"Aye."

She almost wished she hadn't asked. Why was Adam having her followed? Didn't he trust her? Did he think she was still pining for James? Did he, despite his insistence to the contrary, believe the nasty rumors about her that cropped up from time to time? It would certainly explain why he had gotten so furious when he learned she had been seen with James. She took an unsteady breath. "Did you follow me to Izzy's?"

The men pounded on the door. "Open this door, McLean!"

McLean stood. "I dinna carry tales to your parish priest, lass, if that's what ye're wondering. My job was to assure your safety, not judge your morals. But the next time you decide to cavort with your lover, make sure his cousin isn't watching you from an upstairs window."

Before Regina could respond, McLean was gone. Over her head, she heard his footfalls on the stairs.

She leaned her head back against the cold stone wall as the ugly truth behind Duncan McLean's words sank into her mind.

Izzy!

She should have known! Izzy was never going to forgive her for marrying Adam, and this was her way of paying her back. Through no fault of her own, she had lost a dear friend. But through her own stupidity, she had forfeited her husband's trust as well. She squeezed her eyes shut. "Adam, I'm so sorry," she whispered. "Please forgive me."

It was then that she smelled smoke.

For several seconds, she sat without moving, trying to discern where the smell was coming from. Her first thought was the kitchen, which was only a few yards way, but it didn't smell like a cooking fire, or a laundry fire, or a smokehouse fire.

Where was Bertie? Why hadn't she come downstairs? Surely she hadn't tried to go out the front door?

And where was Duncan McLean?

The sound of splintering wood only a few feet away brought a strangled scream to her throat. She clamped her mouth shut to keep from crying out.

The nauseating sound reverberated through the air, louder this time, followed by angry shouts. "We're coming in, McLean!"

Dear God, they were trying to break down the door!

The third splintering crash drove her from her hiding place. She bolted up the stairs.

A blue haze engulfed the dining room. Regina dashed through the dining room and into the hall. "Bertie! Where are you?"

In the hall, the haze was thicker, making it hard to breathe. Regina ran into the study, skidding to a stop when she saw the fire. Adam's books and ledgers had been dumped into the middle of the floor and set ablaze. Flames had spread from the burning pile and were dancing across the polished wood floor.

Horrified, Regina backed from the study. A loud *pop* followed by a deafening roar brought her around just in time to see the beautiful paneled walls of the reception room explode into flames.

She looked frantically around her. *"Bertie!"*

A huddled form at the landing caught her eye. She started up the stairs. "Bertie, is that you? Oh, my God!"

She knelt by the old woman. Bertie's eyes were closed, and her mahogany face was a pasty shade of gray. Blood seeped from a gash near her temple. "Bertie, what happened to you?" Smoke burned her eyes and choked her throat. With a shaking hand, Regina felt Bertie's neck for a pulse, and finally found one.

Regina's breath burst from her lungs in a sigh of relief. "Thank God you're alive—" She doubled over in a coughing fit.

Suddenly a large hand gripped her shoulder, startling her. "What are you doing here, lass?" Duncan McLean demanded. "I told you to stay put."

Bertie groaned.

"She's hurt," Regina managed to get out between spasms of coughing. "We have to get her out of here."

McLean pushed Regina out of the way. Bending down, he effortlessly scooped the old woman up and tossed her over his shoulder. "Stay close to me," he ordered Regina.

Regina followed him down the stairs. She ran to the front door and opened it.

McLean carried Bertie out onto the portico.

Regina started after him.

Without warning, a hand clamped over her mouth from behind.

Halfway back to the house, Adam encountered Arthur Randolph, his son, John Sandhurst, and Edward Lee on the road. They had been riding toward the waterfront as quickly as he had been riding away from it. They reined in their horses.

"We saw the smoke," Lee called out. The men were armed with muskets.

"The fire has been put out," Adam said, trying to catch his breath. "But we need to get to the house. Regina and Randolph's daughter are there."

"Beatrice came home this morning," Randolph said. "But your wife could be in danger. Some of my men are calling for Langley's head. If they can't find him, they may go after her."

The men rode at breakneck speed toward Summerhill. *God, please let me get to her in time*, Adam prayed silently.

When they reached the clearing, Adam's worst fears were confirmed. Smoke and flames billowed out the downstairs windows of the house. Smoke was just beginning to curl from the upstairs windows. He saw several men run from the house and head toward the woods. From their clothing, they appeared to be indentured servants. He gouged his heels into his horse's sides, sending the animal lurching forward.

As he neared the house, Adam saw the front door open, and Duncan McLean emerge from the house, carrying a woman's body over his shoulder. *Regina!* He urged his horse to go faster, then reined in sharply, bringing the animal to an abrupt stop in the front yard. He dismounted.

McLean carefully lowered the body to the ground beneath the oak tree.

Adam recognized the woman. It was Bertie.

Behind him, gunpowder exploded in his ear. He watched in horror as Duncan McLean pitched forward and collapsed on the ground.

He swung around in time to see Edward Lee lower his musket, and something inside him snapped. Quickly closing the distance between himself and Lee, he swung hard, knocking the weapon from his hands. Lee cried out in surprise and pain and stumbled to one knee. "What the hell was that for?" Lee cried out.

Fury blazed in Adam's eyes as they drilled into the other man's bewildered gaze. Without a word, he pivoted and hurried to the oak tree. McLean was struggling to sit up. His face was pinched with pain and he was clutching his left shoulder. Blood oozed between his fingers. On the ground beside him, Bertie stirred.

"Are you all right?"

"I'll be fine." McLean fought for air. " 'Tis only my shoulder."

Adam knelt beside Bertie. "Bertie, can you hear me?"

The old woman clutched clumsily at Adam's sleeve. "Mister Richard," she murmured. Her voice was slurred.

"It's Adam," he said, gently turning her head so he could better see the gash on her temple.

"No, no," Bertie protested weakly. "It was Mister Richard . . . He started the fire . . ." Her voice trailed off.

Adam leaned closer to her. "Bertie, are you certain?"

She nodded. "I seen him. That's when he . . . hit me . . ."

He had not been able to find Richard's body in the smoldering shell of the warehouse. While assured that Langley had not perished in the blaze, he had been left with an uneasy feeling that he was overlooking something. "McLean, where's Regina?"

McLean glanced around him, his black brows drawing together in bewilderment. "I dinna know . . . she was right behind me."

Adam's gaze riveted on the burning house. Randolph and the other men had dismounted and were trying to beat out the flames with their coats, but the blaze was already out of control. Flames licked along the eaves, catching quickly on the dry shingles and spreading. The younger Randolph ran toward the house, carrying the bucket from the well. Water sloshed from the bucket.

A gut-wrenching horror unlike anything Adam had ever felt before surged through him. If anything happened to Regina, he would never forgive himself! He jumped to his feet.

Randolph stepped in front of him, blocking his way. "You can't go in there!" he shouted over the roar of the fire.

"Regina is still in there!" Adam thrust the other man aside.

"Burke, don't be a fool!" Randolph yelled after him.

Adam plunged into the smoke-filled hall. "Regina!"

Dear God, where is she?

He quickly searched his study and the dining room, but she wasn't there. He started toward the reception room, but immediately recoiled from the tremendous heat. His stomach knotted. He prayed to God she wasn't in there.

Then he heard her scream, a piercing, bone-shattering shriek of terror.

She was upstairs.

He took the stairs two at a time.

The smoke was worse upstairs, burning his eyes

and lungs. He frantically began searching the upstairs bedchambers.

She screamed again.

Adam came to an abrupt stop just inside the
doorway of his bedchamber, and for several agonizing seconds, his heart stopped beating.

Richard Langley, his face and clothes blackened
from smoke, was holding a knife to Regina's throat.
His other hand was clamped over her mouth. Regina squirmed and tried to pry his hand away from
her mouth. Richard pressed the tip of the blade into
her throat, and she whimpered against his hand.
Her dark eyes, wide with terror, pleaded silently
with Adam.

"Let her go, Langley," Adam said, trying to keep
his voice at a normal pitch.

"Bloody hell!" Richard spat. "I'm not going to
let you have her, any more than I'm going to let
you have Summerhill. It's mine. Do you hear me?
It's *mine*."

"We can talk about this. Just let Regina go. This
is between you and me."

"There's nothing to talk about. You've stolen
everything that ever belonged to me. My land, my
home, my ships. Well, you're not going to get any
of it, Burke. I'll see it burn before I let you have it."

Adam started walking slowly toward him. "Let
Regina go," he repeated, his voice deceptively
calm.

Richard began backing across the room, dragging Regina with him. There was a wild, glazed
look in his eyes, and he was shaking, like a man
desperately in need of a drink. "Stay away from
me. If you don't want me to kill her, stay away."
As if to emphasize his threat, he gouged the knife

into the soft hollow at the base of Regina's neck, breaking the skin.

A muffled cry tore from Regina's throat. She clawed frantically at the hand covering her mouth.

Adam steadily closed the distance between them. "Let Regina go, and I'll give Summerhill back to you. All of it. The house. The shipyard. Tell me what you want, and it's yours."

Richard laughed harshly. "You must think I'm stupid, Burke, if you expect me to fall for that. But then, you never did think very highly of me."

"That's not true," Adam said, careful to keep his gaze fixed on his brother-in-law, while at the same time watching Regina. Blood trickled down her neck where Richard had cut her with the knife. "I would never have entrusted a share of the shipping company to you if I thought you were incapable of making it profitable."

"What you *thought*, Burke, is that you could buy your way into our world. You thought you could buy yourself a wife. You thought you could buy—" Richard yelped and jerked his hand away from Regina's mouth. He stared in disbelief at the tooth marks on his hand. "You goddamned little bitch!"

Richard drew back his hand and struck her hard across the face, sending her reeling. She hit the wall with a sickening *thud* and slid to the floor.

Adam lunged. He hit Richard head on, knocking him off his feet. Both men crashed to the floor. Blinded by rage, Adam fixed his hands around Richard's neck and slammed his head against the floorboards, again and again. "Don't you *ever* . . . strike . . . my wife . . . again," he ground out between blows.

Still clutching the knife, Richard stabbed the air wildly. The blade sliced through Adam's sleeve and into his upper arm. Adam swung, knocking Richard's arm aside. The knife clattered across the floor.

Richard brought his knee up between them and thrust hard, shoving Adam away from him. Adam gripped the front of Richard's shirt, carrying him with him as he staggered backward.

Dazed, Regina half rose on one elbow. The room spun around her. Beneath her, the floor was hot to the touch. Smoke curled between the wide pine floorboards. A white hot pain stabbed behind her eyes, making her head pound, and a wave of nausea welled up inside her. In the center of the smoky blur, she saw Richard and Adam, locked in a death grip, rolling over and over across the floor. "Stop it!" she cried out, but her voice seemed oddly thin and far away.

Adam broke free and rolled to his feet. Oblivious to the blood pumping from the gash in his arm, he seized the front of Richard's shirt and hauled him to his feet. Richard took a swing at him and missed.

Adam drove his fist into Richard's stomach, causing him to grunt and double over. Before he could recover, Adam brought his fist up hard under Richard's chin in a savage blow that sent him crashing into the wall.

Regina felt as if her stomach crowded her throat. "Adam, don't!"

Richard's eyes rolled back in his head, and his knees buckled beneath him.

Adam stood over him, fighting for air. Blood saturated his shirt from the gash in his arm. He was beginning to feel weak from loss of blood. He stared down at Richard's unconscious form, and was filled with disgust at the man's self-serving cowardice. For a fleeting second, he was tempted to leave Richard to die, then decided against it. Regina would never forgive him.

He would never be able to forgive himself.

From the corner of his eye, he saw Regina get to her feet. Her face was void of color and her movements were awkward and unsteady. He quickly closed the distance between them, catching her just as she started to sway.

She pressed one arm against her roiling stomach. "I think I'm going to be sick," she gasped.

"Not here, you're not." Adam's hand closed around her arm. "Come on. I'll get you out of here."

She glanced at Richard, lying in an unconscious heap against the wall. "Richard—"

Half running, half walking, Adam steered her toward the door. "Don't worry. I'll come back for him."

Smoke, thick and black, choked the hallway. Adam started down the stairs, then stopped short. Flames consumed the entry hall and the stairs below the landing. Gripping Regina's arm, he pulled her back up the stairs and into the bedroom, slamming the door shut after them.

"Adam! What are we going to do?" Regina's voice rose in panic.

He released her.

Richard moaned and stirred.

Going to the bed, Adam dragged the coverlet from the bed and carried it to the window. Below him, Randolph and the other men were staring in dismay at the house. They were no longer attempting to extinguish the blaze. Randolph's son pointed up at him and let out a shout. The men's attention riveted on the bedchamber window. Adam bent and shouted out the open window, "Everyone, stand back!"

The men scrambled to get out of the way.

Protecting his shoulder with the coverlet, Adam threw his full weight against the window, shattering the glass and splintering the wood muntins. After several attempts, he managed to break out both the upper and lower sashes, creating an opening large enough for an adult to climb through. "We're going to have to jump!" he shouted to the men below. He threw the coverlet out the window. "I'm sending Regina out first, then Langley. Langley is unconscious."

Randolph signaled his comprehension.

Adam turned to Regina. "Hurry, there's no time to lose."

Regina went to the window. Tears glittered in her eyes. "Adam, I'm so sorry," she whispered.

"You'll be all right," he said, sounding more calm than he felt. "All you have to do is shove away from the house with your feet. The men will break your fall with the blanket."

She started to shake her head. "That's not what I meant."

Fastening his hands around her waist, Adam lifted her up and set her on the window sill. "Turn around," he ordered.

"Adam—"

"Now!"

Fighting back tears, Regina obeyed. Adam held her steady around the waist while she turned around on the window sill, wedging her feet through the narrow opening, until she was facing outward. Below her, she saw the men holding the coverlet stretched taut among them, and she knew that somehow she was supposed to land in the middle of it.

"Ready?" Adam asked.

She nodded jerkily.

"Remember to push away from the wall."

"I remember." Her voice cracked.

"Regina—" He took hold of her chin and turned her face toward his. His hand shook as he grazed his thumb across her cheekbone. His throat constricted. "I love you," he said thickly.

His face blurred and swam before her eyes. "I love *you*."

Adam released her.

Before she lost what remained of her courage, Regina jumped.

Adam watched, his heart in his throat, as Regina hit the bedcover, bouncing once. She scrambled to the ground, unhurt, and he released his breath in a sigh of relief.

He turned back to get his brother-in-law, then abruptly stopped.

The door to the bedchamber stood ajar. Richard was gone.

Regina lay in the unfamiliar bed, staring up at the ceiling of the Randolphs's guest bedchamber. Night had long since fallen, but even the cloak of darkness was not enough to eradicate the smell of smoke from Regina's memory. For as long as she lived, she would never forget that smell, or the losses associated with it.

Adam lay on his side, one arm draped protectively around her middle, watching her. "You're very quiet tonight," he said.

"I was thinking about Richard."

"Regina, I'm sorry. If I could bring him back, I would."

She turned her head to look at him. His face was hidden in darkness, but she could feel his gaze burning into her. "It wasn't your fault. You tried everything you could. Had you stayed in the house a minute longer, I would have lost you too." She hesitated, then continued in a low voice. "What troubles me is that I have no tears for him. Instead, I feel angry. I've tried to figure it out, but I just don't understand why he had to run back into the fire. There was nothing in the house he could have saved, nothing he was even very fond of. It was as if he *wanted to die*."

"Perhaps he did."

"But, why? Did he hate us that much?"

"I think, love, that your brother hated himself. He couldn't differentiate between the man he was and what he owned. And if he couldn't have what he wanted, then he didn't want anyone else to have it either."

Regina was quiet for a long time, thinking over what Adam had said. Her brother was not the same Richard with whom she had grown up. Something had changed him. Losing everything to Adam had changed him.

No, she thought, remembering. Richard had begun changing even before that. He had begun changing the day he inherited Summerhill. The day he went from being the son of a landowner to being a landowner in his own right. It was as if the money and the power that accompanied owning one of the largest and oldest tobacco plantations on the Northern Neck had gone to his head.

She sighed. "I guess we've lost everything now. The house. The warehouses. This year's tobacco crop—"

"No," Adam said, more harshly than he had intended. "We'll rebuild. And replant. As long as I have my health and two good hands, there is nothing to stop us from accomplishing everything we've set out to do." His voice gentled. "Besides, we still have what's most important; we have each other. I meant what I said earlier, Regina. I love you. More than you can possibly know."

He leaned over to kiss her, but just then her stomach took a particularly nasty turn, and she quickly pulled out of his arms. "I love you too."

Adam frowned, wondering what had gotten into her. "You have a peculiar way of showing it," he said, not quite succeeding in keeping the hurt from his voice.

She swallowed hard, and tried to will her stomach to return to its proper place. Taking hold of Adam's hand, she moved it downward until it lay over her abdomen. She smiled shyly. "Adam, there's something I should tell you . . ."

Epilogue

~~~~~~~~~~

William Langley was half a glass of port away from being under the table. "I hav'ta admit," he said, slurring his words. "When Burke bought your term of indenture, I thought he had gone mad. But he was right about you. You're a good man . . . Duncan McLean."

"Ye're a good man yerself, sir. For an Englishman."

William and McLean and Adam enjoyed a hearty laugh. William raised his tankard in a salute. "To freedom. May it always taste so sweet."

The three men drained their glasses. "I have both of ye to thank for clearing my name," McLean said. His accent was more pronounced than usual. "I'll always be grateful to ye."

They were sitting in the study in Langley's Williamsburg house, drinking port while they awaited news from upstairs. After the fire, Adam had taken Regina to stay with her aunt and uncle while he rebuilt the house at Summerhill. She had protested vehemently, wanting to stay in St. John's Parish. But Adam had been equally adamant. He had come close to losing Regina once; he wasn't going to risk losing her—or their unborn child—again.

Not wanting to be away from his wife for too long at a time, he returned to Williamsburg at least once a month. On his last visit, he had received news from Miles that McLean's sentence had been commuted; the Scot had been acquitted of all charges against him.

He had given McLean the fifty acres he would have been entitled to had he served out the remainder of his term, with the promise of an additional fifty acres should he marry. McLean had other ideas however; he wanted to see a bit more of the new world before settling down. Adam knew he would miss him; during the months since the fire, McLean had become more than a loyal servant. He had become a valued friend.

Although it was seldom spoken of, Richard's death continued to haunt them all. Regina sometimes awakened in the middle of the night from terrifying dreams. On other nights, he would awaken to the sound of her sobbing in her sleep. William and Caroline Langley held no resentments, but the sadness he sometimes saw in their eyes told him that they still felt keenly the loss of their nephew.

As for himself, many nights he had lain awake, going over and over in his mind everything that had happened and wondering what he could have done differently to prevent the tragedy that scarred their lives. He could think of nothing. Richard's demons had been of his own making. Richard Langley was the creator of his own demise.

The ear-piercing wail of an infant jolted him back to the present. He jumped to his feet, but William put a restraining hand on his arm. "Settle down, son. That one's mine. I'd recognize his screams anywhere. It must be time for dinner. The only time he yells that loud is when his stomach is growling."

Adam sat back down, but his heart refused to return to its normal pace. Regina had been in labor since yesterday evening. He didn't know how much more she could endure.

He didn't know how much more *he* could endure.

Caroline Langley had given birth three months ago to a healthy boy. Now Regina was upstairs, in the same bed, trying to give birth to—

"Adam?" Caroline touched a gentle hand to his shoulder, causing him to start. He hadn't even heard her come into the room.

He got to his feet. "How is she?"

Caroline smiled. "Come upstairs and meet your daughter."

William Langley let out a hoot. "I don't envy you, having a daughter. You're going to have your hands full."

Caroline flashed her husband a silencing glance. "I think it will be delightful to have a sweet little girl around the house."

Adam didn't hear them; he was already halfway up the stairs.

He found Regina propped up on pillows in the middle of the bed, holding their infant daughter in her arms. She had changed into a fresh nightgown and brushed her hair. Her face was pale and there were dark shadows beneath her eyes, but she was smiling. Bertie was adjusting the pillows behind her back. "If you need anything at all, Miss Regina, you just yell."

Bertie cast Adam a warning glance on her way

out of the bedchamber. "Don't you tire her out now," she ordered. "Miss Regina needs her rest."

Adam approached the bed. Regina was adjusting the blanket around the baby's face. She glanced up at him, wonder shining in her dark eyes. "Oh, Adam, isn't she beautiful?"

Adam leaned over the bed to peer into his daughter's red, wrinkled face. Beautiful was not the word that came to mind, but he had been fore-warned that newborns were often a disappointing sight to everyone except their mothers. Besides, his daughter was already showing signs of having in-herited Regina's black hair, rosy mouth, and stub-born chin. "Yes," he said at last. "She's going to be a charmer."

"Do you want to hold her?"

"I'm not sure; my hands are shaking." In proof, Adam held out his hands to show her.

"Sit down. You'll do fine. You're not half as nervous as I was when Aunt Caroline first handed her to me."

Adam sat down on the edge of the bed, and Re-gina passed the tiny, squirming, blanket-wrapped bundle to him. Cradling the infant in his two hands, Adam fought to control the bout of uncer-tainty that gripped him. Raising a child was a weighty responsibility, one he hoped he could ful-fill with integrity and compassion.

As she watched him hold their daughter, his touch incredibly gentle, Regina felt her heart swell with pride. She knew instinctively that she was giv-ing her children a most rare and precious gift: a good father. "Is Duncan still here?" she asked.

"He's downstairs. He wanted to wait until he was certain you were going to be all right. And, of course, to find out if the baby was a boy or a girl."

"Have you told him what we decided?"

"No. I thought you might want to tell him yourself." Handing his daughter back to Regina, Adam got up and went to the door. "McLean?" he called out from the top of the stairs. "My wife wishes to speak with you."

A minute later, Duncan McLean appeared in the doorway. The grin he gave Regina was almost boyish. "Congratulations," he said.

"Do you want to hold her?" Regina asked.

Shaking his head, he approached the bed. "I dinna think that's a very good idea, lass. I might drop the wee thing. But I'll take a look."

He bent down and peered into the baby's face, and shook his head in disbelief. "I'm jealous of you, Burke, having not one, but two, beautiful females to brighten your days. You're a lucky man."

"That I am," Adam agreed from the doorway.

Regina watched the awe and delight that passed over the Scot's face as he stared at the baby, and she could not help wondering how she had been so mistaken about him. "Duncan, there's something I want to tell you."

He held up a hand, silencing her. "If you're going to apologize *again*, lass—"

She shook her head. "No, not again. You're probably tired of hearing it anyway." She hesitated, then added softly, "We decided to name her Jenny."

Duncan's gaze riveted on her face. He stared at her for several speechless seconds before letting his attention drop to the baby in her arms. "I-I don't know what to say," he muttered in a choked voice. "My sister would have liked that very much."

Regina glanced over his shoulder to where Adam stood in the doorway, watching her. Tears glittered in his eyes.

In that instant, Regina knew that she had found what she had spent her life searching for.

She had everything she'd ever wanted.

Avon Romances—
the best in exceptional authors and unforgettable novels!

Avon Romantic Treasures

Unforgettable, enthralling love stories,
sparkling with passion and adventure
from Romance's bestselling authors

LADY OF SUMMER *by Emma Merritt*
77984-6/$5.50 US/$7.50 Can

TIMESWEPT BRIDE *by Eugenia Riley*
77157-8/$5.50 US/$7.50 Can

A KISS IN THE NIGHT *by Jennifer Horsman*
77597-2/$5.50 US/$7.50 Can

SHAWNEE MOON *by Judith E. French*
77705-3/$5.50 US/$7.50 Can

PROMISE ME *by Kathleen Harrington*
77833-5/ $5.50 US/ $7.50 Can

COMANCHE RAIN *by Genell Dellin*
77525-5/ $4.99 US/ $5.99 Can

MY LORD CONQUEROR *by Samantha James*
77548-4/ $4.99 US/ $5.99 Can

ONCE UPON A KISS *by Tanya Anne Crosby*
77680-4/$4.99 US/$5.99 Can